MW00653732

THE NURSERY

The Bayou Hauntings
Book Three

Bill Thompson

Published by
Ascendente Books
Dallas, Texas

The Nursery: The Bayou Hauntings, Book 3
All Rights Reserved
Copyright © 2018
V.1.0
Published by Ascendente Books
ISBN 978-09992503-0-3
Printed in the United States of America

Books by Bill Thompson

The Bayou Hauntings
CALLIE
FORGOTTEN MEN
THE NURSERY

Brian Sadler Archaeological Mystery Series
THE BETHLEHEM SCROLL
ANCIENT: A SEARCH FOR THE LOST CITY
OF THE MAYAS
THE STRANGEST THING
THE BONES IN THE PIT
ORDER OF SUCCESSION
THE BLACK CROSS
TEMPLE

Apocalyptic Fiction
THE OUTCASTS

The Crypt Trilogy
THE RELIC OF THE KING
THE CRYPT OF THE ANCIENTS
GHOST TRAIN

Middle Grade Fiction
THE LEGEND OF GUNNERS COVE

This book is dedicated to a friend I've known since before we were in kindergarten together.

Wesley Chapman Moore and I grew up in a little town in Oklahoma. We ended up in business in the same place — Oklahoma City — but on different career paths. We didn't see each other for years.

Five decades later we were together at a class reunion in our home town. We realized we lived less than twenty miles from each other in the Dallas metroplex. Our wives enjoyed each other's company and we rekindled an old friendship. Today there are frequent martinis, lunches and get-togethers for one event or another.

In addition to being a great supporter of my work, Wes offers constructive criticism and insight that help me shape my books into better stories for my readers.

Thanks for the memories, Wes. May there be many more good times with you and Nancy.

CHAPTER ONE

The Arbors
Two Months Ago

"No! God, no! Get away from me! Stay back!"

The old mansion's enormous rotunda reverberated with the screams coming from upstairs. On the ground floor a group of tourists looked up towards the dome fifty feet above them. The second and third floors had hallways with beautiful wood banisters that encircled the rotunda. Two floors up, a girl stood with her back against the railing, shouting and throwing her arms about. She looked to be in her twenties and wore a tank top and shorts.

She held her hands in front of her, as if she were pushing someone away. "I'm sorry. I made a joke, okay? Please leave me alone!"

There was an architect's office on the ground floor. When the people who worked there heard all the commotion, they leapt from their desks and joined the tourists, craning their necks to see what was happening.

One of the five was architect Jordan Blanchard, the man who owned the house. He walked to a handsome African-

American woman dressed in period costume who had just finished a tour of the Arbors.

"What's going on, Penny?" he whispered as another horrifying scream echoed throughout the vast room.

"That girl was in our group, but she got separated somehow. She was a problem during the tour, mouthing off and all. She appeared up there a moment ago, mocking the ghost story I told them."

Another shout from the third floor. The girl flailed her arms about. "I'm sorry! I'm sorry, okay? I believe! I believe, I promise!"

The young man she'd arrived with shouted up to her, "Erin! What's wrong?"

"She's pushing me toward the railing! Get away!

The girl's back pressed hard against the banister as she fended off an unseen assailant. Everyone watched her push and shove against nothing. There was no one u there except her.

"Jack! Help me! I made fun of her and she's mad! She's going to kill me! For God's sake, help me!"

Her friend sprinted up the stairs two at a time, but he wouldn't arrive in time to save Erin. Before he could reach the second floor, the girl struck out hard with her arms as she bent further and further backwards. The witnesses below would recall they'd never seen someone contort their body like that. It looked as if she was being pushed, but no one else was there.

She tumbled backwards over the railing with a horrifying scream. In seconds that seemed like an eternity to the group below, her body plummeted forty feet and struck the parquet floor with a resounding thud.

Jack gave a bloodcurdling yell and rushed back downstairs. As he cradled her body, one of the architect's staffers called 911. An ambulance would respond, but this was a job for the coroner. No one could have survived that fall.

She was the second person to die in this house in the same manner. The first tumbled over the third-floor railing at that exact spot in 1945, over seventy years ago. There would be speculation about the similarities between the deaths, and like the first one, the authorities would call this a tragic accident, even though it was anything but.

An eye for an eye, as the Bible verse went. This involved retaliation. Payback for an offense.

CHAPTER TWO

Present Day

"I want to take you to Beau Rivage next weekend."

Cate had heard of the place. She squeezed Landry's hand, grinned and teased, "An old mansion built before the Civil War? A bed-and-breakfast complete with its own ghost? What on earth would entice Landry Drake, my intrepid ghost hunter, to visit such a place? I was sure you'd suggest the beach."

Her comment made him laugh out loud. A day doing nothing on the beach would have driven her boyfriend crazy. Landry's captivation with haunted venues in southern Louisiana was often the subject of frivolous banter between them. He called it part of his job, but she knew better. Nothing piqued Landry's interest more than getting a lead about paranormal activity. He believed in the supernatural — after what he'd seen first-hand at the Asylum in Victory, anyone would. Now that he was convinced, his reports and documentaries on New Orleans's Channel Nine took on his own personal flair. He enthralled his listeners with stories about phantoms, eerie phenomena and unexplainable mysteries.

Many leads he investigated turned out false. Some property owners wanted the publicity and tourism dollars that accompanied unexplained activity. With no solid evidence, they fabricated backstories. Landry's station gave him free rein to pick which leads he followed, and by now he had learned which ones were worthless and which weren't.

There were a lot of places to look. In Louisiana's Cajun parishes, there were hundreds of venues where the supernatural and unexplainable really happened. Houses, barns, buildings and even cars had turned out to be haunted — if that was the right word to describe the mysteries — and Channel Nine's ratings soared every time it aired another episode of Landry's *Bayou Hauntings* series.

He slipped his arm around Cate Adams's waist as they walked into their favorite lunch venue, a comfortable seafood restaurant called Kingfish. It was conveniently situated in the French Quarter at the corner of Chartres and Conti Streets a few blocks from Channel Nine, and he and Cate came here often. Their romance had ignited at Kingfish during many happy hours, lunches and dinners.

The bartender greeted them by name and poured two Chardonnays without asking. He knew the couple well, especially Landry, who had become a regional celebrity in the past few months.

"How's the ghost-hunting business?" he asked, and Landry jested that it beat working for a living. They made casual conversation and then moved to a quiet table in the back for lunch and a discussion about Landry's suggestion they visit Beau Rivage.

He told Cate what he knew about the plantation. The three-story antebellum mansion had been built in 1835 by Henri Arceneaux, an ancestor of the present owner, Calisto Pilantro, who inherited the house from her grandmother just over a year ago. She'd spent a lot of money refurbishing the place, and it had been open to overnight guests for only a few weeks.

"Okay, tell me," she said with a smile. "What's going on at Beau Rivage? Knowing you, I'm sure there's something paranormal there or you wouldn't spend your time going."

"You know me too well. There are several things I'd like to know about. There's the apparition of a young girl dressed in a frilly blue dress. Apparently the owner has seen her many times. Sometimes the child is standing down by the river, and at other times she's inside the house. There's a secret staircase and a hidden room. Oh, and there was a murder there — the owner's uncle, who was a prominent attorney in Opelousas, was shot to death. The perpetrator was arrested, but he bailed out and disappeared. No one knows where he is. That adds to the mystique of the place, don't you think?"

She shuddered. "Not the last part. I have enough trouble waiting around to see a ghost. I don't need any real-life murderers hanging out where I'm spending the night."

"Apparently he's long gone. Mark Streater is his name; he fled before his trial, so I couldn't find out much about him or why he killed the lawyer. I'm hoping Miss Pilantro can tell us."

Despite Cate's apprehension, her boyfriend's enthusiasm for this kind of adventure was infectious. The more he told her about his plans for their weekend, the more she looked forward to it. Spending time with him was the biggest attraction, she reminded herself, but she also found his searches for the supernatural interesting and sometimes downright fascinating.

"We'll go on Friday. If we leave the city by three, we can beat the weekend traffic. We can be at Point Charmaine in two hours, meet the owner and eat a gourmet dinner that's part of the experience. We'll have all day Saturday to explore the place, and we'll be home by dark."

As Landry had predicted, the traffic was manageable that Friday afternoon, and by five p.m. they had found the sign for Beau Rivage, turned off the main highway, and were driving along a gravel road toward the river. They came to a black wrought-iron fence that marked the property line. The family name "Arceneaux" in ornate metal letters spanned two eight-foot brick columns, one on each side of the entry gate. Tall, lush magnolias lined the driveway that ran nearly half a mile, and Cate gasped as the three-story mansion came into view.

"It's beautiful," she whispered. "What a grand old house this must have been!"

"And this is just the back side. The front faces the river, and it's really spectacular. Apparently it was in serious disrepair when Calisto Pilantro inherited it. She spent more than a million dollars on the place; I guess that kind of money can make anything look good!"

"No kidding," Cate replied, wondering where the owner had made her fortune. She guessed she'd learn all about her since Landry tended to ask a lot of questions. Now that she'd seen the place herself, she was looking forward to spending the weekend at Beau Rivage and learning more about its spooky history.

Theirs was the only car in the designated parking area. They retrieved their luggage and followed signs to the office. As they walked onto the porch, a girl a few years older than Cate came through the door and shielded her face from the late afternoon sun.

"Welcome to Beau Rivage. You must be Landry Drake!"

"That's me. This is my friend Cate Adams."

The girl stuck out her hand and said, "I'm Callie. Callie Pilantro."

This is Callie Pilantro? Cate's face showed her surprise and Callie said, "Is everything all right?"

"Yes, it's fine. Having heard a little about you and your inheritance from Landry, I expected you to be…well, quite a bit older!"

Callie laughed and waved at the house. "Thirty-one going on sixty, with this albatross to keep me busy! Come on inside. You're my only guests tonight, so let's get you unpacked. Then please join me for a glass of wine on the veranda."

Their second-floor room was bright and airy thanks to twelve-foot windows that opened onto a porch and gave them a gorgeous view. In front of them lay two hundred feet of freshly mowed grass that ended at the shoreline of the Atchafalaya River. When these mansions were built, the huge windows doubled as doors, allowing air to come in and people to step outside onto the shaded porch. While Cate unpacked, Landry opened a window and called her over to watch a riverboat meandering downstream toward the Gulf of Mexico.

Cate and Landry went downstairs and walked to the riverbank. They turned and took in the front side of the beautiful old home. Its majestic columns and three stories of porches made it truly spectacular. They came back to the house when they saw Callie appear on the veranda with a bottle of wine and three glasses.

They toasted their new friendship and Callie told them about the house. She had spent summers here as a child, but years had passed until she returned for the reading of her grandmother's will and learned she had inherited the place. "After Mamère Juliet died, it sat vacant for several months, and it had begun to deteriorate by the time I got it."

"Did you know immediately you wanted to make it a bed-and-breakfast?" Landry wondered.

Callie laughed so hard she almost choked on her wine, and he asked if he'd said something funny.

"No, I'm sorry about that. If you knew how dirt poor I was when I inherited this run-down old house, you'd be amazed we're sitting here today."

"That's a story I'd love to hear," Cate interjected, and Callie replied that she'd be happy to tell them about Beau Rivage.

"We have a spiel for the tourists. We talk about the coffin we found in the wall. We show them our hidden room and our secret staircase. That stuff is on our website, and if that's what got you interested in my place, Landry, then I'm flattered.

"I'll give you a tour tomorrow morning. Beau Rivage holds deep and personal memories for me — some pleasant, others disturbing. Publicity is a good thing, but there are secrets at this house I can't reveal. If that changes your mind about being here, I'm sorry."

She paused. "Oh, hell, I've done it again. I get too passionate sometimes and I start rambling without thinking first. I made an assumption as to why you came when maybe all you wanted was a serene weekend at a quiet B&B in the country."

Landry and Cate had taken to their hostess from the start, finding her warm, sincere and appealing. He explained that this visit was a combination of a weekend getaway and a fact-finding mission about how the house had avoided being burned by the Yankees.

"Most of the places I visit never end up on TV, and if your house did, you'd approve everything in the show beforehand. There has to be enough mystery to entertain our viewers, so the more spooky stories, the better. Speaking of stories, there was a murder here not long ago, correct?"

There was a barely perceptible change in her expression. "That was my uncle Willard Arceneaux. That's one of the things I was talking about. It's personal —

family. There was nothing supernatural about his death, so leave it alone."

He apologized for the faux pas and she said she was sorry for snapping at him. "My relationship with Uncle Willard was complex and full of the same dynamics every family has. He had no use for me, and vice versa, to be perfectly frank. That's enough about him. Why ruin a pleasant conversation?"

Cate was surprised at the woman's very strong feelings about her uncle, a man who had died in this very house less than a year ago. No love lost there, she mused as Landry explained more about his work.

"As you said, every old house has its tales. Some of them go back decades, others are well-documented and include eerie sightings by respected people, but I've found that most are pure fiction, contrived to create tourist traffic. I've been doing investigative reporting — specifically paranormal research — for long enough to figure things out. The owners who offer me a free weekend in exchange for publicity about their spooks aren't the ones I'm looking for."

As he paused for a sip of wine, Callie agreed with him. Too many plantation owners were vying for the same tourism dollars, and some weren't above inventing mysterious stories to increase business.

"The ghost of Beau Rivage truly exists, and she's actually a relative of mine from a long, long time ago. If it weren't for Anne-Marie, I might have ended up being a ghost too."

"Really?" Cate said. "Anne-Marie was a child, correct?"

Callie nodded. "You'll hear more on the tour. Landry, I'd like to know about the fact-finding mission that brought you here."

"We're considering a segment on Louisiana mansions that were spared by the Union soldiers, and I was surprised at how few there are. Your place is one of them. I got no answers from your website, so I thought I'd ask the person who might know what happened. That's you, and here we are."

Callie explained that her ancestor Henri Arceneaux built the house in 1835. She discovered his journal and learned that his daughter became frightened when Yankee soldiers came to the house. She ran across the yard, fell into the river and drowned. Even more tragically, it was her tenth birthday. Overwhelmed with grief, her father walked into the kitchen just as a thoughtless Union soldier cut himself a piece of the girl's birthday cake. Enraged and crazed, the child's father pulled out a gun and killed the soldier. Rather than retaliating, the leader gathered his troops and left. Apparently he issued orders to leave Beau Rivage untouched, because nothing happened here for the rest of the war."

"Is that child the spirit who haunts this house — Anne-Marie?" Cate asked.

Callie said it was more complicated than that but offered no further explanation.

Landry and Cate drank their wine in silence, looking toward the river where the girl had died on her birthday and thinking how horrible it must have been for her parents. Callie was lost in thought as well, and then she noticed something at the far end of the porch.

A girl in a frilly blue dress was standing behind Cate and Landry. She smiled at Callie and got a smile in return. Then she was gone.

CHAPTER THREE

Dinner was served in the home's elegant dining room. They occupied three chairs at one end of a long table that seated fourteen. Cate said she felt like the queen having dinner with Prince Philip at Buckingham Palace. Callie explained that like many of the house's furnishings, this table once belonged to Henri Arceneaux.

Callie introduced her chef, Annie, who came from a long line of great Cajun cooks. When guests stayed overnight at Beau Rivage, Annie came in from town to prepare the evening meal and a sumptuous breakfast. The meal was extraordinary — a rich seafood gumbo, crawfish étouffée and bread pudding. They lingered at the table until almost nine, when Cate declared herself stuffed and ready for bed.

They opened the window onto the porch and burrowed under the covers, falling asleep to the hooting of an owl somewhere down by the river. The next morning dawned cool and crisp, and they stayed in bed until almost eight. Downstairs, they had coffee on the veranda and then gorged themselves on Annie's incredible eggs Sardou with gulf shrimp on the side.

Later that morning they toured the mansion. Callie took them from room to room, explaining that the last person to live here was her grandmother Juliet Arceneaux. The house and furnishings had been much different when she inherited it. Everything needed work, but fortunately the house wasn't vandalized as it sat empty for months after Juliet's death. Callie had recovered couches and chairs, refinished beautiful tables, breakfronts and other pieces, and now the public areas of the house looked as they had in the late nineteenth century.

The tour fascinated them. The staircase concealed in the wall was interesting, but hardly unique. Many antebellum homes had those narrow stairways so that servants could get from floor to floor, and even for the master to sneak downstairs for a forbidden rendezvous on occasion.

Landry was most impressed by the room hidden behind a bookcase in the library. The things she'd found that helped her save the house and understand its secrets captivated him. Even better, her resident ghost, Anne-Marie, was the one who had shown the room to Callie.

"Depending on how much you're willing to talk about Anne-Marie, this house could be a candidate for a segment on *Bayou Hauntings*," he said as they sat in the parlor for one more glass of wine. "She would be the focus of our story, and you've probably heard what happens after my shows air. You'll get a lot more tourist traffic, most of them trying to catch a glimpse of Anne-Marie."

"And that is one reason why I won't do it. She's special to me, more than I can explain. I'd be ashamed to commercialize our relationship. Maybe someday I'll feel differently. Maybe something will happen that'll change my mind. In the meantime, I'll keep taking guests through the house, but I won't talk about her."

Callie and Cate spoke about Callie's ancestors Joseph and Henri Arceneaux, both of whom were buried in the family cemetery on the property. They discussed the ways in which the Civil War had impacted wealthy Louisiana families and how fortunate she was not to have lost the house herself, all these years later. Thanks to Henri, her great-grandfather, Beau Rivage remained in the family.

She changed the subject, asking if either of them had been to St. Francisville. They hadn't, and she told them about the quaint river town an hour's drive north of Beau Rivage.

"I know that the Myrtles Plantation is the town's primary tourist attraction," Landry said. "Some say it's the most haunted house in America." As a ghost hunter, he was well aware of the Myrtles even though he hadn't visited it.

Callie nodded. "Right, and that kind of publicity brings a lot of tourism to a little town on the Mississippi River. The Myrtles is a beautiful place, but it's just one of a dozen prewar mansions in St. Francisville. Rosedown Plantation is also open to the public, and there are several beautifully restored Victorian homes there. It's a small town now, but long ago it was the largest port on the Mississippi between Memphis and New Orleans. Why have you never done a show about the Myrtles, Landry?"

"Because it's a good example of what we're *not* looking for. Nothing against the Myrtles; it's a beautiful place with a fascinating history. Lots of people claim to have had eerie experiences there. The problem is, it's a little too well-known. We want new things — bayou towns with spooky tales, haunted houses and eerie legends that people haven't heard about."

She said, "I had a reason for bringing up St. Francisville. A friend of mine owns an antebellum mansion there called the Arbors. He's my architect and we worked together on the upgrades here at Beau Rivage. He bought his place a couple of years ago, poured money into it like all of us crazy owners do, and now he has his office on the first floor and living quarters on the third. They give tours a few days a week."

"I haven't heard of it."

"I'm not surprised. The house belonged to a woman named Olivia Beaumont, the granddaughter of a sugar merchant who built it before the war. She died without heirs. Her will left plenty of money to maintain the house, but it couldn't be occupied or sold until she had been dead fifty years. Why she did that, nobody knows. My friend Jordan Blanchard bought it in 2015, fixed it up, and moved in. I was up there recently, and he told me some interesting stories."

She'd gotten Landry's attention and he leaned forward, eager to hear more.

"Several strange things have happened, all apparently having to do with Miss Olivia, the matriarch. Her first husband fell over a third-floor railing and tumbled forty feet to the rotunda. She married a much younger man, who left on a business trip one day and never returned. Olivia lived alone a few more years until she died in the house. Jordan could tell you more; if you're interested, I'll give you his number."

Landry took Jordan Blanchard's contact information. He was grateful for the tip, but he knew from experience how often things didn't work out. "Don't get your hopes up," he said. "Sometimes a lead turns out to be something really important, but oftentimes it doesn't, unfortunately. Either the stories aren't verifiable, whatever's going on can't be caught on camera, or it just isn't bewitching enough to devote a half-hour segment to it."

After lunch they toured the cemetery. She showed them the old stones of her ancestors and the child's marker for Maria, who died on her tenth birthday and whose casket they had found in one of the walls. Callie pointed to her own mother's stone and the one of Leonore Arceneaux, who owned the house in the late nineteenth century.

Callie wasn't surprised that Landry homed in on Maria. Her story was a tragedy, although it wasn't the only one.

There was a story about Leonore too — one that could have cost Callie her life. That was a tale she kept to herself.

"Maria's the child who died on her birthday, right?"

"Yes, after which her father killed a Union soldier in the kitchen."

"I asked you last night if Anne-Marie haunted Beau Rivage and you said it was complicated. Is that because Maria's somehow involved too?"

"In a way. There's much more to this story, and it's not something I'm comfortable discussing. Maybe sometime down the road we can talk about it."

Late in the afternoon they said their goodbyes. They'd become friends already, and Cate said she hoped they'd get together again soon. As they drove back to New Orleans, Landry commented that Callie never mentioned Mark Streater, the man who had killed her uncle at Beau Rivage.

"Why would she have brought that up?" Cate replied with a smile. "You all were jumping from one subject to another like jackrabbits. Even I couldn't keep up. She probably couldn't get a word in about Mark with all the questions you kept asking!"

CHAPTER FOUR

Jordan and Claire Blanchard set up an architectural practice in 1999 after graduating from Tulane University. The newlyweds were from Baton Rouge, and they established Blanchard Designs in downtown St. Francisville, a town near the Mississippi border that was the seat of West Feliciana Parish. The tiny community couldn't support an architectural firm, but most of their projects were in the state capital just thirty miles away. They chose the serenity of a river town over the traffic and hubbub of Baton Rouge. St. Francisville was a perfect place to raise a family and enjoy life.

They borrowed money from their parents and took out a bank loan to start their practice, and they bought large life insurance policies on each other in case the unthinkable happened. With twin girls and a lot of obligations, Jordan wanted to ensure Claire would not only be debt-free but have plenty extra if he died.

As things sometimes happen, the future turned out to be Jordan's, not Claire's. One morning four years ago, she drove to Baton Rouge for a meeting. That afternoon she was on Highway 61, less than twenty miles from home, when the driver of an oncoming tractor-trailer rig dropped a lit cigarette into his lap. He veered left of center and Claire Blanchard didn't even have time to turn the steering wheel. At age thirty-one, Jordan was a widower with four-year-old twin girls and an empty place in his heart.

In the years since her death, Jordan's practice had grown significantly thanks to some lucrative state contracts. With a growing staff, the office he and Claire had rented was too small now. He looked for an old house, one where he could put offices downstairs and living quarters above. St. Francisville had a plethora of beautiful nineteenth-century homes. Because of the insurance proceeds, he was in the enviable position of being a cash buyer.

He heard about the Arbors, a pre-Civil War house on the river that had just come on the market after sitting vacant for half a century. He called a real estate agent and was shocked when he learned the asking price.

"You're serious?" he said. "I can buy an eighty-two-hundred-square-foot house and four acres on the Mississippi River for two hundred and seventy thousand dollars?"

The Realtor had expected the question. Every person who inquired about the Arbors asked it. "That's correct, Mr. Blanchard."

"So what's the catch?" Being an architect, Jordan knew more than the average guy about houses. He'd worked on other nineteenth-century homes in the area. Something wasn't right, more than the fact that the rambling three-story antebellum mansion had been sitting vacant since 1965. The acreage alone was worth almost what the seller was asking.

The agent's answer sounded scripted, and in fact it was. An attorney — the trustee for the Arbors — had told the Realtor what to say.

"I have to make disclosures when selling a property. I'm happy to take you through the Arbors, and I'll give you the standard disclosure sheet the state requires. The place has the typical problems you'd expect in a house built in 1850. The electrical and plumbing need updating. The good news is that it sits high enough not to have flooded, even in Katrina and Harvey. When the owner died in 1965, she instructed the house remain vacant for fifty years. She left funds to keep it up, but the buyer will have a lot of work to do."

Jordan replied, "I want a fixer-upper, but you're not telling me everything. Why's the price so low? You've shown it to other people. Why didn't someone snap it up already? What else do you know about it? What are you not *required* to disclose?"

She paused. "It's a stigmatized property. Under Louisiana law, there's no obligation to disclose that, so the seller has chosen not to. I'm a Realtor. I have a code of ethics, so I'll tell you what it means.

"People around here tell stories about the Arbors. If you've lived here a couple of years, I'm surprised you haven't heard them. This house is no different than a dozen others up and down the Mississippi. They're all stigmatized properties."

"I don't know what that means."

"It's a legal term. It means there's an issue that might concern a buyer, something that's not related to the property's features, condition or physical state of repair. It might mean that someone died there, by natural causes or otherwise. Take the house in California where the Manson family killed five people. That's a stigmatized property because of the horrific crimes that happened inside. Some states would require it be disclosed every time the house changed hands. Others might require it for several years, and in states like Louisiana, there's no duty to disclose that fact at all.

"The Manson murders are an extreme example. Less horrific ones might be criminal activity on the premises —

maybe a meth lab in the basement — or that the owners believe the house is haunted. Really, it's anything that might make a potential buyer think twice."

"And you don't have to tell a prospect about them."

"A seller can't lie. As the seller's representative, neither can I. If you asked me if the Arbors was haunted, I would tell you some people believe so. But if you didn't ask, I have no duty to disclose. You kept pressing me, and I'm telling you now."

"So that's it? People say it's haunted? No Manson murders? No meth lab? The price is so low because of a ghost story?"

"A ghost story and a mysterious death. Olivia Beaumont's husband fell over an upstairs railing in 1945. He plunged three floors to his death."

Jordan didn't understand. Many buildings in Louisiana — hundreds in the New Orleans French Quarter alone — were supposedly haunted. They were tourist destinations and moneymakers for their owners, and every time one came on the market, somebody quickly bought it. Why would Olivia Beaumont's estate offer this one at a bargain? And why hadn't the first looker taken it?

"There has to be more. What you're telling me makes no sense."

"There's one more thing — an odd deed restriction."

Jordan was familiar with deed restrictions; he dealt with them often when he was designing a house or a building. Neighborhood covenants often decreed a minimum size for homes, or no outbuildings, or brick veneer construction instead of frame. Utility companies obtained easements — the right to cross a property — and owners couldn't build on that land. If they built something anyway and the electric company needed to dig up a line, the structure would have to come down.

"You're telling me there's an easement?" he asked.

"No. This one is different. Nothing you've ever heard of before, I'm certain. I hadn't, and I've been selling real estate for fifteen years. There's a room in the house that can't be changed. It's locked and has been since Miss Olivia died in 1965."

"Why am I just hearing this now? Isn't this something you should have disclosed when we first talked about the Arbors?"

"I explained the disclosure obligations earlier."

"I've never heard of anything like that. What's in the room?"

"I don't know. I haven't seen inside. I don't think anyone has."

I can live with a locked room if I get the house at the right price. "Okay, now I'm wondering what's next. What else is wrong with the place? Why did the woman's will keep it off the market for fifty years?"

"I don't know. The Arbors is a spooky old house, Mr. Blanchard. Ghosts or not, it's an eerie place that gives many people the creeps. Its biggest drawback is how long it's been empty. It's going to take money — far more than the purchase price — to bring the house to code and make it livable. I don't know how the executor came up with the price. All I know is this. I've shown it a few times since it came on the market, and there have been no offers so far."

The first time Jordan visited the Arbors, he'd spent twenty minutes walking through its halls. Two days later he'd spent almost two hours inside the massive old house, checking the floors, climbing on the roof to look for leaks, noting the deficiencies in plumbing and electrical, making a to-do list with cost estimates. The agent was right; the renovations would certainly exceed the purchase price.

He found the place in better shape than he expected. Although the house had been unoccupied for half a century, someone had done basic upkeep and maintenance. The roof and shutters had been replaced, and someone cleaned house now and then. Beautiful old pieces of period furniture filled the rooms, and the ornate crown moldings, paneling and banisters were in good shape. Jordan began to think of the Arbors as his own; he decided he'd save most of the original decoration and restore the house to its nineteenth-century grandeur.

Each floor was nearly three thousand square feet in size. There was plenty of room for his architectural firm to operate in several ground-floor rooms, and he and the girls could live upstairs. He'd even capitalize on the ghost by opening the second floor and part of the third — several bedrooms, parlors and maybe even the locked room — to the public. The antique furniture would stay, and maybe he could make money promoting his haunted house as a tourist destination like Myrtles Plantation, a thriving bed-and-breakfast on the north end of St. Francisville.

There was the intriguing matter of that locked room. It was on the second floor, next to what had been Olivia's master bedroom. He'd have to honor the restriction preserving the room — *undisturbed* was the exact word she had used — but if he ended up with the property, that locked door would be open at last.

Jordan made a lowball offer and expected a counter, but the attorney accepted it the same day. At closing he was handed a large ring of keys. Curious, he left the closing, went straight to the house, and tried each key in the locked door. None worked. He refused to damage the fine old door, so it would remain an enigma until the key turned up. He put it out of his mind as his work crew began refurbishing the mansion.

A few months and a lot of money later, Jordan and his twins, Ellie and Violette, moved into the Arbors along with Jordan's architectural business. The girls found the huge old mansion a never-ending source of enjoyment. They searched rooms, found long-forgotten nooks and crannies, explored the grounds, and watched steamboats filled with tourists drift down the Mississippi in front of their house. They'd wave to the captain and get a loud toot-toot in reply.

Jordan found Penny Bishop, an articulate, outgoing and pleasant woman who had been a tour guide at nearby Rosedown Plantation. Now tourists visited the Arbors Tuesdays and Thursdays from ten until four. What Jordan had thought might be a distraction for his employees became just the opposite; they enjoyed having guests, and the visitors appreciated seeing a mixture of old and new in the mansion.

Everything seemed to go well as the family settled in to life in the old house, and Jordan's architectural firm took on one new, profitable account after another. Tourists loved the mystery of the locked room, so Penny made it a highlight of the tour. She explained the two odd instructions in Miss Olivia's will. The house had sat empty for fifty years after her death, and the room behind the door would remain undisturbed forever.

Visitors asked Penny her thoughts about what lay behind that door. She'd just shake her head, shrug and smile. To tell the truth, she had no idea either.

CHAPTER FIVE

Two weeks after Callie told Cate and Landry about the Arbors, Landry drove up to St. Francisville. He'd searched the web but found little information about the old house. Deciding it was worth a day trip, at the moment he stood in the vast rotunda of the house as Olivia Beaumont's grandfather clock solemnly rang ten times.

Landry had decided to take the house tour before speaking with Callie's friend Jordan Blanchard. He wouldn't be incognito — his popular *Bayou Hauntings* TV series ensured someone would recognize him.

Guide Penny Bishop collected a fee from five of her tourists, and when she came to Landry, she looked at him in surprise.

"I know you! You're Landry Drake, the ghost hunter! What are you doing here?" The others pointed his way; now they recognized him too.

He said he was in the area with some free time and had heard about the house. His answer didn't appear to satisfy her because she asked everyone to wait a moment. She walked away and came back with a man she introduced to Landry as Jordan Blanchard, owner of the house. Jordan

BILL THOMPSON

ordered Penny to begin the tour, and he asked Landry to come to his conference room.

"May I ask what you're doing here?"

Landry thought Callie would have contacted her friend by now, but Jordan seemed taken off guard for some reason.

"I'm sorry. Callie Pilantro gave me your name and number —"

"I see. You had my number. Instead of calling me, you show up unannounced and sign up for a house tour. Were you hoping I'd be away so you could look around without my knowing it?"

Why the hell is this guy becoming belligerent? "The tour is open to the public, and I decided to see the house before I stopped by your office."

"You didn't call, so it made no difference to you whether I was here. You're trespassing and I want you off my premises."

This was getting stranger every minute. "Hold on! You advertise tours of the house, and I paid to take one. That's not trespassing. What's your issue with my being here?"

"*You* hold on! You want to know my issue? I don't want this place on your damned TV show. There's nothing spooky here. It's simply another old house on the Mississippi. I allow tours so the public can see how an antebellum mansion looks. If you put this house on your show —"

"Please let me explain. Callie said strange things have happened here."

"She was way out of line telling you that. I'll speak to her, don't you worry."

Landry remained calm. "May I finish? She described several things that happened here. Not paranormal things, but normal ones. And historically accurate ones, from what little I found on the internet. She said Olivia Beaumont's first husband fell from the third floor to his death in the rotunda, and her second husband disappeared. She never remarried after that, and when she died, she kept the house off the market for fifty years. In 2015 you bought it. If that's all accurate, then there's nothing supernatural going on. So why would I want to put the Arbors on my show? Is there something you aren't telling me?

He ignored the questions. "So why did you come?"

"Two reasons. First, my girlfriend and I enjoyed meeting Callie very much, and I promised her I'd consider visiting your place. Second, I like to nose around in small towns where I haven't been. Now and then I find something interesting. St. Francisville has the Myrtles — that's your town's big claim to ghostly fame. But as Callie pointed out, there are other beautiful homes in West Feliciana Parish, and yours is a real showplace. And there's another thing. If I had a personal encounter with a ghost right here and now, it wouldn't end up on my show unless you agreed to it. We never feature a house without permission."

This seemed to relax Jordan, and he apologized that Landry had missed the tour. "I don't often get upset," he added. "I have two daughters to raise, and I worry about calling attention to the house where they live." He pulled a bill from his wallet and handed it over. "Here's your ten bucks back. Come on; I'll show you around myself."

Jordan took him to the top floor and showed him the house's ornate cupola. The view from the railing down forty feet to the floor was spectacular. He pointed out the spot where Olivia Beaumont's husband Charles Perrault fell through the railing to his death, a place included in the tour because it was a tragic and well-known fact about the Arbors.

"Penny calls it our ghost story," he added, "but it really was just an accident. Ghosts sell tourism, I guess. Facts not so much. You'd know more about that than I."

Several rooms on the third floor — the family's living quarters — were not open to the public, but Landry saw the others, and they went down the broad staircase to the second floor.

"Seven rooms on this floor are open to tourists," Jordan explained as they walked through bedrooms, parlors and dressing rooms. "Most of them have original furnishings from the late nineteenth century. Our guests get a feel for how palatial these old mansions were."

They came to a closed door along the hallway. "What's in there?" Landry asked. As a trained investigator, he saw Jordan's momentary hesitation before he answered.

"It's a room we haven't restored. It's the only room on this floor that isn't open."

"May I see it?"

"No, you may not."

"I hope you don't mind, but seeing an unrestored room would give me a feel for how the place looked in the old days. Just a quick peek —"

"I said it's not possible. There's no key, and I'm not about to ruin a beautiful nineteenth-century door. I've never been in there myself. Come on, I'll show you the ground floor."

"You've never been inside? Don't you wonder what's behind that door? Not knowing would drive me crazy, and I'd end up jimmying the door if I had to."

"Let it go," Jordan snapped. "I see what you're doing. Don't make a mystery out of nothing. It's just a locked door. When we find the key, then we'll know. If there's a ghost inside, I promise I'll call you." His anger was showing through again.

They walked down the wide circular staircase to the rotunda. As Landry followed Jordan to the front part of the house — Jordan's architectural office — he glanced upstairs. He saw something interesting and paused. The door to that room was open now, and in a moment it closed.

Someone had gone inside.

Jordan didn't notice Landry look upstairs. Landry wanted to ask about it, but with Jordan's sudden change, he knew now wasn't the time. Jordan's anger made Landry wonder even more what he was hiding.

With all pretense of hospitality gone, the rest of the tour was over in no time. He quickly showed Landry the office area that had once been a music room, a parlor and a forty-by-twenty living room. Today it was as modern as one would expect a workplace to be. They walked through a remodeled kitchen at the back and saw the remaining rooms on the ground floor that were included in the house tour.

"That's it," Jordan said, guiding Landry toward the front door. Landry decided he had nothing to lose at this point.

"May I ask you a question?"

The man gritted his teeth and tensed his facial muscles. *What is making him so angry?*

"Why not? I'd rather answer questions now than have you go around saying the Arbors is haunted."

"I hope you don't think —"

"What I *think* doesn't matter, Mr. Drake. I'm busy and I'm sure you are too. Ask your question so we can both get back to work."

He pointed up. "That door on the second floor. I saw it open and close a few minutes ago."

"No you didn't. How hard is it to understand? The door hasn't been open since I moved in. Penny's group is gone; there's no one up there anyway."

"I believe you, but I know what I saw. The door was open, and then it closed. Do you mind if we take a look for a moment?"

He shouted, "Do I mind? Yes, I mind! Is that clear enough for you? I tried to be accommodating, and you got your tour. But you just won't stop, will you? That room is off-limits, period. I have two young daughters and my job is to protect them. I'd do anything to keep them safe. Anything. Do you understand?"

"Of course, but what does the safety of your daughters have to do —"

"I don't want the kind of publicity you generate. This is an antebellum home, not a haunted house. There's nothing here for you, and you're no longer welcome. If you so much as mention the Arbors on TV, you'll hear from my lawyer. Do you understand?"

Landry looked at him in amazement. The man was so upset he was shaking.

Jordan opened the front door, ushered Landry out, and slammed it behind him.

CHAPTER SIX

That was the worst dressing-down Callie ever received. Jordan's attitude astonished her; he'd never so much as raised his voice before and now he seemed furious.

"What the hell gives you the right to tell someone about what's going on at my house? Not what *really* happened, but your damned *theory* about it!"

"Calm down. I'm sorry; I didn't think you'd mind —"

"You didn't think at all! You know who Landry Drake is. He's a reporter for a TV station. Not just a reporter — a ghost hunter, for God's sake! I'm trying to do damage control up here, and you of all people sic him on me. You told him there's something supernatural at the Arbors. Why are you trying to stir up trouble for me? Stop it, Callie. Leave me alone!"

The phone went dead and Callie stared at it in disbelief. Jordan was not only her architect, but as he said, they were friends. If she'd had any idea he would feel this way, she would never have told Landry and Cate about the Arbors. But she had, and she'd also suggested Landry call him. That had clearly been a mistake.

Her phone rang. It was Landry.

"Hi. I think I know why you're calling. I just spoke with Jordan. To be more precise, he hung up on me after a two-minute shouting session — his, not mine. I hardly got a word in."

Landry said he'd heard from Jordan too. "I'm sorry I caused all this. Visiting his house was a mistake, and I got an ass-chewing myself. He emphatically said that he wasn't interested in talking to me. I think his exact words were, 'If you set foot on my property again, I'm calling the cops.' I got the message. My stopping by for a chat wasn't such a good idea."

Landry apologized again, but Callie told him to let it go. "Jordan's a nice guy. He's also a good friend, and he'll get over it. I think he's up to his you-know-what in alligators, and I should have thought things through before stirring the pot, especially now."

CHAPTER SEVEN

Callie, Landry and Cate sat at a window table at Café Pontalba in the French Quarter. The forecast called for intermittent showers that afternoon. When the first drops began, they watched street artists remove their works from the wrought-iron fences around Jackson Square as tourists sought shelter in nearby bars and restaurants.

When she called to ask them to join her for lunch, Callie had said, "I'm paying. No discussion. I owe you one for your experience at the Arbors."

They were glad to see her again so soon. Despite their five-year age difference, Cate and Callie had quickly become friends, and Landry felt a camaraderie too. She had inherited a decaying old mansion, but with dogged determination and some fortunate breaks, she had transformed it into a beautiful B&B that tourists and locals alike visited.

As they dived into a plate of oysters on the half shell, Callie disclosed an ulterior motive for asking them to lunch.

"I talked to Anne-Marie," she said, "and she agreed I should tell you our story."

Landry looked up in surprise and almost dropped the oyster shell in his hand. "Anne-Marie? Your resident ghost? You talked to her about us?"

"I certainly did! You're in the ghost business, so why does that surprise you?"

He struggled to find an answer. Most of the hauntings he'd investigated involved malevolent spirits — friendly ghosts like Casper didn't raise ratings like evil ones did.

"I guess it seems odd talking about conversing with an apparition."

"I don't see her as often as I did, but she saved my life. I didn't mention it, but she was there the other night when we all sat on the veranda. She stood at the far end of the porch and smiled at me. I knew she approved of you two because I've seen how she reacts when she doesn't."

Now that they were back together, Callie felt comfortable enough to ask them back to Beau Rivage. Maybe Anne-Marie would appear, she said. She couldn't promise a sighting, but at least two other people had seen her. One was her deceased uncle Willard. The other was Mark Streater, the man who had disappeared after killing her uncle.

"I'm sorry that your trip to St. Francisville was a waste of time," she continued. "I understand that Jordan wants to protect his children, but I wish he hadn't acted that way. Since he lost his wife, Claire, he's been protective of the girls. They're all he has left. I'll tell you this — there are strange things going on at the Arbors. He told me that himself, but if he wants to keep his ghost a secret, that's his call. Maybe I can make it up to you by introducing you to a wonderful spirit at my place."

Landry replied with his standard "no guarantees" spiel, but she laughed and waved him off. She didn't need publicity, she assured him. There was plenty now that the secrets of her mansion were on public display. All she wanted — presuming Anne-Marie cooperated — was to introduce Landry and Cate to her friend. His curiosity aroused, Landry checked his calendar; they chose a Friday afternoon two weeks away when they could come for the weekend.

Callie wanted time alone with her new friends and once the date was set, she cut off reservations for that weekend. One couple had already made theirs, an older man and his wife from Tennessee, who were there when Landry and Cate arrived around five.

They sat once again on the front porch, the Atchafalaya River just across the broad expanse of lawn. The other couple joined in casual conversation and wine. They didn't recognize Landry, and he found it refreshing to be anonymous.

Landry said he was a reporter for a New Orleans TV station and introduced Cate as his friend, a medical records specialist from Galveston. The man and his wife were Warren and Judy, retired professors from the University of Tennessee on a road trip through Louisiana. Whenever they could, they overnighted in old houses.

Warren said he'd looked up Beau Rivage on the internet and asked if they might hear about her ghost. Callie related the story of the tragic death of a ten-year-old girl in 1863, a Yankee soldier shot dead for eating the dead child's birthday cake, and a house spared from destruction by a remorseful Union soldier.

"Does she ever appear?" he asked. Landry and Cate were interested in Callie's casual answer.

"Some folks who own houses down here in Cajun country will promise you a ghost if you pay to spend the night. That's not how it is at Beau Rivage. Do I believe my ghost is real? Yes, I do. Have guests ever seen her? Not that I've heard."

"Have *you* ever seen her?" Judy asked.

"When I inherited this place, it was in sad shape. After my grandmother died, it was vacant for months. I spent many a night here and even rode out a hurricane in the dark. The wind whistled through every crack, the house creaked and groaned like an old man getting out of bed, and there were lots of things that appeared in the shadows. Some might have been real, and others not. That's a long explanation to say yes, the house has strange things that happen here and, yes, I've seen her."

"Does she haunt the bedrooms?" Judy giggled. "Warren, I'm not sure what I'd do if I woke up with a ghost in the room!"

"You have nothing to worry about," Callie replied with a smile. "Let me refill your wineglasses. It'll be dark soon, and Annie will want to serve dinner by seven."

While Callie gave her new guests a tour, Landry and Cate stayed on the porch, watching shadows encroach on the trees and the river as darkness fell. Forty-five minutes later the five of them sat around Henri Arceneaux's antique dining room table, enjoying a wonderful pork tenderloin served with grits, biscuits and gravy. As if they needed more, Annie created flambéed cherries jubilee.

Warren and his wife went upstairs after a strawberry dessert. Callie asked Landry and Cate to join her in the library. She opened the hidden door — they'd seen it on their last trip, but it was fascinating to watch the bookcase swing back, revealing the secret room Callie's great-great-grandfather Henri Arceneaux had included when he built Beau Rivage.

It was here that Callie had found Henri's private journal and the answers to many of Beau Rivage's secrets. It was here that she had opened a strongbox filled with Confederate currency, worthless when Henri tried to convert it after the Civil War but today worth a fortune to currency collectors. Her ancestor's cache of money from a defeated South had saved Callie from financial ruin. She'd kept a few bills to display and sold the rest for almost two million dollars, enough money to do everything she needed to make Beau Rivage a showplace.

Callie said the real reason she'd brought them back to the library was to show them something tourists never saw. She pointed to a recess next to the massive fireplace — a place so well concealed they'd have never noticed it. There was another set of stairs, a small one with only three or four risers, that went down.

"This stairway leads to the yard through a small door hidden behind the shrubbery. When I found it, I thought I knew how Anne-Marie came into the house without using the doors." She laughed. "Now I know better. Doors aren't an impediment for her!"

Landry asked if this was where Callie expected they might see the child, and she shook her head. Anne-Marie could appear anywhere, but typically she came to the veranda.

"I wanted to show you this stairway because this is where she and I escaped from Mark Streater. Anne-Marie saved my life. She means a great deal to me. When she's here, she's real. I won't commercialize her, Landry. I want you to meet her. If you're lucky enough to do that, I want a promise you won't disclose what you've seen unless I approve it."

"You have my word."

Callie poured three more wines in the kitchen. She flipped off the lights and they went back to the porch, sitting in darkness as the light of a crescent moon illuminated the river and shimmered on the dewy grass.

"It's so peaceful here." Cate sighed. "I can see why you enjoy it so much."

"It was worth fighting for. There was a time I thought it would never happen —"

She paused and her voice dropped to a whisper. "There she is. Standing in the tree line about a hundred yards from the house. Do you see her?"

They could see something, but if Callie hadn't pointed her out, they would have overlooked it. Cate concentrated and said, "Is she wearing a light blue dress?"

"Always."

The figure was wispy and hard to see. Landry wasn't sure it was there. It could be moonbeams in the trees, he suggested, but Callie smiled and shook her head.

"That's where she often stands. I know it's hard to see her in the dark, but that's my Anne-Marie." From the porch, they watched Callie walk down the stairs. It was a bewitching scene: a twenty-first-century woman walking through the moonlit grass and a child dressed in old-fashioned clothing strolling to meet her.

They walked up the stairs to the veranda; Callie sat while Anne-Marie stood silently beside her.

The vision captivated Landry. He'd experienced some amazing, terrifying and bizarre things as an investigative reporter, but this was truly a first, and he could hardly believe it was happening.

"Anne-Marie, these are my friends Landry and Cate."

As she gazed into their eyes, hers blazed with an intensity that caused them to look away. "The lady wanted babies," she said in a low monotone.

"What lady?" Callie asked.

"She wanted them, but they died."

"May I ask her something?" Landry said, but Callie shook her head.

"Is it the woman I told my friends about? Miss Olivia, the lady at the Arbors?"

"Are you talking about the ghost?" Landry interjected, and Anne-Marie knitted her brows.

"We don't use that word," Callie whispered. "She doesn't like it. Let me do this, please."

She looked at the child. "I'm not sure what you meant. Is it Miss Olivia you're talking about?"

Without a word, Anne-Marie walked out into the yard. Within moments she disappeared into the shadows.

"I'm sorry —" Landry began, but Callie shushed him.

"Don't worry about it. She's odd — I know that. Many times you can't understand what she says, and she comes and goes at will. The only thing I've seen that upsets her is that word — the word *ghost*. I don't know what she considers herself, but that's a term she doesn't like at all!"

Comfortable with Landry and Cate now, she told them the background about Maria, the child who had drowned on her birthday, why her casket was placed into a wall instead of the cemetery, and how Anne-Marie was involved. Landry was fascinated, but he refrained from asking questions. It was clear how much the child meant to Callie, even if she was a spirit.

They left on Saturday afternoon. Landry had seen his share of paranormal manifestations, but the things he'd learned at Beau Rivage were fascinating. The highlight was something they hadn't expected — seeing Anne-Marie. Landry considered it the most interesting thing he'd ever experienced.

At the station on Monday, Landry searched for information on Olivia Beaumont and her children. He found very little about Olivia and nothing about offspring. Anne-Marie's cryptic comments had been hard to follow. Maybe he'd misunderstood her.

He turned his attention to Jordan Blanchard. Landry had shown up at the Arbors, which made Jordan so angry he'd yelled at his friend Callie. Why did he do that?

Maybe because he was hiding something.

CHAPTER EIGHT

Ellie and Violette were eight-year-old identical twins. Every time Jordan looked at his daughters, he saw his wife, Claire. She'd been gone four years, but she lived on through her girls. Their blond hair, blue eyes, and saucy dispositions were Claire all over again, and although he was sometimes wistful, he loved how much they were like their mother.

Vi was the serious, methodical twin while Ellie was the impulsive one. Always the risk-taker, her sister constantly tried to curb Ellie's penchant for coming up with things that got them both into trouble.

Although they loved school and did well in the second grade at Bains Elementary, like all children, they lived for the three p.m. bell on Friday that signaled the weekend.

The girls had the run of the upper floors at the Arbors. Other than the kitchen, the first floor was off-limits; that was where their dad's architectural office was, and his people worked Saturday mornings. If the kids were quiet and didn't bug their father, they could play and explore upstairs or outdoors or even in town.

Everywhere but that one room.

Since it was Saturday morning, they slept late. Vi stretched and yawned and looked over at the other twin bed. Ellie glanced at her sister and said, "About time you got up. Wanna know what we're doing today?"

"I just woke up. Leave me alone for a minute."

Ellie hopped out of bed. "Okay, sleepyhead. You'll be excited when I tell you!" She opened their bedroom door and padded down the hall to the bathroom. In a minute Vi heard the shower turn on.

She stayed in bed, glad not to have to jump up, get dressed for school, and run downstairs to eat breakfast and catch the bus. Her sister always got up first so she'd get the hottest water. Ellie made everything a competition — even being first in the shower — and Vi accepted it without a word. She couldn't out-argue, outwit or outlast her sister when Ellie got on a tear about something. It was easier to be quiet than to get in a fight, and conflict seemed to be what Ellie enjoyed most.

As usual, Ellie already had today's plans decided. It would be nice if she'd ask once in a while what Vi wanted to do, but Ellie ran the show and Vi went along with it.

After Vi finished in the bathroom, they crept down two floors and went to the kitchen in the back of the house, where a girl named Lauren, who worked for their dad, was refilling her coffee cup. She was always nice to them, and they talked a minute before she returned to work. Ellie made toast while Vi got out jam, peanut butter and honey. As they ate, Vi asked what the plan was for today.

"Exploring."

"Exploring what?"

"I want to look in the locked room."

"Ellie! You know we can't do that! Dad said —"

Her impetuous sister interrupted. "Dad says lots of things. Dad said we couldn't go into the woods, but if we hadn't, we wouldn't have found that cemetery, would we?"

"No, but I thought it was weird there. I got scared, and so did you, except you won't say so! You always have to act like you're so brave."

Her sister laughed. "You're a scaredy-cat. I'm going to look in that locked room. Don't you wonder what's in there? We can open the door, look inside for one minute, and close it."

Right, Vi thought. Things were never as simple as Ellie said. "We can't get in. The door's locked. You know that. It's always locked."

Ellie's voice became as conspiratorial as an eight-year-old's could be. "I found where Dad keeps the keys to everything in the whole house!"

"Ellie! We can't do that! You're going to end up in big trouble!"

"Not me. *We.* We're going in there together. And anyway, he won't find out. We'll take the keys, peek inside, and put them back. He'll never know. Haven't you wondered what's in that room and why Dad won't let us go there? It's the only place in the house we can't see, and I want to know why."

"I'm not going."

As usual, Vi ended up going along with the plan. As they tiptoed past the office, they could hear people at work. Ellie opened the door to a closet that held brooms, mops and a shelf full of cleaning supplies. They stepped inside, pulled the door shut, and turned on the light. Ellie pointed to a nail in the wall high above them. A ring with a lot of keys hung on it.

"How do you know the right key's on there?" Vi whispered.

"I don't, but look how many there are. I'll get them down." There was a six-foot ladder standing against one wall, but the room was small and they couldn't open it with the door closed. She found a step stool instead, moved it into place, and turned a tall bucket upside down on top. "Help me get up here," she ordered her sister.

"You can't climb that! You'll fall!"

"Shut up!" Ellie whispered, grabbing her sister's arm for balance and climbing up on the teetering pyramid. Just as she grabbed the keys and stuck them in her pocket, a mouse ran across the floor in front of Vi, and she screamed.

Ellie jerked backwards and the shaky tower started to fall. Ellie fell against the door and ended up in the hallway with a thud. Vi screamed again, and seconds later their father ran around the corner and knelt beside Ellie.

"Are you hurt? What are you all doing?"

Ellie was okay; her lower lip quivered for a moment, but she didn't cry. She stood up and declared herself just fine.

Sobbing, Vi babbled, "Dad, this wasn't my idea, honest. I told her she could get hurt. Tell him, Ellie!"

Ellie glared at her sister. As clever as she was, Ellie had never outright lied to her dad. Vi had ratted her out, and she struggled to invent a story that would make everything all right.

"We were looking for something in the closet."

"In the janitor's closet? What were you looking for?"

"Uh, I spilled something upstairs. We can clean it up. Come on, Vi."

A tiny tear rolled down Vi's cheek, and her father said, "Why don't you tell me what's going on, honey?"

"She took a ring of keys. Ellie wants to go in that locked room."

Jordan frowned. "Is that right, Ellie?"

She lowered her head, took the key ring from her pocket, and handed it to him. "Yes, sir."

"I'm disappointed in you both. You know that room is off-limits to everybody. It makes me sad that you told me a story, Ellie. No matter how bad things are, you must always tell the truth."

Now they both were crying, and he hugged them. "I love you girls more than anything in the world. If you wanted to see the room so much, why didn't you ask me? I would have told you the truth. I've never seen it myself. There's no key, so no one can get inside."

"Don't you wonder what's in there?"

"Sure I do. The day we bought the house, I tried every key on that ring, and nothing worked. Remember I told you that a lady owned the house and she died a long, long time ago? She wrote something I had to agree to when I bought the house. I can't disturb anything in that room."

That didn't satisfy Ellie. "Come on, Dad. Aren't you still curious? Couldn't you take the door off or something?"

"I guess I could have gotten a crowbar and knocked it down," he answered with a smile. "But that wouldn't be fair. Maybe someday the key will turn up. If it does, then we can see what's inside. All of us, not just you two! Until then, leave it alone, Ellie. That's an order! Now come on; I'll fix you some hot chocolate."

CHAPTER NINE

Ellie sat straight up in bed with the covers pulled up to her chin. Her little body shuddered.

It was just a dream.

It *was* just a dream, she told herself again. It hadn't really happened. It couldn't have.

Beads of perspiration gathered on her forehead as she recalled it. In the dream — because that was what it had been, just a dream — a scratchy sound woke her up. The night-light across the room illuminated the door that went into the hallway. The doorknob was turning ever so slowly, making a creaking sound.

The door opened and a person came in. It was a woman — a tall, thin lady wearing a black dress that hung to the floor and had long sleeves. Her dress reminded Ellie of the witch from *The Wizard of Oz*, but she wasn't ugly or bent over or riding a broom. She was pretty, but her face wasn't friendly. She was frowning and looked mad. Ellie recalled that she stood very straight. The woman was old enough to be a grandmother, but Ellie didn't think she'd be a nice one.

The woman was in their bedroom, at least in her dream. Ellie glanced over at Vi's bed in hopes she'd seen the woman too, but Vi was sound asleep. It had seemed completely real, but it couldn't have happened. Dad locked the outside doors every night and then he double-checked them. Nobody was in the house but them. It was just a dream, even though it felt so real. She wanted to stop thinking about it, but she couldn't get it out of her head.

Ellie was the twin who didn't play with dolls, didn't like make-believe stuff like tea parties and dress-ups, but instead wanted to explore things. Usually it was stuff she shouldn't be exploring, but that was how Ellie Blanchard was. Her sister was just the opposite, and that worked fine. Ellie told herself she couldn't have seen a lady standing at the foot of her bed. The door was closed and no one was in here except her and her sister. It had been a dream.

Shaking off goosebumps, she fluffed her pillows, lay back, and thought more about it.

The lady spoke to me. She said something important. What did she say?

Ellie struggled to recall; then it came to her. The lady asked if Ellie wondered what was in the locked room.

I dreamed that because I got caught taking the keys today. That's what the dream was about. Plus, I fell asleep thinking very hard about where the key might be. No wonder I had a dream like that. But who was the woman?

Ellie didn't go back to sleep for a long time. She went room by room in her head, as she had done earlier, thinking of places where that key might be. They'd been here two years and Dad hadn't found it yet, but she was determined that she would.

She awoke when rays of the morning sun peeked through the curtains in their third-floor bedroom and fell upon her face.

"Vi! Vi, wake up!"

Her sister groaned, turned over and grunted.

"Wake up. I want to ask you something!"

Vi stretched and groaned. "Why do you always have to wake me up on weekends? What do you want anyway?"

"Did you see someone in our room last night?"

"What are you talking about? There was nobody in here. Right?"

"I had a dream that someone turned the doorknob and opened the door. It was a tall woman all dressed in black, and she walked to the end of my bed. Did you see her?"

"You woke me up for *that*?" She put the pillow over her head and snuggled back under the covers.

Ellie jumped up, flopped down on Vi's bed, and pulled off the pillow. "Listen. This is important. She asked me if I wanted to see what was in the locked room!"

"It was a dream, Ellie. We don't have a key, remember?"

"Listen to me for a minute. *Was* it a dream? Think hard, Vi. Did you see her too? Maybe it really happened!"

Vi sat up and frowned. "Stop it, Ellie! Stop trying to scare me. Why are you doing this? Nobody came in our room last night. Just stop it."

Over the next few days Ellie couldn't stop thinking about what she'd seen. It hadn't felt like a dream, even though it probably was. She'd spent the day thinking about that locked door, and she must have dreamed about it. At last she forgot about the incident.

Four nights later it happened again.

CHAPTER TEN

Ellie's eyes popped open as she heard the knob creaking. As before, the door opened and the figure in black entered quietly. She walked to the foot of Ellie's bed.

Who…who are you, ma'am?

Do you want to know what's inside the locked room?

Yes, ma'am. I want to know. But are you real, or am I dreaming?

Ellie realized they weren't actually talking. She was *thinking* the words, and the lady was responding with thoughts, but it felt like they were talking to each other.

Weird, she thought, surprised she wasn't afraid. The lady looked a little scary and was very tall, but Ellie didn't feel threatened by her. She only wanted to tell Ellie how to get into the room.

Am I dreaming? Ellie asked in her mind, but the woman didn't answer her.

My father's desk sits in the master bedroom downstairs. There is a secret panel in the back of a drawer. Look there.

Yes, ma'am. I know the desk and I'll look there. Who are you?

This is my house.

It's our house —

This is MY house! MINE! The unspoken words rang angry and harsh in Ellie's mind.

The lady turned and left. Ellie thought she was floating rather than walking, but for some reason that didn't seem odd.

She laid her head on the pillow, wishing she could go downstairs and look in the desk right now, but if Dad woke up, he'd be mad. This had to wait until morning.

From the bed next to hers came a quiet voice. "Aren't you going to look for the key?"

Ellie jumped up and turned on the lamp that sat on the nightstand between their beds. "You heard her too! But how? She wasn't really talking, was she?"

Vi said, "I woke up when she came in. I could hear you both talking in my head. What is she, Ellie? I feel like this should scare me, but I'm not afraid. What did she mean that this is her house?"

"I don't know about all that. But since we're up, do you want to go see what's in the secret panel in the desk?"

"Dad'll kill us…"

"Vi, I know you want to go look. And if we're quiet, Dad won't wake up."

They crept out into the hall and tiptoed to the broad, circular staircase. The house looked different at night, kind of creepy and a little scary. Moonlight shone through the stained-glass windows in the dome above them, casting eerie shadows everywhere. They glanced over the railing into the rotunda forty feet below. Someone had left a light on in the office, and a faint yellowish glow illuminated the parquet floor. Theirs was a huge old house that was frightening at night.

Ellie and Vi gripped each other's hands as they hurried down the second-floor hallway to what had once been the master bedroom. It was next door to the locked room, and it

54

was full of furniture that Dad said had been there for more than a hundred years.

They opened the door slowly so the hinges wouldn't creak. The room was pitch-black inside.

"Go upstairs and get the flashlight in the nightstand," Ellie ordered, but Vi shook her head.

"No way I'm going back up there by myself! I'm scared!"

Ellie gave her a snort of disgust, quietly shut the door, and flipped the light switch. An ornate chandelier that once held gas lamps had been retrofitted for electricity long ago, and the room was flooded with light.

Good thing Dad's sleeping upstairs, Ellie thought as she walked to an oversized rolltop desk with eight drawers. She and Vi opened one drawer after another, but they were all empty. And there was no secret panel.

"What am I missing?" Ellie mused out loud, and Vi, the thinker of the duo, suggested taking the drawers out. That worked; in the back of a middle drawer they found an inch-deep hiding place. Tucked inside it was a large rusty metal key.

Ellie stuck it in her nightgown pocket and told Vi to put everything back. They went to their room.

"Why didn't we go to try the key?" Vi asked.

"It's too dangerous to do it in the middle of the night. Nobody's opened that door in years, and who knows what's on the other side? Let's wait until tomorrow." Ellie admitted that she also had the creeps after finding a key right where someone in a dream said it would be.

"Can I sleep in your bed?" she asked Vi, who was thrilled that her always-brave sister wasn't so brave after all. She had been terrified during their little journey downstairs, and she was glad to know Ellie was scared too.

They snuggled under the blanket and talked about the mysterious lady in black. She was weird, but something about her seemed friendly.

Ellie whispered, "It wasn't a dream, then, was it? It couldn't have been, because we found the key."

"I guess not." Vi yawned. She turned her back to Ellie and was asleep in seconds.

Ellie's mind churned with ideas and possibilities. She wondered if they would see the woman again. She forced herself to sleep so the morning would come more quickly.

Vi was gone when Ellie awoke. She heard the shower and knew she had a few minutes until it was her turn, so she picked up the key and turned it over and over, getting tingly at the thought of putting it into the lock. At last that door would open, and everyone would know what was behind it.

Vi came into the bedroom wrapped in a towel and got dressed. Ellie asked again if her sister had heard the words, since they weren't spoken aloud.

"I already told you I heard both of you. How else would I know you should look for the key?"

"Who do you think she is?"

Vi paused. "She's not real, right? At least I don't think she is."

"But she opened and closed the door. If she was a ghost, wouldn't she float through the wall or something?"

Vi said, "I always thought you could see through ghosts. I couldn't see through her, so maybe she *was* real." That thought made Vi nervous, and she told Ellie it scared her that someone could get into the house at night and come in the bedroom. "We have to tell Dad about this," she said, and Ellie agreed.

More than anything, Ellie wanted to go downstairs, put the key in the lock, open the door, and see what was inside. But she knew better. Dad said that room was off-limits, so they went downstairs to find him.

"Good morning, sunshines!" he said as they peeked around the door to his office. He was sitting behind his desk, drinking coffee and studying a large drawing. "What are you guys up to?"

Ellie told him about the woman. She explained that the apparition had visited their bedroom a few days ago and then again last night. "It was a dream, but it felt real. Know what I mean?"

He nodded.

Vi chimed in. "Dad, it was a dream, wasn't it? Nobody can come in our bedroom at night, can they?"

"No, honey. And I unlocked the doors myself this morning. They were locked tight all night long."

"Then how did a dream person tell Ellie where to find something?"

"I'm not sure. Ellie, what did she say?"

"She said this was her house, and she told me where to find the key. You know that desk in the master bedroom? She said it was her father's desk. One of the drawers had a secret place in the back. We found it just where she said!" She put the old key on his desk.

Jordan forced a smile, but he was concerned. Ellie had dreamed about a woman who owned his house, who said her father's desk was in the master bedroom. That could only be Olivia Beaumont. What was that about?

"A person in a dream told you where it was? Are you sure?"

Ellie screamed, "Dad, I'm not lying!"

It didn't make sense, but here they stood with an old key. He put his concern aside and said, "Well, how about we take a look behind that door?"

They screamed in delight and scampered up the stairs. He got there a moment later and handed the key to Ellie.

"You get to do it, since the lady told you where it was."

Grinning from ear to ear, Ellie inserted the key into the hole and tried to turn it. It moved a little but not all the way. She used all the strength she could muster. Finally her dad fetched a can of WD-40, sprayed the lock, and tried it himself.

The key turned with a resounding click as the bolt withdrew. Jordan stood back and said, "Ellie, go for it!"

She turned the knob and pushed the door open. Hinges that hadn't moved in over five decades responded with loud creaks, and they stepped into the room. Except for light from the hallway behind them, it was totally black. Jordan found a light switch on the wall beside the door and flipped it on.

In a testament to 1950s technology, one of twelve bulbs in the ornate chandelier fourteen feet above them flickered on, struggling to do its job after more than fifty years. The effort lasted only a moment until it gave up the ghost, as its companions had done long before.

Jordan went downstairs and returned with a powerful halogen work light from the janitorial closet. He set it up and soon they could see.

He walked to some tall windows across the room and took hold of the drapes. He gave a mighty tug on one, and its heavy fabric, untouched for all those years, ripped into long shreds that hung to the floor as clouds of dust flew into the air. The girls laughed, but their laughter turned to alarm when a chilling breeze swept through the room.

"What was that, Daddy? I'm cold! Is it coming from the window?"

"No," he told them. It was a balmy spring morning. That blast of frigid air was something else. He was more careful pulling the other drapes apart, and at last rays of sunshine filtered through the grimy windows. Spiderwebs ran along the frames, and a layer of dust covered everything in the room, but as the girls looked around, they forgot about the cold air as they stared in wonder at a place locked in a time capsule. A room for children. A nursery.

Vi cried, "Look! Two cribs, Daddy! Just like Ellie and I used to have!" She ran across the room and touched the lacy linens hanging on the side of one crib. A puff of dust rose into the air, and she asked her father why they were dirty.

"We're the first people to come into this room in fifty years. That's longer than I've been alive!"

His statement astounded them. To a kid of eight, adults are the oldest things imaginable, and it amazed them that this room had been closed off since before their dad was born.

"Look at this great table!" Ellie squealed, brushing away the dust from a child's table that sat in front of a massive fireplace. "It's all about *Alice in Wonderland*!" She and Vi pulled out four small wooden chairs, each one gaily decorated with scenes from the Mad Hatter's tea party, and sat down. "Daddy, can this be our playroom? Please say yes!"

Vi chimed in. "Please, Daddy!"

Jordan hadn't known what was behind the door, but this was the last thing he expected to see. He knew little about Olivia Beaumont, whose grandfather built the house in 1850. The locals said she was reclusive and domineering and she stood straight and tall when she walked through the town. Frightened children ran away when they saw her coming.

There seemed to be no heirs. She died in 1965, leaving money for upkeep and instructions that the house not be sold for fifty years. Today as he stood in the locked room, he thought about the other deed restriction, her directive that no one could "disturb" this room.

If Olivia had no offspring, then why did this room exist? She'd grown up here herself, but these weren't her toys. They were old, but no child had touched anything in this room. One thing was unmistakable. This was a nursery, and it was meant for two children. There were two cribs, a child's table and chairs, dozens of stuffed animals and dolls, and even a brand-new, 1950s-vintage Radio Flyer red tricycle.

What happened to the two children? Had someone taken them from their domineering mother? Did something terrible happen to them?

The girls brought him out of his thoughts. "Daddy! Answer us! Can this be our toy room?" He laughed as Vi tugged on his sleeve and Ellie danced around him.

"Okay, here's the deal. The lady who owned the house before us left some instructions. It sounds like we can't make big changes or sell the furniture or anything like that. I think I'll ask Mrs. Patrick to give it a good cleaning. Maybe I could switch out the drapes since they're so brittle that I've already torn one —"

Another rush of cold air swept around them for a few seconds. Vi began to cry as Ellie squeezed her father's hand.

"What's going on, Dad? Why did it get so cold again?"

"I don't know, but it's gone now." Although it seemed the chilling breeze happened in response to his comment about changing the drapes, he kept his thoughts to himself. There was no need to scare his kids when they were so excited about what they'd found.

"Okay, here's what we'll do about the room. I don't want you guys playing in here until Mrs. Patrick cleans it up. All this dust isn't good for you, so until then I'm going to lock the door and no one comes in. Once she's finished, I guess it can be your playroom."

They were thrilled and Vi asked if he was going to let the tourists see it. He said he didn't know, and he wondered if he'd said yes, would another cold breeze have swept through the nursery?

CHAPTER ELEVEN

It was a good thing Vi and Ellie had a week of school to pass the time, because they could hardly wait until Mrs. Patrick came on Saturday. All of them went to the second floor and waited until their dad unlocked the door and opened it.

The room was dark once again, and the girls voiced his unspoken thought.

Ellie asked, "Who closed the curtains? We left them open."

"I don't know what happened," he replied, trying to appear unconcerned. Something about this room made him uneasy. "I guess a breeze blew them shut."

"Come on, Dad. You locked the door and said no one could come in. *You* came in, didn't you? *You* closed the curtains, right?"

"Yeah, you caught me," he lied. "I closed them to keep the sun from hurting all this old furniture and stuff." That satisfied the girls, but it damned sure didn't answer his concerns. This room was creepy as hell. Something wasn't right. The curtains hadn't closed themselves, so how did it happen?

He opened them and showed the ripped drape to Mrs. Patrick, who said she could repair the heavy fabric without taking it down. The job wouldn't be perfect, but it would do until he decided to replace them.

She spent most of her day cleaning the nursery. Jordan hauled the ladder upstairs and replaced the bulbs in the chandelier while the housekeeper vacuumed, dusted and scrubbed every surface. By five p.m. the room was as presentable as could be without bringing in a professional crew.

Despite nagging questions, Jordan couldn't deny his kids the pleasure they'd been waiting for all week. He declared the nursery ready for occupancy by two thrilled girls. They ran inside, scurried from place to place, opened doors to the armoire and breakfront, and discovered toys, a child's china tea service for twelve, and drawers packed with baby blankets, infant gowns and sleepers.

"Who were those clothes for?" Mrs. Patrick asked.

Jordan shrugged. "I have no idea. You grew up in St. Francisville. Did you ever hear that Olivia Beaumont had children?"

Everyone in town knew about Olivia Beaumont, including Mrs. Patrick. The woman had been eccentric, and she hadn't seemed to have any friends. One husband had died right here in this house, and the other one left town, but she'd never heard a word about children.

"So if she never had kids, who was all this stuff for? Apparently Olivia was single when she inherited the house from her father in 1931. Later on she got married, and then her first husband died here."

Ellie cried, "Here in the house? Someone *died* in our *house*?"

He'd made a huge mistake. This was no conversation for his children to hear. They were preoccupied with everything new they were discovering, but his precocious daughter Ellie, ears always tuned to what adults were saying, had overheard his comment.

"The man who owned the house fell down and hurt himself so much he died," Jordan said, understating Charles Perrault's fatal fall through the third-floor railing.

"Wow," Vi said. "Where did he die? It wasn't in here, was it?"

"No, not in here, and don't worry about it. It was an accident that happened a long, long time ago. You girls need to get comfortable in your new playroom!"

There was a closet filled with boxes of dolls, books and clothing. A playpen was ready for setup so a baby could use it. Everything was brand new — it seemed nothing had been touched once it was placed where it lay today.

Vi got the china tea set out and arranged four place settings on the *Alice in Wonderland* table. "I'm Alice," she said with a curtsy. "Would you care for a cup of tea?"

"I need to finish up a few things downstairs, and I'm sure Mrs. Patrick is ready to go home after hours in this dark, dusty old room. You girls pour the tea and I'll see you in a while."

As he and the housekeeper reached the stairway, he heard a creaking sound. He turned and watched the nursery door close. It surprised him that the girls were comfortable enough to close the door this soon.

As was her custom on Saturdays, Mrs. Patrick had left a casserole in the oven. She had never asked if he wanted one — she did it one day, and everyone raved about it so much that it became routine. In reality it was the best meal they got all week. Jordan could cook, but it wasn't something he enjoyed. He gave his kids nutritious meals, but everyone loved Mrs. Patrick's Saturday night dinners and leftovers on Sunday.

Jordan answered a few emails, worked on a proposal he had to submit next week, and when he looked up, he saw the sun had gone down. He glanced at his watch — the girls had been up there for two hours without a peep, and that was unusual for them. Ordinarily they'd have been bugging him, since on Saturday afternoons they were allowed to come into the office whenever they wanted, so they must be having fun.

He took out the casserole and dished chicken and rice on their plates to let it cool. He walked upstairs and stood quietly by the door, listening.

He heard conversation, but the thick door muffled the words. It sounded like Vi and Ellie were talking to each other, but then he heard something else. Another voice. Maybe a deeper one.

He opened the door and stepped inside. His daughters looked up in surprise; they were sitting at the table by the fireplace. Three chairs were there; the fourth was against a wall. An empty chair rested between the ones the girls sat in.

"What's going on, kiddos?"

"Hi, Daddy! We're having a tea party! Want to come?"

"Can I sit in that empty chair?"

"No, silly." Vi giggled. "That's our friend's chair. Pull up the other one."

"Who's your friend?"

Ellie answered quickly, "No one, really. Vi just made it up."

"No I didn't!" But she stopped talking when her sister gave her a stern glance.

Jordan let it go. Kids will be kids, and imaginary friends are part of every childhood. "Ready for dinner? You guys have been in here for a long time."

"Sure! This is the funnest room we've ever had, Daddy. Thanks for letting us play in here!" Vi seemed so happy that it made his heart feel good. Ellie too; they were having a blast in their new room, and it seemed as if the locked door had hidden something his daughters would be enjoying a great deal. God knew they needed something to keep them occupied in this drafty old mansion. Now they had it.

At dinner they laughed and whispered to each other, and their antics made Jordan smile too. Since Claire had died four years ago, there had been enough tears to last a lifetime, and it was good to see them so happy.

Between mouthfuls of dinner, Vi said, "That man who died in the house was a bad man, Daddy."

Ellie slapped her arm and told her to shut up.

"Ellie! Stop hitting your sister! What do you mean, Vi? How do you know that?"

Ellie was staring a hole through Vi, and her sister hung her head and said, "I don't know. I just made it up, I guess."

"Vi, I don't think you're telling me the truth. Come on, how do you know about the man who died?"

"We were just having a tea party. That lady came too, and she told me."

Ellie interrupted to say the lady was make-believe. They were the only ones at the tea party.

"Is that right, honey?"

Vi averted her eyes and nodded. "I made it up."

The children got their first real parental lecture. Ellie had lied once before, and Jordan said telling the truth was the most important thing they could do. He loved them, and part of his job as a dad was to take care of them, and they had to always tell him everything. They sat with their hands in their laps, lips quivering and eyes downcast, as he said how much he trusted them. He said make-believe was fine, and they could play that way anytime they wanted, but when he asked them something, the answer had to be true, not made up.

After he'd tucked the kids into bed, Jordan went down to the nursery. The door was closed again, although he had left it open earlier. He tested it to see if it would close by itself, but it seemed too heavy for that. He looked around the room and wondered what this place was about. Everything had been lovingly prepared for children — two of them, it seemed — but until today, no child had touched a single thing in this room.

Jordan clicked off the overhead light, walked into the hall, and climbed the stairs. He passed the girls' room and paused at the door, but there was no sound from inside. That didn't surprise him; after all that excitement, he was sure they'd sleep well tonight.

His bedroom was next to theirs. As he opened the door, he heard a faint scraping noise. He knew what it was because he'd half-expected it. He ran to the hallway across the rotunda from his bedroom and looked over the railing to the floor below.

This time there was no mistake. He had left the nursery door wide open to see what would happen.

And now it was closed.

CHAPTER TWELVE

The school year ended and the girls were excited about three glorious months of summer. Other kids had iPhones and iPads, but Jordan's girls didn't. He encouraged them to read, to explore, and to use their minds instead of playing games all day. Jordan had played outdoors when he was a kid in Baton Rouge, and he insisted Ellie and Vi spend a lot of time in the sunshine. It was hot and sticky, but nobody cared. That was summer in Louisiana.

St. Francisville was more village than town, a homey, comfortable place where people knew each other well and said "good morning" to friends and tourists alike. Its Southern charm was irresistible, and Jordan let his kids ride their bikes all over town. He'd never have allowed it in a city, but this was St. Francisville, and Jordan was glad Ellie and Vi could grow up in a small-town environment.

He finished work one afternoon around five, walked into the kitchen, and found his daughters sitting at the table, drinking juice, giggling and whispering.

"What have you guys been up to today?"

Vi answered, "Just playing."

"Did you see any other kids in town?"

"We didn't go to town today."

"You played in the nursery all morning. When I saw you at lunch, I thought you were going to town this afternoon."

"We decided to stay here."

"And play in the nursery?"

"Yes. We had a lot of fun, Daddy!"

Jordan asked them what on earth they had done up there all day long. The girls glanced at each other, and Ellie said, "We were doing pretend things. Playing house and stuff. We played with those dolls we found."

"And Cherry," Vi murmured.

"Vi!" Ellie said with a sharp glance in her direction.

Their father asked who Cherry was.

Ellie said, "She's our imaginary friend. She comes to our tea parties sometimes."

"Is she another little girl? What does she look like?"

Vi shook her head. "She's not a little girl. She's a grown-up."

Ellie pinched her sister and whispered, "Vi, shut up!"

Jordan stood and said, "Okay, girls. Remember our talk about telling the truth? Come with me. We're going upstairs."

"Why, Daddy? We're telling the truth."

"Because something's going on and I want to know what it is. Maybe what you said is the truth, but you're not telling me everything. There's no reason to stay cooped up in the house all day when it's gorgeous outside. I want to know about these parties in the nursery."

Now there were four chairs around the table, each with a cup, saucer and spoon in front of it. In one chair was a large stuffed rabbit, taller than the girls and wearing a fancy checkered top hat, a vest and short pants with a carrot sticking out of one pocket. He had an unusual face for a toy; his lips were curled into a grimace and his buck teeth were so large they seemed grotesque even for a rabbit. His arms were positioned on the table as if he were about to pick up the cup in front of him.

"Who's this guy?" Jordan asked, and Vi explained that it was Peter, who had joined them for their tea party today.

"I haven't seen Peter before. Is he nice? Where did you find him?"

Vi glanced at Ellie and said, "He's very nice. We found him in a box in the closet. There are lots of boxes in there full of dolls and things, Daddy. There are a lot of toys for the babies who were going to be in this nursery!"

Despite his surprise, Jordan maintained his composure. He asked the names of the babies, and Vi said, "They didn't really ever come here. They weren't actually born."

"So they're make-believe, right?"

She paused. "I guess so."

"Vi, why did you say these toys were for babies?"

Ellie piped up. "Who else, Dad? Babies love toys!"

Despite her evasiveness, he let it go. He had more questions, but he'd put his girls on the spot by accusing them of lying. He told himself these were kids playing make-believe games in a fantastic nursery full of brand-new toys. Children's minds raced with imaginary experiences, and he shouldn't allow his concern to dampen their enthusiasm. There had been a lot of sadness in their lives, and he didn't intend to take this exciting new place away from them over things he couldn't get his mind around.

That night in bed he considered the tangibles — the real things he knew were factual.

One. There was a new toy in the room — a large fearsome rabbit taller than his children. A nice rabbit, according to Ellie, but he didn't look nice to Jordan. They hadn't told him the full story about Peter, but what backstory could a toy have anyway?

Two. The table had four place settings. The rabbit sat in one and the fourth was for the make-believe grown-up Vi had told him about. Who was that imaginary friend?

Three. The door to the nursery would not stay open, no matter what. He'd even tried a doorstop; the girls said they didn't move it, but somehow it got moved and the door swung shut. If it hadn't been for the tours, he'd have fixed the door so it couldn't close, but he didn't want tourists in that room. It was for his family.

Four. There was something odd about that room. Olivia had created two unusual deed restrictions. The house couldn't be sold for years, and in perpetuity the nursery couldn't be "disturbed," whatever that meant. Were those two strange provisos meant to solve a single problem? Did she keep the house off the market for half a century to hide something in the nursery? Nothing else made sense, but that didn't either. Why go to such lengths to secure one single room in a huge house?

Five. Who had the nursery been built for? It was clear to see the love that went into the detail and the amount of money spent on furnishings, wall murals and toys — but was that all make-believe too? No babies ever slept in the cribs or crawled in the playpen. Did Olivia Beaumont, who by all accounts had no children, create a room where she and her imaginary children had tea parties and played with a rabbit?

Jordan fell asleep, his head full of questions with no answers. He didn't sense that his children were in any sort of danger, but there was something unsettling — something creepy — about that room. The girls were comfortable there, happy to play in the nursery for hours on end. He would keep a close eye on things.

Sometime in the night he awoke with a thought. Could the mystery of the nursery be a part of something he had seen in the woods?

Before he bought the Arbors, Jordan had walked the property. A few hundred yards from the house, he found a cemetery. Many antebellum mansions had them; in those days, families buried relatives nearby instead of in municipal graveyards.

What had once been a wooden fence now lay in pieces around the serene quarter-acre plot nestled within a grove of majestic oak trees. The sun's rays didn't penetrate the dense foliage, which kept the place cool and breezy even on the hottest summer day.

There were seven headstones, some far older than others. Jordan took pictures of all the inscriptions. Six had names and dates. The seventh stone — neither the oldest nor the newest — was a tall statue with nothing engraved on it. It was a guardian angel.

This was what had awakened him tonight. He'd seen guardian angel gravestones in other cemeteries — always marking the grave of a child. That fact hadn't come to him when he stood in the woods that day, but now he had to find out why the tombstone was there. He told himself he'd work on it tomorrow.

The records at the West Feliciana Parish courthouse dated back to 1810. At that time it had been Feliciana Parish, a part of the Territory of Orleans. Two years later the state of Louisiana would be created, and in 1824 the parish was divided into east and west. The courthouse had been heavily damaged during the Civil War, but fortunately the parish records remained largely intact.

Once Jordan had explained what he wanted, a helpful clerk guided him to a desk where he sat while she retrieved two large leather-bound volumes. On the spine of the first were the words "Cemetery Records — West Feliciana Parish, Louisiana — 1850–1899." The second book was the next half century, ending in 1950.

He opened the first volume. As he turned the oversized leaves, he found that from oldest to newest, each cemetery had its own section. In pen and ink, often using flourishing handwriting, clerks had meticulously recorded burials for the past two hundred and eight years. It surprised him that the parish had over twenty cemeteries. Some were public, others were on church grounds, but the majority were family plots adjacent to the decedents' homes.

Jordan was looking for the one on his property. He flipped pages until he found it. "Beaumont Family Plot, The Arbors, St. Francisville." He was excited to see it; he'd half-expected this search to end up with nothing.

The huge sheet had only six entries. Jordan looked on his phone at the pictures of the stones he had taken that day, and he compared the writing on the grave markers to the entries before him.

The first burial had been Francois Beaumont, who was born in 1816 and died in 1891 at seventy-five. Jordan knew that he was Olivia's grandfather, the man who built the Arbors.

The next listing was Francois Beaumont's wife, Grace. Born in 1828, she had died in 1858. When he was in the cemetery, Jordan had wondered what took her at the young age of thirty, but sitting here now, looking at lines on a page, the answer was clear.

Burial number three was Olivia's father, Jean-Paul, born in 1858, who died in 1931, at seventy-five like his father. He was born on the same day in 1858 that his mother, Grace, died. The newborn lived, but the mother died.

Surprisingly, it happened again. Jean-Paul's wife, Marthe, was born in 1879 and died in 1900 at age twenty-one on the day Olivia was born. Jordan paused and considered what a tragic situation it must have been that in this family both Olivia's grandmother and mother died immediately after giving birth. Maybe that was why Olivia never had children; she was afraid of what might happen. Or maybe she wasn't afraid at all. Maybe there had been offspring. Maybe the guardian angel was protecting them. He continued to study the entries.

Next came Charles Perrault, Olivia's first husband. He was born in 1896 and died at age forty-nine in 1945, when he fell through the third-floor railing.

The last name on the page was Olivia Beaumont's. She was born in 1900 and died in 1965. When she was born, her father had been forty-two and her doomed mother half his age.

Her maiden name was shown, although she was married to Charles Perrault for twelve years and to Bruno Duval for several years after that. For some reason she had taken back her maiden name after Charles died.

That was it. According to the official parish record, six people were interred at the Arbors. Jordan had seen those six stones, but there was another. Why had someone erected a seventh stone, a guardian angel? Had Olivia's grandmother or mother borne other children? Had Olivia?

He left knowing that parts of this puzzle were missing. Today he had learned about the tragedy of deaths in childbirth that haunted this family for at least two generations. It hadn't happened to Olivia. She died aged sixty-five of natural causes, unlike her mother and grandmother.

He wondered even more about the nursery. Olivia cherished the room so much that she had made it a shrine. There were two cribs, and his twin girls played with toys bought for someone else, in a sanctuary where make-believe grown-ups had tea parties with children.

It pained him to take away the thing his girls loved most — that special room — but it was coming to that. There was no rational explanation for any of this, but the more he thought about it, the greater his concern. Something was wrong and he had to deal with it for the children's sakes.

CHAPTER THIRTEEN

Vi, Ellie and the rabbit sat at the small table. They had positioned dolls all around them on the floor, and each had its own china cup and saucer. The teapot, sugar bowl and creamer were in front of the girls, and the party would begin once someone took the fourth seat.

The door opened and the lady entered the room without a sound. She closed it, walked to the table, sat in the small chair, and arranged her long black dress just so.

"Good morning, children."

"Good morning, Cherry." The first time she came, she had asked them to call her Mama, but they refused. They had their own mama, they explained, and she was in heaven.

"Twin girls — *you* girls — are all I ever wanted," she had protested, but they wouldn't use the name.

"Call me by my nickname, then," she said, and she told them what it was. It was funny and it made them laugh. She pronounced it a different way, but to them it sounded like Cherry.

Vi poured make-believe tea for everyone while Ellie went around asking who wanted sugar and cream. The woman smiled when she saw the dolls who ringed the table; it pleased her that the children liked to play with these toys, because she had picked them out especially for the twins.

She warned Ellie and Vi never to mention her to their father. "If one of you tells him we play together, he will never let you come back in this room. If you don't keep this a secret, we will never see each other again."

"He wouldn't care, Cherry," Ellie had protested, and the woman had said *no* so loudly it had scared them. They loved playing with her because she was different, like somebody from a long time ago who was still here today. As much as they enjoyed playing with a grown-up, they never felt as comfortable around her as with their father. She was a little scary looking, being so tall and dressed all in black. But Cherry was always friendly. Well, not always, but most of the time she was.

So she remained a secret, one that Vi had more difficulty keeping than Ellie. After Dad's talk about always telling the truth no matter what, Vi was upset. She was more of a play-by-the-rules girl than her adventuresome sister. They agreed Ellie would answer Dad's questions about the nursery. It didn't bother her so much — she said it wasn't lying, it was just protecting their friend.

The lady told them wonderful stories about this house in the old days. They asked if she still lived here, but she didn't answer. She didn't like what their father had done to the first floor. The Arbors had been a grand home. Changing rooms into offices was something she didn't care for at all.

Although the girls never asked, when odd things happened in the house they knew it was her. Kitchen cabinets sometimes flew open in unison, a room had cold spots, a wet spot on the floor that wasn't really there — those were ways she showed she wasn't happy about something.

Today's tea party was well underway, complete with a story about the Queen of England joining them in the garden this afternoon for a party, when the door opened and their father stuck his head in. He did that more often now.

"Everything okay, kids? Why don't you go outside? It's a beautiful day." He smiled when he looked at the table, with dolls carefully arranged around it, each with a cup for tea. He noticed the rabbit and saw that the fourth chair was empty as always.

Ellie said, "In a little while, Dad. When we finish our tea, we'll go. I promise."

Jordan left, thinking how difficult it would be to tell the children they couldn't play in the room they loved so much. There didn't seem to be anything wrong in there, and he convinced himself that keeping a closer eye on things was the answer.

As soon as their father left, the lady rose from the fourth chair and said, "Well, then. I suppose you had better run along, my dears. I'll come back and see you another day."

Vi cried, "Not yet! Please don't go!"

"I must, darling. I love you twins very, very much. Don't forget to keep our visits a secret!" She walked across the room, opened the door and left.

CHAPTER FOURTEEN

Weekdays at the Arbors were hectic because everything happened at once. Jordan's people showed up for work, the girls grabbed breakfast while they loaded their backpacks for school, Dad fixed their lunches and pecked their cheeks, and they rushed off to catch the bus. Saturdays were better — the girls often slept late — but the office was open from eight to twelve, so the three of them were never alone as a family except on Sunday.

Sundays were quiet days just for family. Vi and Ellie named their Sunday ritual "Brunch with Daddy." The kids joined Dad in the kitchen at nine. He would have been cooking for over an hour, preparing sausage, biscuits and gravy, grits, crispy apple-smoked bacon, warmed-up cinnamon scones from the deli, toast with luscious creamery butter, and fresh-squeezed orange juice. It was a meal worthy of company, but it was a special treat just for him and his girls.

They sat around the table and talked about whatever anyone wanted to bring up. The children enjoyed discussing grown-up things with their dad. He talked about his work and what was going on in town. He answered questions they threw at him, even though some required careful explanation so an eight-year-old would understand.

He asked his daughters about school, friends, activities and things that were on their minds. He kidded them about what he called their love lives — and they snorted in disgust every time he asked them if they had boyfriends. They talked about their mother and how much they still missed her. "Do you remember what she looked like?" he would ask sometimes, and they would say yes. They had a picture of her on their nightstand, and Jordan knew that helped keep her memory alive. She'd been gone four years, half of his girls' lives. It didn't seem that long sometimes, but time passes quickly when you're a single parent raising twin girls. That was why Brunch with Daddy was such an important part of their routine. It was often the only time in a week when they bonded as a family unit.

Today their father threw out a proposition to them — a plan to redo the nursery. He'd given it a lot of thought. Even after the cleaning, that room was the gloomiest in the house. Although the heavy curtains were always open now, they covered enough of the windows that much of the light couldn't get in. He would hang sheers to make the room sunny and bright.

Murals were painted on every wall, rural scenes with colts and lambs frolicking in pastures of green that had been beautiful once, but today they were faded and dull. He suggested painting the room a light color to brighten things up.

As he talked about changing the room, he could see concern in his children's faces. When Vi's lower lip trembled, he asked what was wrong.

"Don't change anything, Daddy!" she screamed, bursting into tears.

Ellie agreed with her sister. "You aren't supposed to change anything in that room. That's what the lady said."

Jordan was astounded. Why were two eight-year-olds so concerned about decorating? He hadn't forgotten about the restriction on "disturbing" the room — in fact, he'd consulted an attorney about what that vague word meant. The man said a deed restriction created over fifty years ago by a long-dead owner with no heirs could be interpreted as broadly as Jordan wished. There was no one around to protest anything he did. "Go for it," the attorney counseled. "Do whatever you want; it's your house."

Despite the breadth of the advice he'd received, Jordan felt obligated to abide by Olivia's wishes. He created a work order that in his professional opinion satisfied the intent of the deed restriction. He would not remove the plaster or wainscot on the walls, replace the chandelier or change out the floors or ceiling. Everything else was fair game, and that was what he had presented to the girls. But it wasn't going well at all.

Ellie said, "You can't change the walls. Cherry painted those pictures herself."

"Cherry? Your imaginary friend? What are you talking about?"

Ellie had made a mistake. She poured out words to correct it. "Uh, right. Our imaginary friend. We pretend she painted the walls, that's all. But you can't change things, Daddy!"

"Yes I can, Ellie. I asked a smart man — a lawyer — what I can do here. I can repaint the walls because I want your playroom to be bright. The murals are old and faded and no one knows who painted them. The owner probably hired an artist; that's what people usually did."

We know who painted them, Ellie thought. *It was Cherry. She told us so.*

Today he was fighting a losing battle, but he intended to win this one. He'd let it go for now, give them time to digest his ideas, and then break the news that he was going to do the project, like it or not.

After brunch the girls did what they always did. They cleared the table and loaded the dishwasher while Dad put things away and cleaned up the mess he'd made. Then they went upstairs to the nursery.

Cherry was sitting in her rocker and she looked angry.

"I've been waiting for you."

Vi said, "Aren't you going to say, 'Good morning, children,' like you always do?"

The lady ignored her, and Vi became nervous. "What's the matter, Cherry?" she whimpered.

"You know what's wrong. I'm angry with your father."

Vi's eyes widened in fear. "Don't be mad at Daddy. He didn't do anything to you."

"And he will not, my dear. I won't allow it. He will not disturb this room that I created for you two darling girls."

Ellie chimed in. "He says it's old and dark —"

"It's wonderful," Cherry said in a voice that sounded mean. "It's *your* room. Don't you understand that?"

Vi shook her head. "I don't know what you mean. This isn't our room. This house is very old. You didn't know us then."

The lady broke into a rare smile. She rocked back and forth, lost in thought, until Ellie and Vi gave up. They went to the table and prepared it for this morning's tea party. She had scared them, and the girls weren't sure if she would come to the table, but eventually she took her seat and drank her pretend tea with the rabbit, the dolls and two confused little girls upset about how mad their grown-up friend was.

In bed that evening, Ellie and Vi whispered about Cherry. Was she real, or was she make-believe? She seemed real enough; she could open the door, talk to them, and hold a teacup, but when their dad came into the nursery, he couldn't see her even though she was sitting right there.

Ellie said, "I think sometimes she's real and sometimes she's not. She's not a ghost or something. Ghosts are see-through, but she's not."

"Why can't Daddy see her?"

"Because she's our special friend. I guess she's make-believe, all right, but who cares? I love playing with her."

"She scared me today. Were you scared too, Ellie?"

Ellie nodded. She didn't say so, but she had been *really* scared today. Cherry had never acted like that before, and she wondered if they should tell their dad.

If they did, they might never see her or the nursery again. Cherry would have to stay their little secret.

CHAPTER FIFTEEN

Tuesdays and Thursdays were always hectic. While architects worked at huge drafting tables in the former salons on the first floor, Penny Bishop showed tourists around the mansion.

The house, built in 1850 on a broad expanse of land fronting the Mississippi River, boasted an architecture found nowhere else in the area. There was a central atrium ringed on two upper floors by hallways and dark wood banisters. From the rotunda on the ground floor, one could see the dome fifty feet above. Sunlight shimmered through stained-glass windows and bathed the interior in a rainbow of color.

Today six tourists climbed the ornately carved circular staircase that stood in one corner of the rotunda. Their footsteps caused each riser to creak and groan in testimony to over a hundred and fifty years of service.

Beautiful railings lined the hallways on the upper floors. On the top floor, an elderly lady on today's tour peered over and gasped. The drop to the ground seemed like a mile to her, and she pulled back in fear as her husband and the others laughed.

Penny enjoyed giving these tours as much as the guests liked taking them. She regaled visitors with the history of the Arbors, and her love of the house was clear to everyone.

Her voice became eerie and mysterious as she gathered the group around one place on the third floor. She cautioned the guests to stay back from the railing while she told them about the ghost of the Arbors.

She spoke of the matriarch Olivia Beaumont and her two husbands. She told about the terrifying end to Charles Perrault, the husband who fell three stories to his death, "tumbling over the banister railing directly in front of you."

Several people gasped as she recounted the awful tale of his lifeless body grotesquely spread-cagled on the elegant parquet floor forty feet below. One visitor — a girl in her mid-twenties wearing too-short shorts and a tank top — sneered at Penny's story.

"Give me a break," she said to her boyfriend, mocking the guide's remarks. "So the guy fell over the railing. Now he's a ghost? Big f-ing deal, if you ask me."

Others shot her looks of disapproval, and Penny said in a stern voice, "This was Charles Perrault's house too. They were married twelve years and he was only forty-nine when he fell to his death. Was it an accident, or something else? The ghost isn't her husband; it's Olivia. She's been spotted on the third floor, standing in this very spot. Did she push her husband over, or is she simply mourning his death?"

The girl retorted, "How about this? He had a mint julep or two, got drunk as a skunk, and fell over the railing. It's not as good a story as yours, but you have to tell a spooky one to sell tickets. I say that's what really happened. We're not stupid, you know. You have a great line of bull, but nobody believes in ghosts."

Penny's voice was quiet. "I believe. I've seen Olivia Beaumont with my own eyes." She turned and guided the group down the hall to the next room. Fifteen minutes later the tour was over and everyone gathered in the rotunda.

Someone asked about Olivia's second husband. Penny said he simply disappeared one day. He was much younger than she was, and he left on a business trip, never to return.

"That's a little mysterious too," another person said, and Penny half-expected the rude girl to put her two cents in. That was when the group realized she wasn't there.

Her boyfriend said, "I don't know where she is. I'll go look for her."

Penny was upset. That impertinent girl had created enough trouble already. "No, stay here. I'll go," she said, but at that moment there came a shout from the third floor. The girl — Erin — was up there, leaning over the railing and laughing.

"Look! Look at me! I'm right where the spooks are! Think the old lady wants to push me over? Bring it on, Olivia! I'm not afraid of a stupid ghost!"

Penny ordered her to come down and, appearing to comply, the girl walked toward the staircase. Those on the first floor were chatting among themselves when they heard a terrifying wail and a plea for mercy.

That brought people who worked in the architect's office to the rotunda, and the girl screamed again. She appeared at the railing, her body pressed backwards against it.

The people were dumbfounded as the girl shouted to someone they couldn't see. In a frightened voice, she promised she believed and again begged for someone to leave her alone. She yelled to her boyfriend, Jack, but Erin's time had run out.

Everything happened in seconds, and the witnesses would recall later how her contorted body twisted further and further back over the yawning rotunda until she tumbled through the air with a terrifying scream that would be etched forever in their memories. "Who pushed her?"

police would ask, and every single observer would give the same answer. No one pushed her. She was the only one on the third floor. The girl appeared to be hallucinating, and she had leaned further and further back until she fell.

Pandemonium erupted in the rotunda as Erin's body slammed into the floor next to the elderly couple. Penny fainted, as did two visitors and one of Jordan Blanchard's draftsmen. His assistant, Lauren, ran to call 911 as Jordan knelt first beside Erin, whom he quickly determined was beyond help, then Penny. He was fond of her and she'd given him a lot of history about this place he hadn't known before hiring her.

She was awake in a few seconds, and he cradled her head in his lap as she whispered, "You realize what this means."

He knew what she meant. "The police will be here in a minute," he replied quietly. "We don't know she did this."

Penny understood. She'd keep her ideas to herself. He helped her sit up as they heard sirens coming down Ferdinand Street toward the old ferry dock, the sound growing much louder as two police cruisers and an ambulance turned into the parking lot.

Chief Norman Kimes commanded a small cadre that made up the St. Francisville police force. The town had less than two thousand people. There hadn't been an unexplained death in decades, and Kimes and his team were unprepared to handle the situation they found at the Arbors. The EMTs checked the dead girl and covered her with a sheet. After ensuring the others were okay, they returned to the station. Chief Kimes called the coroner and assembled the witnesses in Jordan's conference room.

Jordan's shaken but steady assistant, Lauren Baxter, passed out bottles of water to everyone. Twelve people had seen the entire thing — five tourists, including Erin's boyfriend, Jack; the tour guide; and six people who worked in the architect office on the main floor, one of whom was Jordan, who owned the house.

The police chief explained that he would go around the table, asking each person to provide identification and explain why they were there, and then he would take a statement from each of them in private. He didn't suggest what would happen after that, because at this point Chief Kimes had absolutely no idea.

Kimes allowed people to leave after their interviews, and by one p.m. the only ones left were Penny, Jordan and the dead girl's companion, Jack. The stories were consistent — everyone heard and saw exactly the same thing, and no one had a clue how or why it could have happened. On Penny's tour the girl had laughed and mocked her ghost stories, but Erin's rude behavior didn't explain the tragedy that had befallen her. Jordan couldn't add anything. He had come to the rotunda only after Erin's screams, and he saw what the others saw.

Her boyfriend's interview took longer because he was the only one who had known the dead girl before she came to the house. Jack told the policeman he was from Kenner, a suburb of New Orleans. He was a laborer who couldn't hold a steady job because of a drug habit. He'd met Erin two months ago at a concert in Metairie and they "decided to shack up together." Today they were finishing a two-day trip that had begun at Destrehan Plantation fifteen miles from New Orleans. Last night they had stayed at the Myrtles just up the road, because they wanted to experience a haunted house.

He admitted they'd spent the evening smoking pot and drinking — they'd done a lot of both, he confessed — and they slept so soundly at the Myrtles that they wouldn't have heard a spirit if it had been in bed with them. They came to the Arbors because of its rumored ghost — after which they were heading south to Napoleonville and then to his house in Kenner. That had been the plan, but now she was dead.

Jack's lack of compassion surprised the chief at first, but it turned out the kid didn't know her that well. They had met, smoked and drank and slept together for a couple of months, but he knew hardly anything about her past and nothing about any relatives.

Chief Kimes asked if Erin had ever had hallucinations or visions. They hadn't been together long, but he'd never seen anything like today.

When the interview was done, Jack rose from his seat and said, "What if it really was a ghost? Erin made fun of the guide when she told us there were ghosts. The lady said some guy fell off the railing a long time ago, and Erin laughed at that. She said maybe the guy had a few too many drinks or something. What if the ghost got mad?"

Chief Kimes wondered if he was serious. The paranormal was something that came up often in conversation in these parts of Louisiana, and although he didn't believe in ghosts himself, Norman Kimes was smart enough not to insult others who might truly think they had encountered a spirit in an old mansion.

"Do you think that might be it?"

"I don't know," the kid admitted, "but something went on up there that none of us could see. Erin wouldn't have fallen backwards over that railing for no reason. She was scared to death — we all saw it."

"I'll keep it in mind," Kimes replied. "I have to eliminate the physical possibilities before I go out in left field for ideas, but I promise I'll keep it in mind."

The chief added his observations about the witnesses to the notes he had made, and he closed his portfolio. Then he called the state police in Baton Rouge. This case was an enigma, and this small-town cop wasn't above asking for help.

It turned out there were traces of illegal drugs in Erin's bloodstream, enough to allow the coroner to rule her death an accident. She was high, she was hallucinating, and she lost her footing and fell over the railing. Case closed, without officials having to consider such outlandish theories as the one offered by the dead girl's boyfriend. Ghosts, indeed. This was the twenty-first century, after all.

CHAPTER SIXTEEN

As Landry pulled into the parking lot at the River View Restaurant, he laughed at its name. It had neither a river view nor the look of a proper restaurant. Located at the end of a dirt road off Highway 61 on the outskirts of St. Francisville, its metal roof and walls adorned with old Dixie and Jax beer signs told tourists that this wasn't a place for them. It had four one-star reviews on Yelp, all from hapless visitors who for some unknown reason had entered the exclusive domain of the working class. The men who drank here — and they were almost all men — had never heard of Yelp and they weren't the kind to post reviews. They were fishermen and mechanics, men who worked on lawn crews and highway projects, salt-of-the-earth people, second- or third-generation residents of West Feliciana Parish.

There were two dozen vehicles in the parking lot, all pickups, some jacked up and most with huge tires. A few were clunkers, but most were late-model Ford F-150s and Dodge Rams.

Landry had been in places like this before. An investigative reporter often ended up on the seamier side of town. The River View wasn't the worst dive he'd ever been in, but it ranked right up there.

He had returned to St. Francisville two days ago, the day after the girl died at the Arbors. Her death changed everything, and Jordan couldn't dodge his questions this time. But before he saw Jordan, Landry had another lead to track down, a man named Ox Fedder.

The last time he was in town, he had visited the parish courthouse to trace the ownership of the Arbors from the beginning. It had been a stroke of luck that the clerk who helped Landry was nearing retirement age; a younger one wouldn't have known the things that man did. He hauled out the records and asked Landry what he was looking for.

After his confrontation with Jordan, Landry didn't need more controversy, so he said he was doing research on Olivia Beaumont and her family, principally Francois, her grandfather who had built the Arbors.

The clerk offered the name of someone Landry might speak to, a man who had worked at the house before and after Olivia died. He was a simple man, the clerk added, and smiled when he advised the best place to find Ox Fedder was on Saturday afternoons at a local tavern called the River View. "Here's a little advice. Don't go down there dressed like you are now. You'll stand out anyway — the place is like *Cheers* — you know, where everybody knows your name. Except it's not *Cheers* — it's a dump. But you don't want to go in there looking like a city slicker. Dress down; that's my advice."

Landry wore the grungiest T-shirt, tattered shorts and tennis shoes he had. He wore a stained Saints ball cap backwards, and a pack of Camels protruded from his T-shirt pocket, even though he didn't smoke. He'd learned that the offer of a cigarette often loosened the tongue of a man who knew things Landry wanted to hear.

The bar was packed on a rainy Saturday afternoon. Smoke collected toward the ceiling and there was a stale odor of beer. Heavy rain pinged the sheet-metal roof, and the LSU-Ole Miss game blared from TVs around the room. The patrons, all in various stages of intoxication, shouted to be heard. It all came together in a cacophony of sounds that somehow seemed natural in a place like the River View.

A waitress pointed Landry to the man he'd come to see. The burly guy had greasy hair and greasy hands, one of which gripped a glass of bourbon. An Abita Turbodog chaser was within reach. Landry was fortunate to find an empty stool beside him. Bellying up to the bar was tough; even though the man was aware Landry was trying to squeeze onto a stool, he didn't move.

Ignoring Landry, the bartender checked on his regulars, engaging them in conversation highlighted by intermittent outbursts of laughter and curses. Landry watched him wipe his brow and hands on the same bar towel he used to dry the glasses, and he forced himself to get past the thought he could end up with dysentery — or worse — if he had a drink in this sleazy place.

He raised his hand once, then again, and eventually the bartender sauntered over and stood before Landry without saying a word.

"I'll have a Turbodog," he said as the giant next to him drained the last of his.

"I'll have the same," Ox Fedder said, "and another Jack." He pointed at Landry without looking his way. "Put it on this feller's tab."

The bartender laughed and said, "That all right with you, buddy? Best thing for strangers is to buy the regulars a beer or two."

That was what Landry wanted, and he gave a thumbs-up. He thought about sticking out his hand, but he had no desire to touch the man's nasty fingers, so he said, "How's it goin'?"

Ox looked straight ahead and said nothing. In a moment the bartender set the man's beer and whisky in front of him, removed the empty glasses, and walked away. After five minutes, Landry raised his hand again and the barkeep returned.

"I ordered a Turbodog earlier."

"Oh, yeah? I guess I forgot." Everyone around Landry laughed as the bartender turned to the other man and said, "Ox, you need anything else?"

"Sure, boss. I'll have another round."

The bartender said, "Ox is having another round on you."

Landry played the game. He was a native Louisianan born and raised not two hours from here, but in this place he might as well have been from New York City. He couldn't hold his own in this environment, and it was time to get down to business, if there was any business to be done here.

The beer arrived and he turned to the man next to him, held up the bottle, and said, "Cheers."

Without speaking, Ox raised his bottle and took a long draw.

"Ox. Is that your name, or is it short for something else?"

The man shifted his bulk to the right, and for the first time he looked Landry in the eyes. A long scar on his left cheek ran from his eye to his lip, pulling it up in a perpetual half grin, half grimace that revealed yellow teeth. He hadn't shaved in days and his face was as dirty as his hands.

"It's short for something else. It's short for 'none of your goddamned business.'" He turned away.

Landry had paid for two rounds of drinks, and he pressed on despite thinking it might be a bad idea. "I'm looking for information about a house in St. Francisville. A house where you used to work."

Ox said nothing.

"I want to know about the Arbors."

A mighty belch and another long draw of whisky.

"I'll pay you fifty dollars if you can tell me what I want to know."

Nothing happened for what seemed like forever, and then Ox said, "What do you want to know?"

"I want to know what you think is going on there. The owner's husband fell over the railing back in the forties and died. The other day a tourist fell over the same railing in the same place. Was that a coincidence?"

"You a cop? I don't talk to no cops."

"No. I'm a reporter."

Ox grunted, turned and looked at Landry again. "I seen you on the TV. You're that ghost-hunter guy."

"Right. I'm Landry Drake."

The huge man had difficulty putting his thoughts into words. Maybe it was the alcohol and maybe it was genetic. Most likely it was a combination. At last he said, "The old woman had another husband after the one that died."

This was what Landry had come to hear. "Two husbands? Tell me more."

"I never seen him, but there was two. My old man worked for Miss Olivia. He knew the guy."

"What's his name? Is he still alive?"

"Hell if I know what his name is. Who knows? Who cares? He left town one day, far as people say. He ain't been seen since. Some people think Miss Olivia killed him, know what I mean?" He raised his eyebrows and broke into a nasty smile, as if the thought of killing someone was exciting, and Landry wondered if the man might have had experience in that field.

"What else do you know?"

"My old man always said the place was haunted. When we was kids, we would go there and poke around. He'd whip my ass with a strop when he caught me, but that wasn't no big deal. Happened all the time. People claim they saw the old lady looking out the windows, but I never saw her. Heard stuff, though. Heard some screamin' one night when me and Bobby Field snuck in. Comin' from upstairs somewhere. Scared the shit out of him and he ran off. I wasn't scared of nothin', but he pissed his pants, know what I mean?" He laughed and belched in Landry's face.

Landry held his breath for a moment and said, "When did you work there?"

"I hurt my back workin' at the mill and they fired me. My old man was ready to retire, so the lawyers hired me to work at the Arbors. I kept the place up until some guy bought it. She left it empty for fifty years, ya know."

"Why did she do that?"

"Who the hell knows? She was crazy, my pa said, walkin' around in black clothes all the time like a goddamn witch or somethin'. She'd sneak into a room when he didn't know she was there. She'd be standin' there when he turned around and stuff. It spooked the hell out of him. When I worked there, I never went inside after dark, but even in the daytime it was kinda creepy with all that furniture and stuff just sittin' there with sheets draped over everything. But I never was scared or nothin'. I ain't afraid of ghosts."

"So you think Olivia Beaumont's ghost is in the house?"

"I didn't say that. Who knows what's in the house. I never saw no ghost when I was in there. My pa said he did once, but he said a lot of crazy stuff."

"What do you think about the tourist who fell over the railing the other day?"

"I don't think nothin' about it. Ain't none of my business, and ain't none of yours either. I'm gettin' tired of talkin' to you, mister ghost man. Gimme my fifty dollars and leave me alone. I'm thirsty too. Before you leave, I'll take another round."

"I'd like to talk to your father. Is he still alive?"

The thickset man belched a laugh that ended up as a cough. "Alive? Yeah, I guess the old fart's alive, but he ain't in his right mind. He can talk for hours about when he was a kid, but he cain't remember what he done this mornin'. I ain't seen him in a while. You won't learn nothin' from him, but go for it, mister ghost hunter. Carlton Fedder's his name. Last I heard, he lived in a shack down on Bayou Sara somewheres."

Landry walked out with more information than he'd arrived with. He wasn't sure if it was worth fifty dollars plus the bar tab, but he had so little at this point that anything helped.

On Monday morning he went to the offices of the *St. Francisville Democrat*, the local newspaper that had been printing since the late nineteenth century. He was shown to a desk with a computer, and he searched for Olivia's husbands.

The name Charles Perrault yielded just two results, the first from 1933. At age thirty-seven, he married thirty-three-year-old Olivia Beaumont, daughter of sugar merchant Jean-Paul Beaumont and his wife, Marthe, both deceased. They married in Our Lady of Mount Carmel Catholic Church in St. Francisville and honeymooned in Barbados, where her family owned a large sugar plantation.

The only other entry about Charles was his death in 1945 at age forty-nine. He fell three stories at home in a tragic accident.

In a town as small as this, Landry wondered why there weren't other articles about the two. They were wealthy and lived in a beautiful mansion on the river, but it appeared they had no social involvement. A lot of parties were written up in the society column, but the Perraults neither attended nor hosted.

He saw Olivia Beaumont's obituary. Born in the house in 1900, she died there in 1965 and was buried in the family cemetery on the grounds. There was no service and no list of relatives, including her husbands.

The final listing for the matriarch of the Arbors was posted a few weeks after her death. It was a legal notice by Olivia's executor — a local lawyer — calling for presentation of claims against her estate.

There was nothing about her second husband, but there was no reason there should have been. If Olivia hadn't publicized her marriage, or if she had married somewhere other than this parish, there would have been no notice or story in the *Democrat*. She was a private person and he had to leave it at that.

CHAPTER SEVENTEEN

Locating Carlton Fedder was more difficult than finding his son Ox, who occupied the same barstool at the same establishment every Saturday and Sunday from the time it opened until he fell off the stool and someone took him home.

Landry asked around town about the man, but no one remembered him. Not unusual, Landry thought. It had been decades since Carlton worked at the Arbors. Landry had to use his investigative skills to find someone who knew the old man. According to Ox, Carlton Fedder did everything Miss Olivia needed; he was a handyman, yardman and errand boy all rolled into one, so Landry began at the hardware store, where a handyman might be a frequent customer.

The young clerks would be no help, so Landry asked for the owner. He was glad when a man in his seventies stepped out of a back office. It would take age, not youth, to find Carlton Fedder.

The proprietor recognized the well-known paranormal investigator. He also remembered Fedder. "Odd sort, that fellow," the owner said. "But then, so was Miss Olivia.

Maybe they were a good fit. She hardly ever came to town; she'd send Carl in to fetch whatever she needed. She had an account here that he paid once a month."

"Any idea where he is now?"

"I can't help you there. A few years back I heard he had Alzheimer's and was living in a shanty down on the river. I haven't heard a word since."

Landry said Carl's son mentioned he might be living on the Bayou Sara, and the man snapped his fingers. "That's right; I remember now. You know those fishing shacks off Old Ferry Road? No, you wouldn't; you're not from around here. Old Ferry Road will take you as close to the bayou as you can get, and you must walk the rest of the way. There used to be five or six shanties down there for fishermen to use. If old Carl's still alive, and if he hasn't wandered off, that's where he might be."

Landry walked through tallgrass toward the bayou and the three structures that remained standing. The other two had collapsed into a heap of unpainted boards when the last hurricane blew through. He was amazed the ones left hadn't fallen too. They were wooden structures with holes where windows belonged and roofs made of sheet metal. There was a single outhouse that had served all of them, although in their dilapidated conditions, Landry couldn't imagine that anyone still lived here. He figured this trip was a waste of time.

He walked to the first house and called out, but he heard nothing. The front steps had rotted long ago, so he climbed up on the porch, avoiding holes where boards were missing, and looked through the empty doorframe. There had been squatters — he saw a pile of grimy clothes on top of a filthy brown mattress, and cigarette butts littered the floor. But the place was empty now.

The other two shanties were the same. If Carlton Fedder had ever been here, he was gone now.

As Landry was about to leave, he heard an outboard motor and turned to watch two men in a bass boat heading toward the bank a hundred feet away. One waved, and Landry walked to the river as they got out and tied the boat to a tree.

"Morning," one said. "Anything I can help you with?"

"Is this your land?" Landry asked. "I was looking for someone. People in town told me he might be here."

"You're Landry Drake, aren't you? The wife and I love your specials. Since you're in St. Francisville, I suppose you're working on a story about the Myrtles — right?"

"No, I'm doing a little research, that's all."

"Yeah, in your business, I guess you run into a lot of leads that end up being nothing."

Landry nodded and asked if they knew a man named Carlton Fedder.

The second man, who had stayed in the boat, said to his friend, "He's talking about Crazy Carl. He lived in that middle shack for a long time. When we were fishing on the bayou, we'd stop and give him a stringer of fish and a couple of beers. Everybody called him Crazy Carl because he talked to himself all the time. I think it came from living alone all those years, because every time we showed up, he'd greet us like we were his long-lost friends. He didn't make much sense, but he sure was glad to have someone to talk to."

The first man asked why Landry wanted to find Carl, and he said he was hoping the old man could give him some information on a place where he used to work.

"Where would that be?"

Landry hesitated; the men knew who he was, and every time he was in this situation, revealing the location he was investigating made for a lot of gossip.

"I can't say right now. I'm in the early stages of checking out a story, and I don't want to get any rumors started. I hope you understand."

The guys did, and he gave each of them a business card. "Please call me if you hear anything about Carl," he said, and they promised they would.

Landry drove back into town, not surprised that his clue led him to a dead end. Clues often did in this business. It was time to return to New Orleans and the real world. He enjoyed the investigative part of his job most of all — it was like being a detective, following clues and hoping for results — but the reporting part — the routine stories he covered every day — was what paid the bills.

Before he left this quaint community, he had one last stop to make. It was odd that a tourist had fallen to her death just like Olivia's husband had. Maybe it was a coincidence, but he didn't believe in them. His documentaries got produced because he did what he loved, investigating threads to see where they led.

He turned on Ferdinand Road, drove into the lot, and parked next to the sign that read *Blanchard & Blanchard, Architects*.

Jordan's assistant, Lauren, stuck her head into the boss's office. "Landry Drake's here to see you."

"Shit," he muttered, knowing he couldn't dodge the reporter now. "Okay, bring him in."

Jordan motioned to a chair across his desk and Landry sat. "I guess I can't throw you out this time," he snapped.

"I have an open mind and I'd like to hear your thoughts on the similarities between the death last week and Charles Perrault's death in 1945."

"I have no thoughts about it. All I know about the first death is what I've heard. As for the girl who died last week, she fell over the railing."

"The others in the group say she was having some kind of struggle up there. She was trying to fight something off. You saw it too, right?"

"Yes. I heard her shouting and I ran out just as she fell. I'm sure you know she and her boyfriend had been drinking and doing drugs the night before. They were still in her system. The cops say she was hallucinating, and I believe it. There's no story here, Landry. Look at the facts and don't invent something supernatural. She wasn't pushed over the rail by an evil spirit; she was hungover or strung out, she got too close to the railing and she fell. I'm sorry that it happened, but it wasn't my fault, and there's nothing more to it."

Landry stood and thanked Jordan for his time. The man seemed relieved to be off the hook so quickly. Making small talk, Jordan asked him what he intended to do next, and Landry said he was going back to New Orleans.

"I'll be honest with you, Jordan. I'm not finished with your house yet, and if you wish, I'll keep you advised on anything new. I'd appreciate it if you'd do the same, but I'll understand if you want to keep things to yourself."

Jordan admitted that everything had changed after the girl's death. There was plenty of publicity now, and there was no way he could stop it. There would be no more house tours — they ended on that fateful day. Whatever money it brought in wasn't worth the onslaught of lookie-loos hoping to encounter a ghost.

"Did you ever unlock that door upstairs?" Landry asked.

"Yes. It's a nursery. My girls play in there now."

"Oh, really? I don't want to intrude, but would you mind —"

"It's part of the family rooms now. They're not open to the public."

"I understand." Landry was disappointed, but he didn't want to push Jordan. There might come a time for getting tough, but it wasn't today. He did have one last thought.

"Olivia had no children, did she?"

That was the question Jordan asked himself repeatedly. "Not that I know of. Why did she create a nursery, then? I admit I don't know. It's no mystery, though. It's just a room. There's a playpen, two cribs, children's furniture, toys, books, dolls and stuff. Maybe Olivia had nieces and nephews."

Jordan didn't mention that everything in the nursery had been brand new, never touched by a child's hand. And there were no nieces and nephews. Olivia was an only child and her parents were deceased by the time she married.

Landry was halfway to New Orleans when something Jordan had said hit Landry like a ton of bricks. There were two cribs. That could only mean one thing. Twins.

The nursery, a room that had been closed off for more than fifty years, was meant for twins.

Twins, just like Jordan Blanchard's girls.

CHAPTER EIGHTEEN

Cate was at Landry's French Quarter apartment before he got home. They strolled down to Felix's, ordered a couple of Abita Ambers, and dug into plates of oysters on the half shell. Landry filled her in on the trip to St. Francisville, including how strange Jordan still acted. He told her about the nursery, his theory on the twin cribs, and about his meeting with Ox Fedder.

"I want to talk to Ox's father," he said. "He was Miss Olivia's right-hand man and he may know something important. His son said he has Alzheimer's, although I wouldn't trust that guy's assessment of anything, including diagnosing a disease. The old man used to live in a shack down on the bayou; I went there, but he was gone."

"How will you find him? Does the son know where he lives now?"

"He hasn't seen his father for some time and there's no one else to ask."

"I have an idea. Why don't you ask the attorney that handled Olivia's estate?"

That was an excellent suggestion, and the next morning he asked an associate at the station to make the call. Sometimes these days when people heard his name, they clammed up, hoping to get money or a picture on TV in exchange for information.

Landry's associate was vague without being dishonest; he said he was looking for Carlton Fedder regarding a family matter. He had been in touch with Carlton's son, who couldn't help him. All of that was true, if a little deceptive.

The attorney thought he might be able to help. "For several years after Miss Olivia's death, her estate employed Mr. Fedder to look after the house and grounds. When he retired, his son, Ox, worked there until the house was sold in 2015. My firm administers a modest retirement fund for the senior Mr. Fedder that Miss Olivia set up a long time ago. I'm not at liberty to give you his address, but I'd be happy to forward a piece of mail to him if you'll send it to me."

Landry's assistant sent a note asking Carlton Fedder for information about the Arbors. If he could help, he'd pay up to five hundred dollars for it.

Two weeks later an administrator called from Oak Hills Senior Center in Opelousas, a town about sixty miles from St. Francisville. Carlton Fedder lived there; he had received the letter and he was willing to talk if someone would come over.

She added, "He suffers from Alzheimer's and he has good days and bad. The old times are things he recalls the best. Because of that, he may be able to help. And I'll admit the money would come in handy for him too."

A few days later, Landry sat on a breezy patio under a sprawling old oak tree. In a wheelchair next to him was eighty-eight-year-old Carlton Fedder. The man had once been a stout hulk like his son, Ox, but now his body was bent with arthritis and his bony fingers were curled into fists. He had a head of thick, wavy white hair and a goatee someone kept trimmed for him.

Unlike his son and despite his hardship, Fedder was friendly and wore a smile. "Call me Carl," he'd said from the outset, and then he asked what Landry wanted to know.

Carl had started working at the Arbors in 1954 after he answered an ad in the newspaper for a full-time houseman. "I wasn't sure what that was —" he laughed "— but I soon learned what Miss Olivia wanted was a jack-of-all-trades. I was good with my hands and we got along just fine."

"Did you know Olivia's second husband?"

"Mr. Bruno? Sure I did. He was already there when I hired on. They'd been married a few years, I guess. Her other husband died, you know. May the eighth, 1945. Fell through the banister at the house. I never knew him, of course. Died before I got there."

Amazed, Landry asked how he could recall the exact date of Charles Perrault's death.

"'Cause it's VE Day. The day the war ended in Europe. Mr. Charles died that very same day, or so Miss Olivia said."

"Tell me about her other husband. Bruno, correct?"

"Yes. Mr. Bruno Duval. He was a young feller, half the age of Miss Olivia. He was twenty-eight when they got married and she was fifty. Crazy, ain't it! I suppose he was lookin' for a gravy train, but he had no call to treat her like he did. She was tough as nails to him just like she was to me, but she was always fair. He'd run off to town and hang out at that club. You know the one I mean. Can't think of the name of it right now."

Landry nodded. The name of the club wasn't important.

"He started messin' around with girls his own age, and he was still married to her. He'd come in the house drunk at four in the afternoon when he was supposed to be at the office watchin' over Miss Olivia's affairs. Worthless, that man was, and finally he got his comeuppance. He hit her. Did you know that? There's no call for a man to hit a woman, no matter what she done or anythin' else. I done a lot of stuff in my time, but I never raised my hand to a woman. He hit her hard, right in the stomach. And her nearly sixty years old. Nope. No call for him to do that."

"What happened?"

The old man sat silently for a long time. He smiled occasionally, apparently reliving events from long, long ago. Then his face turned sad, and he said, "She was hurt real bad. She bled a whole, whole lot. Under her dress or somethin', you know? I helped her to the bathroom, but she made me leave. An hour or so later, she came out and said she would be okay."

"Where was Bruno?"

Once again he paused; then he smiled. "People get what they deserve. Do you believe that? I do. Yep, people that does things wrong usually ends up on the receivin' end of justice."

"Was he still in the house when Miss Olivia came out?"

The old man laughed. "Oh yeah, he was still there, all right. He stayed right close 'til I took care of things for Miss Olivia. I guess he's…oh, never mind. That ain't somethin' I can talk about anyways."

Landry stopped him. "What do you mean, Carl? I don't understand."

"Miss Olivia always treated me with respect. She was highfalutin and had fancy clothes and pretty things all over the house, but she never treated me like a servant. We was friends, me and her. I would have done anything for her, especially after Mr. Bruno hurt her like that. He was a bad man. He ran around on her and all she wanted was a little baby."

A miscarriage! That's what had happened when he hit Olivia!

"Did she have her baby?"

"No. She was supposed to, but she didn't. I don't know about that stuff, but she said it wasn't gonna happen after what he done. That's what made her so mad at him."

"What do you mean?"

"Justice. That's what I mean. No man should hit a woman. So he got his."

110

"Carl, what justice did he get?"

"Son, I've enjoyed talkin' to you a whole lot, but we're about done. I promised Miss Olivia back in 1959 that I'd always protect her good name. And I'm a man who keeps his promises. Someone treats me right, I treat them right."

"What did you do for Miss Olivia?"

"I always done whatever she asked. Me and her was friends, like I said."

The discussion was over. Carl said he was tired, and Landry had gotten all he was willing to give. As an orderly wheeled the man back to his room, Landry switched off the recorder in his pocket. He hadn't wanted to take notes, but he didn't want to miss a single word, and now he was glad he'd done it. The old man had remarkable clarity about events from decades ago, and he was harboring a secret that even his addled mind wouldn't give up.

Landry wrote a check to the facility, and the administrator promised to deposit it in Carl's account so they could buy things he needed for his comfort.

On the way back to New Orleans, Landry thought how he might break through Carl's defenses and learn more. This was the first solid information he had on Olivia's second husband, a much younger man she probably married so she could get pregnant. But if Carl was right, she was fifty-eight years old when something happened to Bruno. *Could* she have gotten pregnant at that age? *Would* she have? Apparently so, because it sounded as if she had miscarried when Bruno hit her.

Over the next week, Landry searched the records but found no death certificate in Louisiana for Bruno Duval. She might have thrown him out, or maybe he voluntarily moved away after what he'd done. Only Carlton Fedder knew what had happened that afternoon, and he wasn't talking.

He decided to give it one more try. He called the Oak Hills Senior Center and asked for the administrator. She remembered him from last time, and he said he would like to come see Carl again.

"You haven't heard," she replied gently. "I'm sorry to be the one to tell you, but Carl passed away three days ago. Peacefully in bed, I'm glad to report. Now his body and his mind can be healed again."

With the old man's death, Landry feared that the mystery of Olivia Beaumont's second husband might never be solved.

CHAPTER NINETEEN

There was one person left who might know something about Bruno Duval, but Landry had to find out his name. He searched the web to see who was chief of police in St. Francisville in 1959. He read an article about Chief David Hebert's 1977 retirement party; after thirty years on the force, Hebert was looking forward to golf and fishing.

Hebert was a common Cajun name and there were three Davids in town; Landry hoped one was the former chief. Like Carlton Fedder, the man would be around ninety years old now. He chose one of them and made the call. Thankful for small towns, the wrong David Hebert steered him to the right one, saying the old fellow was as feisty and alert as ever.

A moment later Landry was speaking with the man who was police chief on the day Bruno Duval hit his wife. He explained that he was doing research on the Arbors and that he'd talked to Carlton Fedder, who told him Olivia Beaumont had miscarried after Bruno hit her.

Hebert still recalled the incident, although his version surprised Landry. The chief said he'd never heard the tale Carl related. As far as the police knew, there had been no argument, no fistfight, no miscarriage, and no bloody garments. Bruno Duval hadn't been there either. Olivia had called the station one morning in 1959, maybe in the spring or summer, and reported her husband had gone to Baton Rouge for a business trip a week before and never came back.

The chief had gone to the Arbors himself. He didn't work many cases himself, but Miss Olivia was a member of the parish's upper class and was accorded respect. Hebert said he took Olivia's statement, sent Bruno's picture and information to Baton Rouge, and nothing else ever happened. As far as the former chief knew, he was still missing today.

"How was her demeanor during the interview?" Landry asked. "Was she distraught? Did she cry?"

"She was a hard woman, Mr. Drake. You hardly ever saw her in town, and she was unfriendly as hell when you did. I don't think anyone ever called her a friend. No, she didn't cry. She just sat there stone-faced like she was talking about the weather." He paused and added, "You know about Bruno, right? About the age difference and all that?"

Landry said he did, and the chief continued. "She was more than twice his age. Word around town was she wanted a child. She lost twin babies from her first husband years before, and then he fell from the third floor of the house. The gossips spread rumors about Miss Olivia, like how maybe she pushed him in retribution for having lost her children. People said the husband's ghost roamed the third floor at night. You could hear his pitiful wailing as he fell into the rotunda. Others said it was Olivia's ghost pacing the floor at the spot where she pushed him over. But to me, all that was bull. Police look at the facts, and the fact was, Bruno Duval was way, way younger than Miss Olivia. I always thought she picked him so she had a better chance of getting pregnant, even though she was in her fifties.

Someone who knew her said she was fixated on having a baby, and she put up with Bruno's infidelity to get what she wanted. Far as I know, there never was a baby, and that was that. She was too old."

"But according to Carl Fedder, she did become pregnant again, and she lost the baby when Bruno hit her."

"I never heard that until right now, and I don't know if I'd believe anything old Carl says. I heard he lost his mind. There's no telling what he remembers and what he makes up. The fact was, Bruno was younger, he'd make trips to Baton Rouge often. He'd stay for a week without contacting his wife, and that last time he just never came back. There was no reason to suspect foul play. I don't think Olivia suspected it either. My personal opinion is he ran off with a girl his own age. You really couldn't blame him — being married to Miss Olivia couldn't have been much fun. That's all I know about it, and my personal opinion doesn't matter a bit, just like Carl's doesn't. Bruno's been gone sixty years. Probably dead by now, I figure."

"One last question. Did you search the house when you were there?"

"No, there wasn't any need. Everyone in town knew about Bruno. He was gone, Mr. Drake. That's all there was to it."

Landry thanked the man and wished him well. The chief laughed and said there was a fishing pole in a bass boat waiting for him, and he'd better get to it.

After the call, Landry compared notes from his interview with Carl and the one today. He couldn't understand why Olivia hadn't call the police after Bruno hit her. Instead she had ordered her man Carl to do something about Bruno. Now Carl was dead, and that secret died with him.

CHAPTER TWENTY

One morning Cherry sat in the rocker watching the twins play with their dolls. There was nothing she enjoyed more than these times with her children, in the peaceful serenity of the nursery she'd so lovingly created for them.

Her reverie was broken when the door opened and their father walked in.

"Hey, girls. I've got news for you. The guys are coming this afternoon to paint in here. I need you to clean up all your toys and put them in the closet. You won't be able to play in here for a few days, but when you come back, it'll be great. They're taking down the drapes and opening the windows. I'll bet no one's opened them in years, and the outside air will make it bright and fresh in here."

Olivia glared at him, her face distorted with fury. She crossed her arms and stopped rocking. It frightened the girls to see how angry she was. Jordan saw them look into the corner; he looked and saw an empty rocker moving back and forth as if a light breeze had caught it. *What the hell?* he thought, staying calm so as not to further alarm the kids.

"Girls, what's wrong? We talked about this earlier. It's not healthy for you to breathe all this old dust, and it's not right that you spend so much time in this dark room. It'll be beautiful when we're done!"

"Okay, Daddy," Vi whispered. "I don't want to stay here anymore. Someone else can move the toys and stuff. I want to be with you." She ran to her father and took his hand. Ellie did the same, and he walked them downstairs, wondering what had scared them.

Olivia sat in the room by herself, rocking and thinking. The children's father would regret what he was doing. She knew something that would make him sorry.

One week later, all the furniture was back in place. The nursery was filled with sunshine that poured through clean, clear windowpanes. Sheers replaced the heavy curtains, and the walls glowed in vibrant primary colors. It was a happy room ready for playful children.

Jordan hadn't allowed Vi and Ellie to look inside until the work was finished and the paint odor was gone. He wanted it to be a big surprise, and today, as they stood in front of the door, he was hoping to see happy faces and hear squeals of delight.

"Ready?" he said, his hand on the doorknob. "One, two, three…OPEN!"

They walked in and looked around in shock.

"Daddy! What happened?" Ellie cried.

The *Alice in Wonderland* table was upside down on the floor and the four chairs tossed about. Someone had thrown the dolls everywhere, but the thing that brought tears to their eyes — and to his — was the beautiful china tea set. It was shattered into a million pieces. Not a cup or saucer was intact. Everything lay in a heap in the middle of the floor.

Jordan looked around in disbelief. He'd been in here an hour ago. The workmen left after that, but he knew they didn't do this. Jordan's employees — the only other people in the house — were downstairs, but none of them ever came to the second floor, nor would they have been behind something as awful as this.

The kids sobbed and said, "Why, Daddy? Why?"

He held them close and said he didn't know what had happened, but he would make everything right. "You'll have a brand-new tea set tomorrow if I have to fly to the moon to get it," he promised.

He sent them outside to play while he cleaned things up. He also called the supervisor whose crew remodeled the nursery. Jordan knew he didn't do it, but this was a process of elimination. The astonished man said everything had been fine when they left thirty minutes ago.

No one could have done it.

But someone did.

He cleaned the room, put everything back, and gave it a last look before going to get his girls. While he worked, Olivia sat in the rocker in the corner with a satisfied smirk on her face. She'd done enough for now; it wouldn't be right to alarm the children further, and she'd made her point. This was *her* house, not his.

Thanks to next-day delivery, the new tea set arrived the next afternoon. The girls were back in business, hosting their usual tea party by four. Neither the children nor Cherry mentioned yesterday's fiasco. Cherry had been so mad the kids were sure she had done it, but they were terrified to bring it up, so everyone acted as if nothing had happened.

"I have a marvelous idea for you girls," she said to them as Vi poured imaginary tea for the dolls. "How would you like to see your mother?"

Ellie gasped in disbelief. "Our *mother?* She's dead, Cherry. Don't say things like that!"

"What if I took you to see her?"

Vi whispered, "Wouldn't...wouldn't we have to die? That's what Dad says. Someday we'll see Mom again, but not until we go to heaven."

"He doesn't know about these things like I do. What if we really could go see her?"

Ellie grinned from ear to ear and said, "That would be wonderful! Can we really go?"

Vi, the sober twin, wasn't buying it. "That's not right, Cherry. Why are you telling us stuff like this? No one can see a dead person."

"*You* can if you go with me."

"No, we can't. It's impossible —"

"Want to know a secret, children? You *can* see a dead person. Look at me. I've been dead for a long, long time. But you can see me, can't you?"

Her revelation didn't surprise either of them, nor were they scared. By now they realized what she was, even though they didn't understand. They knew the woman who owned the house had died, and no one had lived there for fifty years until their dad bought it. Cherry said it was her house, that she had painted the walls and bought the toys in the nursery, so she had to be that dead woman. They didn't understand — even an adult couldn't have grasped something that bizarre — so they simply chose not to think about it. They interacted with her even though they knew their father couldn't see her. They kept her secret so they wouldn't lose their friend.

"Do you swear you're telling the truth?" Ellie asked quietly. "Can we really see Mom?"

"Of course, my dears. And you can come right back here afterwards. Don't you trust me? I would never hurt you or tell you something that wasn't true. You love me, don't you?"

She had never asked that question before, and they had never said those words to her. The girls looked at each other without answering.

"I asked you a question. Ellie, do you love me?"

Ellie hung her head. "Yes, ma'am."

"Vi?"

Vi looked at Ellie and grabbed her hand. She nodded her head slowly but said nothing.

"All right, then. Tomorrow we will go on an adventure. I will take you to see your mother."

That night at the kitchen table Jordan knew something was wrong. The girls always told stories about how they'd spent their day, but tonight they were silent and morose. They sat with their heads down and picked at their food.

"What's up, girls? Something's wrong. What is it?"

"Nothing's wrong, Daddy," Vi said. "We're just tired, that's all. May we be excused?"

He let it go and sent them upstairs to play while he cleaned the dinner dishes. When he went into their bedroom, he was surprised to find them in bed, even though the sun hadn't set. It was two hours before bedtime, and something was clearly bothering them.

He asked the child who couldn't keep a secret if she tried. "Vi, is there something you need to tell me?"

"I don't want to, Daddy." She began to cry, which got Ellie started too.

Jordan told Vi to come to Ellie's bed, and he put his arms around them. "Girls, I don't know what you've done or what's happened, but there can't be any secrets between the three of us. We're the only family we have now that Mom's gone —"

Torrents of tears flowed down the children's cheeks.

"Okay. That's it. Confession time. I don't care what it is, and you won't get into trouble, but tell me right now what's going on."

"Cherry's taking us to see Mommy tomorrow," Vi said. "But we can't do that, can we, Daddy? We told her we can't do that until we go to heaven."

Jordan struggled to keep his emotions hidden from the children. What the hell was this about? He knew that Cherry was their imaginary friend, the one who joined them at their tea parties. She was a grown-up and a female. But that was all he knew.

He had a sudden horrifying thought.

She *was* imaginary — right? But what if she was real?

That wasn't possible. There was no way a live person could come and go in this house without his knowing it. He'd barged in on the children many times, and there was never another person in the room. She wasn't real. And maybe that was worse than if she had been.

"You're right," he replied. "Mommy's in heaven, and people here can't just go see people in heaven, even though I wish we could. All we have of your mother now is the wonderful memories in our minds. We have pictures like this one here on your nightstand, and we can remember how much fun she was, even though you guys were little when she left."

He let all that sink in, and then he continued. "Tell me about Cherry."

"She told us we couldn't tell you about her."

Those words hit him like a freight train. This was a parent's nightmare — an adult "friend" who told little kids to keep their friendship a secret. That was the world of child molestation, exploitation and kidnapping.

He took a deep breath and fought off the trembling sensations, the dark thoughts creeping into his brain. He felt goosebumps as he held his daughters close.

"Tell me everything about her. I don't want you to leave anything out. I need to know everything."

The words poured out in torrents. They had kept more secrets than eight-year-olds should have to, and they couldn't wait to tell their father everything they knew at last. They talked about how she looked, what she said, how mad she was when he wanted to change things, and how they were sure she broke the tea set and knocked the furniture over.

"So this is not an imaginary friend, is it? You're saying she's a real person, this Cherry? Is she old like Daddy?"

Ellie shook her head. "She's not a real person. She's dead. She's the woman who put all those toys in the nursery. This was her house a long time ago. And she's a lot older than you are. She's like a grandmother or something, but she didn't have any children. She tells us we're her twins. She wanted us to call her Mama, but we told her we wouldn't."

This had gone far enough. Vi and Ellie would be devastated, but he couldn't allow them to see her again.

"Get dressed, girls," he said. "I'll stay in here with you while you do. We're going to have a little adventure. He took their rolling suitcases from the closet and said, "Put some extra clothes in here."

"Where are we going, Daddy?"

"We're going to spend the night in a hotel!"

The girls clapped their hands with glee. They loved going on trips with Daddy, and they eagerly packed their bags. They were so excited that neither thought to ask why they were leaving right at bedtime.

He booked a hotel room with two queen beds. Thirty minutes later they had checked in and the girls were in their pj's. They had been so upset they'd skipped dinner, so he let them order off the room-service menu, which they absolutely loved to do. They sat in bed eating chicken strips and fries and watched *Despicable Me* for the hundredth time.

Just before bed, Vi asked why they'd left home so fast.

"I don't want Cherry to play with you all again, that's all. She shouldn't have told you that about Mommy, and I'm not going to let her near you."

"Do you think she would hurt us, Daddy?" Ellie asked. "I don't think she would."

"I don't know. I don't know what she might do. All I know is my job is to keep you safe."

"But we get to go back home, right?"

"Yes," he answered, knowing they had to go back again, but wondering how he was going to keep them away from the ghost of Olivia Beaumont.

CHAPTER TWENTY-ONE

Up against hard deadlines on two critical projects, Jordan had to go back to his office. The girls' revelations tormented him, but he put them aside so he could concentrate. Mrs. Patrick had rearranged her housekeeping schedule, and she'd stay at the house with Vi and Ellie today. Tonight would be another story, one that Jordan would tackle later.

Mrs. Patrick had strict instructions to keep the children out of the nursery. He'd also ordered her to never let them out of her sight. Jordan was usually friendly and easygoing, and his commands puzzled Mrs. Patrick. She sensed that something was very wrong. She quizzed the girls, but they said nothing, as their daddy had asked.

At twenty minutes past ten a.m., all hell broke loose at the Arbors. Mrs. Patrick came flying down the stairs, screaming at the top of her lungs. Jordan was on a conference call with engineers in New Orleans; he heard the commotion and dropped the receiver. He and several others ran into the rotunda, and he caught Mrs. Patrick as she reached the bottom stair and fell into his arms.

"Oh my God! Oh my God! I didn't mean to do anything, Mr. Jordan, I promise you! I don't know what happened!"

"Calm down," he said, struggling to keep his composure and help her regain hers. Something was seriously wrong, and he felt that sense of dread again. "What are you talking about?"

"It's the children! I had to go to the bathroom. I'm so sorry, but I couldn't wait any longer. I wasn't gone for a minute, but when I came back, they weren't in the bedroom. I can't find them, Mr. Jordan! They're gone!"

He asked if she had looked in the nursery.

"That was the first place I went. The door was closed, and when I opened it, I thought I heard their voices, like maybe they were hiding in a closet or something. I called out to them, and I thought I heard real quiet laughing, but they weren't there!"

He ran up the stairs and threw open the door. His heart sank as he ran inside, because he heard sounds too, tinkly like a wind chime and with faint words from somewhere far away. He couldn't be sure, but it sounded like a child's voice. *His* child's voice.

Mrs. Patrick was right. They were gone.

CHAPTER TWENTY-TWO

Noise reverberated throughout the house. Everyone was talking at the same time. "I'll call the police!" his assistant, Lauren, screamed, and Jordan nodded. There was nothing the police could do, but not calling them would have raised more questions than doing it. He wondered what he'd tell them. Anyone who heard the truth would call him insane.

Police Chief Kimes and a young sergeant were on the scene in minutes. It wasn't often that the chief came himself, but after the girl's death and now a missing persons report, he thought it best to get involved from the beginning.

Jordan and the chief sat in his office while the other cop interviewed everyone else in the conference room.

Jordan said, "I don't have time for this. I have to find the girls."

"We'll do it quickly, but it has to happen." Kimes wasn't much older than Jordan and he had kids too. He empathized with this man and the gut-wrenching thing that was happening here. A kidnapping — for that was what Chief Kimes assumed had happened — was an awful crime, with an often-tragic outcome.

Kimes had been a cop for fourteen years. He had heard a lot of wild tales, but nothing like the story Jordan related. He learned about the children's imaginary friend, whom Jordan believed had lured away his kids.

"I know how crazy this sounds," Jordan said, "but hear me out. Their friend isn't imaginary. It's Olivia Beaumont."

"But she's been dead for years."

"Makes no difference. She took the girls. I know it!"

Jordan told him about her anger when he changed the nursery. She had retaliated by destroying their china tea set and taking them "to see their mother." He described the tea parties and how she was with Ellie and Vi every day they were in this house.

Incredulous, the chief remained composed. "Let me make sure I understand. You claim your children have a playmate who's the ghost of Miss Olivia Beaumont, and she took your girls to see their deceased mother?"

"That's it. That's what happened."

By now Chief Kimes was good at identifying a liar, and as crazy as the story was, this guy seemed to be telling the truth.

"You think your children actually saw Miss Olivia?"

"I'm sure of it. They carry on conversations. She's real to them. Vi and Ellie don't understand what they're dealing with. They're eight years old, for God's sake. They're just little kids!" He broke down for the first time, putting his face in his hands and sobbing. Then he composed himself, reached for a box of Kleenex, and continued.

"She was furious when I remodeled the nursery. Keeping it the same was so important to her that she put a restriction in the deed that nothing could be 'disturbed.' My lawyer said a little paint and some new drapes weren't a problem, especially since Olivia had been dead more than fifty years and there was no one left to complain. Well, he was wrong. I was wrong too. I had no idea she would do this. I didn't realize she *could*. I would never have touched the room — hell, I would never have bought the house if I'd known then what I saw today."

Kimes wrapped up the interview. His sergeant recounted what the others had said, and his head was full of questions. Most missing persons cases involved family or close friends of the victims. Jordan didn't seem like the kind of guy to kidnap his own kids, but there were crazies everywhere who acted completely sane.

Jordan hadn't been the last one to see his kids — that had been the housekeeper. He was so worried about them that he'd ordered her not to let them out of her sight. She didn't seem the type to kidnap children, and Jordan's alibi made sense. The only reason he'd brought the kids back to the house was that he had a work deadline. He intended to stay somewhere else for the night. It all made perfect sense, except that the father believed a ghost kidnapped his children.

The girls themselves were the enigma. Kimes wouldn't accept the testimonies at face value. In the factual, logical world of police work, there were no ghostly abductions or voices from beyond. The girls had left their bedroom when the housekeeper went to the bathroom. Most likely they had sneaked downstairs and gone outside. He didn't know what happened after that, but he had more faith in his theory than the story Jordan Blanchard told.

He ordered his officers to search the property, look under the house and go into the woods. Maybe someone lurking in the trees had abducted the twins.

The cops found nothing, and Chief Kimes was wrapping things up when a TV news van from Baton Rouge pulled into the parking lot. Jordan saw it out the window and stormed out of his office, screaming, "Dammit! Who the hell called the media?"

Kimes explained that the stations monitored police radio transmissions. They would have heard the initial call and then the second one, when the sergeant radioed for the chief to come interview the father. "They're allowed to do that," he added, "but not on your property without permission."

Jordan's assistant, Lauren, went to the porch and politely advised the crew that they weren't welcome. No one was available for an interview, and if they wanted to shoot video, they had to go off the property to do it.

They moved their van to the highway, and the newscaster filmed his report with the house behind him. As the two patrol cars pulled out, the reporter flagged down one and asked Chief Kimes for a statement.

"It's an ongoing investigation, boys. You heard the radio transmission, so you already know the girls are missing, but I can't tell you anything more right now."

Kimes was correct that they'd heard the transmission, but the radio call was for a 10-57, a missing person. They had come here with nothing, and the chief had just given them valuable information. More than one person was missing. He'd called them "girls," so these were children. This was a big, big deal.

News people on a hot lead can be as tenacious as an alligator in the Louisiana swamps, and the reporter sensed a huge story here. It took a couple of calls and a favor cashed in to learn that architect Jordan Blanchard had twin daughters, Ellie and Violette, and they were missing. That became the lead story on the noon news.

Jordan's critical projects meant nothing to him now; he left them to his staff to complete. Jordan sat at the table in the nursery; he wanted to be close to his girls, and this was the best place he knew. He cried, he prayed out loud, and he pleaded with Olivia to bring them back. He told them he loved them, and he asked them to speak to him, but the sunny, cheerful room was quiet.

———

Landry sat in his office and opened an email from his producer with a link to the news report from Baton Rouge. Police were at the Arbors in St. Francisville, where there were missing children. Neither the police nor the home's owner, Jordan Blanchard, had issued a statement, but people in the community who knew the family confirmed that the children who lived in the house were Jordan's eight-year-old twin daughters, Violette and Ellie.

Landry's first thought was to drive to St. Francisville at once, but he talked himself out of it. He was an investigative reporter, and breaking news wasn't his beat.

He called Callie to be sure she had heard the news. She hadn't; as Jordan's friend, it shocked her that the girls were missing. Thinking he might need support, she drove to St. Francisville.

Someone knocked on the nursery door. Jordan had no idea how many hours he'd sat in the nursery, and Lauren asked if he wanted to come downstairs and eat something. Mrs. Patrick usually prepared lunch, but in her agitated state, she'd gone home. Jordan said he wasn't hungry and he wanted to stay here a little longer.

An hour later he walked down the stairs and into the kitchen. Two co-workers were sitting at the table drinking coffee. Their conversation stopped when he walked in.

"Go on," he said in a monotone. "Don't mind me."

He fixed a cup of coffee and gazed out the window, lost in swirling, dark, awful thoughts as the uncomfortable pair sneaked out. Sinking in a vortex of horror, he stared at nothing and imagined he heard the children's voices. They rang like an echo in his head, and his helplessness made him crazy with anger and fear.

He heard the voices again, more distinct than before.

"Daddy! Daddy!"

Lauren rushed into the kitchen and screamed, "Jordan! Hurry! The girls are up on the landing! They're calling you!"

The staff ran to the rotunda as Jordan scrambled up to the second-floor hallway and fell to his knees. He hugged the girls as everyone sighed in relief.

Lauren called Mrs. Patrick and gave her the news. The woman could rest now that the children had returned. Relieved and thankful, she promised to check in with Jordan later to see if he needed any help.

He was desperate to learn where the children had been, but he didn't want to push them if they were in a fragile emotional state. "Do you feel like talking about where you went?" he asked, and they said they wanted to.

"Can we go in the nursery and talk?" Vi asked.

He snapped, "Why would you want to go in there? That's where —" He paused. That room was hell on earth for him, but not for the kids.

Ellie explained, "We love it there, Daddy. That's our favorite room."

It's her *favorite room too,* he mused, and the thought angered him. But there was no reason to confuse the girls, at least until he understood what had happened. They had disappeared from the bedroom, not the nursery. It might have had nothing at all to do with what had happened. He sat with them and listened.

Children explain things differently than adults do. Whether something is beyond the realm of possibility doesn't matter to them. In the simple words kids use, Vi and Ellie struggled to tell their father what had happened. It had begun the moment Mrs. Patrick left them alone in their bedroom. Cherry had called out to them.

Jordan interrupted. "She called you? From where? Why did no one else in the house hear her?"

"She didn't call us like that. She called us in our heads. I heard her and so did Ellie. She asked us to come see something really neat. She said we could come right back. Why are you sad? And where did Mrs. Patrick go? We came right back. We were only gone one minute."

The words sent a shiver down Jordan's spine. *One minute.* The girls didn't realize they'd been gone for over four hours.

"Where did you see Cherry? What room was she in?"

Ellie said, "She was here. We came to the nursery and she took our hands. She never touched us before and it felt weird. All tingly with little sparks. Did yours feel that way too, Vi?" Her sister nodded, and she continued.

"We didn't really walk or fly or anything. She took us to that mirror in the corner and we all kind of went inside it. I can't explain it. It was like —" She paused. "I want to tell you about it, Daddy, but I don't know how to."

Vi took a try. "It's hard to tell somebody else. It was really crazy. Not mean or bad or sad — just different. There were clouds and a lot of colors and real pretty music. There were nice smells too. We walked like on a sidewalk or something, but my feet weren't touching the ground. Being there made me feel good. Oh, and I could still see the nursery. We were there, but I could see the table, the dolls and even Peter. We were here, but we were also in that other place. Do you believe me, Daddy? It's the truth!"

"I believe you, honey. I really do. Did Cherry tell you why she wanted to take you there?"

Ellie looked at her sister, and Vi averted her eyes.

"Not really. I…I don't remember much about that."

"Ellie? You seem to know something. What did she say?"

"She told us not to tell."

He wanted to lash out, but he caught himself. He paused, took a deep breath, and relaxed. He wouldn't learn anything by upsetting his kids. This wasn't their fault.

"Okay, girls, I'm your daddy. We agreed we don't keep secrets in this family. Cherry's not family. Only the three of us are. Tell me what she said."

"She said that beautiful place we saw is on the way to where Mommy lives now. If we want to go see her, all we have to do is say yes and Cherry will take us."

Vi put her small hand in her dad's. A tear rolled down her cheek as she said, "I want to see her, Daddy. Ellie too. Maybe you can come with us."

He said nothing because he could think of nothing to say. "Then what happened?"

Ellie said, "Vi asked Cherry when we were going back home, and she said all we had to do was let go of her hand. When we did, she left and we were back here. That's when we ran out in the hall and yelled for you! It all happened so fast!"

He took them down to the kitchen for milk and cookies. Lauren popped in to say a news crew from Baton Rouge was here, hoping to get a statement, and he agreed to talk to them. The world knew his kids were missing, and he wanted to say they were safe.

He gave a brief statement. The children had wandered off and lost track of time. They were in the house the entire time and they were never in danger. They reappeared in a hallway, not realizing what a stir they'd caused. He thanked the public for their prayers and said he was grateful things turned out well.

———

As Callie turned off Highway 61 into downtown St. Francisville, her phone rang. It was Landry advising her the children were back. He said the Baton Rouge station would have a full report on the evening news.

The excellent news gave her goosebumps. She told him she had driven to St. Francisville, but now she had second thoughts.

"As much as I want to know what happened, he's about to be inundated. He has to be emotionally exhausted — can you imagine the horror of not knowing where your children are? He must have been sick with worry; then suddenly they're safe. He's been whipsawed from despair into relief.

"I'm going back. If I go there, I'll only add more stress. I'll call and tell him I'm thinking about him. That's all."

"Call me if you learn anything interesting."

She hesitated. "If Jordan says it's okay, then sure. He's an old friend, Landry —"

"Enough said. I shouldn't have asked."

———

As addled as his mind was with everything going on, Jordan had a deadline that was critical to his future. Now that the girls were safe, he had to work on his projects. He put Ellie and Vi in the conference room to watch a movie, instructed Lauren to stay with them every second and joined his co-workers to wrap up the two proposals due tomorrow.

He took only one call that afternoon — Callie's. She told him how glad she was that the kids were okay. He explained he was on a tight deadline, but if she could come on Saturday — the day after tomorrow — he and the kids would love to have her spend the weekend. She said she'd love to, and she hung up without revealing she was five minutes away. Then she drove home.

Lauren interrupted Jordan at 6:30 to say the girls were getting restless. The movie was over, they were hungry, and she needed to get home. He apologized for losing track of time. He sent his staff home too; everyone was tired, and the proposals would easily be done by tomorrow's 4 p.m. deadline.

"How about some chicken nuggets from McDonald's?" he said to Vi and Ellie, who were delighted.

"Milkshakes too?" Vi asked, and he said yes. They'd get everything to go, return to the hotel for one more night, and have a picnic in bed. That thrilled the girls, and he asked them to run upstairs and pick out a few games to take to the hotel. Then he had an alarming thought.

"No! Don't go up there alone! I'll go with you. We'll all go look for the games." It was tragic that he couldn't let his girls out of sight in their own house.

They had a great time in their hotel room. They saw it as an adventure, but being forced out of his house troubled him deeply. At bedtime they asked how much longer they would stay in the hotel. "This is a neat place," Ellie said, "but we like our real bedroom most. All of our stuff's there."

He promised this was their last night here. Now wasn't the time to tell the girls more, because the news would distress them. There wouldn't be any more nights in their bedroom, even though Olivia had only appeared in the nursery and never on the third floor where the kids slept. He knew nothing about what she was, but he was certain she could move freely about the house. He couldn't risk her getting to them again. They couldn't stay at the Arbors until she was gone. He had no idea how to make that happen. If he didn't, they would never spend another night in that house.

He tucked them in bed, they said prayers, and he kissed them goodnight. Vi whispered, "Daddy, Cherry got real mad at you for changing the nursery. She said she loves us, and she calls us her children. But we're not, Daddy, and I don't like it when she says that. She said you'd better not ever disobey her again. Please don't do it, Daddy. I don't want anything —" She stopped, unable — or unwilling — to finish the thought.

Dear God, he thought as he hugged his daughters and got in the bed next to theirs. *Dear God, help me understand what to say and what to do. I don't know what's going on here, but I can't let her get to the children again. Vi's even worrying about me! Protect all of us until I can figure out what to do about all this.*

It was a rough night for Jordan. He couldn't stop thinking about their situation. Tomorrow would be busy with the two project submissions and a hard deadline. More important was where they'd go next. Living somewhere else would be a hardship for him. He had no family or close friends to help with the girls, which was why the home-office arrangement was perfect. His kids came home after school and his staff was there. Since he was just downstairs, he didn't need to take time off or hire a sitter.

One thing loomed large — the cost of living somewhere else. His practice was doing well, but he couldn't afford to rent a second house and another office. The Arbors had been perfect for their needs — until Olivia Beaumont ruined everything.

His eyes popped open every hour or so, and it took a moment to realize where he was. He checked on the kids, making sure they were sound asleep, and at last, around three, he slept too. He awoke to the alarm at seven. He had to get to work; Mrs. Patrick was coming at eight to take the children out for the day. He'd pick them up at her house after work.

One more night had passed with no problems, but shelling out a hundred and fifty dollars a night for a hotel room was an expensive short-term solution. He had to find something else.

They checked out and went to a deli for breakfast. He drove to the Arbors, and when they saw the old house, the girls cheered. His mood was just the opposite; this wasn't his home now. Because of someone who didn't exist, three people were forced to change their lives.

Lauren knew Jordan had stayed in a hotel, and she knew he believed the house was haunted. She was a skeptic, but it wasn't her place to offer an opinion. She hadn't been through what he had. She could tell that her boss was under tremendous stress, and when he asked her to look into short-term accommodations starting that night, she didn't question him. She promised to report back when she had something.

He dedicated his full attention to the projects. His associates had done a terrific job getting everything ready, and he used the remaining hours to add finishing touches and triple-check every single number. In a rare move, he closed his office door, a signal to the staff that he was not to be disturbed. "Only for the kids," he told Lauren. "Only if they need me. Don't interrupt for anything else, period.

CHAPTER TWENTY-THREE

Thirty minutes before the deadline, Jordan put the proposals into a FedEx drop box. He picked up the kids from Mrs. Patrick's house and stopped at a C-store to get two bottles of champagne and a case of Dixie beer. Jordan put the girls in the conference room and asked everyone to join them there. He congratulated his employees on creating two top-notch proposals despite the turmoil of the children's disappearance. He felt certain Blanchard & Blanchard would win at least one bid, and maybe both. Getting either would be a huge revenue boost. Everyone toasted, including Vi and Ellie, who raised glasses of Gatorade.

As kudos and congratulations went around the room, Lauren moved next to her boss and asked what he had decided about tonight. The blank look on his face told her he hadn't looked at the email she had sent hours ago. She'd found a short-term rental on Airbnb, sent him the link, and told him this was the only thing available; if he wanted it, he'd better hurry. He'd ordered her not to disturb him, and she hadn't. He never saw her message; an hour after she sent it, someone else rented the house.

He admitted he'd forgotten and wished he'd told her to rent something herself. "Just book another night at the hotel," he said.

"Not an option, I'm afraid. There's not a room in town. The *American Queen* steamship people invited a group of travel agents on a boat ride down the Mississippi. They're spending two nights here and they've booked everything. I even tried Baton Rouge, but with an LSU game tomorrow, decent places there are full too. I found a room, but trust me, you wouldn't have put Vi and Ellie there. I'd offer my place, but my brother came yesterday for a visit and I'm full!"

There had been nothing more important than finding lodging. *Why did I check out this morning?I should have kept the room just in case. I spent all day doing* my *stuff, taking care of* my *business, and now it's after six and we have no place to go. What dad forgets his children's welfare?*

Frustrated and angry, he went into his office and closed the door. It had been a long day and he couldn't pack up the kids now. Who knew how long he'd drive to find a decent motel? There was one other option — the only one left.

They would spend one last night in the house, in his bedroom, not theirs.

Vi and Ellie were thrilled. The hotel was fun, but home was best. They had no idea their dad intended for this to be the last time.

"We're staying together again!" Vi cried as they sat on his bed while he pulled in a mattress and put sheets and pillows on it.

"Yes, we are. I thought the hotel was fun, so let's do it one more time!"

"Can we sleep in our bedroom, Daddy? Please?"

He shook his head and said, "I've already put the mattress on the floor. We're sleeping in here." He tucked them in to his bed, said prayers, and kissed them goodnight. Just minutes later he heard their soft breathing. It had been a long day and they were tired.

Jordan was asleep as soon as he hit the mattress. Sometime around four a raspy sound woke him. He cocked an ear, and when he heard the faint noise again, he sat up. The room was in shadows as pale predawn light cast a ghostly hue.

There was the sound again. Now he saw what it was. His heart jumped as he watched the doorknob turn to one side, then the other.

As he raced to their bed, he heard a whisper. Each time he'd checked on the girls during the night, they'd been asleep. The covers on Ellie's side were pulled up the way she liked them, and he reached to touch her hair.

She wasn't there.

Bile rose in his throat. *Ellie's moved over to Vi's side! Dear God, she has to be there!* He turned on the lamp and jerked down the covers. The bed was empty.

He heard whispers again, so quiet and distant that they might not have been real. It was Vi's voice. *Daddy, we can't get in!*

He collapsed on the floor and sobbed.

How could he have done this to his children? What did it matter how tired he was, or how far he had to drive to find a room? What difference did proposals and deadlines make when his children's lives were at stake? For the terrible thing he'd done, he might pay the ultimate price this time.

Jordan heard it again — the raspy grate of the doorknob, followed by a knock. He ran to the door and threw it open. Vi and Ellie rushed in and hugged him. They were holding two rag dolls.

"What's wrong, Daddy?" Ellie asked. "Why are you crying?"

"I thought I'd lost you again! Where were you?"

"You forgot to give us the dolls we sleep with. Vi and I went to our bedroom and got them. When we came back, we couldn't make the knob turn!"

"Was everything okay in your room?"

Vi nodded. "Cherry asked us to come to the nursery with her, but we didn't. We told her we were sleeping in here with you."

"Cherry was in your bedroom?"

"No, Daddy. She talked to us in our heads."

Ellie said, "We didn't mean to scare you. We needed our dolls."

He hugged them. "She'll never stop — I know that now. This is it, kids. We can't stay here ever again!"

There it was, laid out before them. Now the children understood what was happening, why they had stayed in a hotel and why their dad slept on the floor. He said he was sorry, but this was the last time they'd be staying at the Arbors.

An arctic blast of air swept through the room. "It's her, isn't it?" he asked, and Ellie nodded.

"Is she here?"

She hesitated. "No, Daddy, but she can hear you and — well, I think she's sad."

Vi shook her head. "Tell him the truth, Ellie. She *is* here, and she's not sad. She's mad at you, Daddy." She turned and said, "Don't be mad at my dad, Cherry. He wants to protect us!"

"Can she hear you?" he whispered.

Vi nodded and pointed across the room. "She's here now. She's standing in that corner."

Jordan ran over. He saw nothing, but he sensed a presence. He stepped into a cold, squishy puddle and jumped. There was something wet on the floor.

"Crap!" he yelled, recoiling. He lost his balance and fell to the floor, landing hard on his bottom.

Laughing, the girls came to him, and their hysterics made him smile too. He had to be careful not to burden his little ones with scary thoughts. They didn't see their invisible friend as a kidnapper — to them, she was a confidante, a special grown-up only they could see. He'd do anything to protect them, but right now he had to pretend for their sakes that everything was okay.

"I guess old Cherry pushed me down," he said.

They chortled, "You fell, Daddy. You fell on your butt all by yourself!"

In a moment Vi said, "Bye, Cherry." The chill in the room left with her.

"Where did she go?"

Ellie said, "I don't know. Into the mirror in the nursery, I guess. That's where she usually goes. Daddy, please, please don't make us leave. This is the best place we've ever lived. We love it here. We don't want to go anywhere else!"

How do you explain unreality to two eight-year-olds? He sat on the floor between them and held them close.

He said Cherry wanted to take them where Mommy was. Did they understand that for a person to go there, they would have to die? "No matter what Cherry tells you," he added, "living people can't go where the people who've died are."

He explained that Cherry was Olivia Beaumont. She had been born in this house and she had died here a long time ago.

"She's dead, girls. That's why everything she does is so strange. That's why I can't see her. Can you understand what I'm telling you?"

Vi wept. "We know she's dead. She told us. That doesn't matter. We can see her and she plays with us! She's just different, that's all."

"I'm sorry. I can't let anything happen to you."

Everyone was wide awake; it was after five, and he had only a few more hours before they could leave.

"How about Brunch with Daddy?" he asked, and Vi said they couldn't do it because today wasn't Sunday. He said this would be a special one — their first ever Friday brunch. On the floor outside their bathroom, he checked emails on his phone while the girls showered. They went to the kitchen, and soon the smell of bacon cooking wafted through the house. The kids stirred up waffle mix and set the table while Jordan downed a cup of black Community coffee, then a second.

Ellie had to use the restroom, so everyone went with her. Cherry was already mad that he was taking them away. He didn't dare let them out of his sight, so he and Vi waited outside the door until she finished.

The sun's first rays peeked through the window. He heard someone call his name.

"In here," he answered as Lauren walked in to find her boss in a T-shirt and boxers and needing a shower and a shave. The girls hugged her.

She laughed and said, "Sorry to startle you guys. Jordan, I knew you weren't happy about staying here, and I thought about you all during the night. I got up early and came over to check on you."

"We spent the night in Daddy's room!" Ellie announced. "He's afraid of Cherry, but she's our friend. He says because of her we can't stay here anymore. Is he going to make you leave too?"

She gave Jordan a shrug and he said, "I'll explain later. Can you keep the kids with you while I shower and shave?"

"I think that's a great idea," she quipped. "I've always worried about having our office in your house. Sure enough, here you are walking around in your skivvies."

He laughed it off, went upstairs and got ready. When he returned, there was a Monopoly game underway. He told Vi and Ellie he had something to tell them.

"Shall I go?" Lauren asked, but he said she needed to hear it too.

"I know you like Cherry, but you must trust me. She's not a real person. You know she's dead because you told me. She may act like your friend, but she wants to take you away from me forever. I know you love this house. So do I, but we can't stay here any longer —"

At that moment every cabinet door in the kitchen — the ones above the countertop and those below — flew open at the same time. The girls screamed and Jordan shouted, "Get away from us! Stay away from my children!"

Lauren stared in astonishment at the open doors, wondering what could have caused such a manifestation. She didn't realize Jordan was facing an adversary he couldn't see, one who was hell-bent on stealing his twins.

Time had run out. This charade was over.

CHAPTER TWENTY-FOUR

The most difficult part had been explaining things to his daughters. Dealing with his staff was a different challenge. They were adults — intelligent people with degrees who dealt with life as everyone does. Things happened a certain way, for a certain reason or for no reason, but events could be explained.

Now their boss, an architect whom they admired and respected, was sitting before them in his conference room, telling them a fantastic tale. Jordan's girls sat on each side of him, and he gripped their arms so tightly it made them squirm. He looked like a lost, desperate man who believed his children were in danger, but his employees didn't know why. They knew Jordan well; they worked side by side with him. Yesterday he'd been one of them, joining them in a beer to celebrate a job well done. Now he was a tormented, paranoid soul.

They found his tale astounding. He explained about Olivia Beaumont, the domineering matriarch who lost two husbands in unusual circumstances. One died in the house and the other disappeared. She died in 1965, leaving instructions that the house remain unoccupied and off the market for fifty years. And so it had sat until Jordan bought it in 2015.

Olivia had wanted children. Why else would she furnish a nursery with twin cribs and fill it with toys and dolls? She had painted murals on the walls and prepared everything for babies who never arrived. Before her death, she decreed that future owners should never disturb this one special room.

Until Ellie and Vi came along, no one had ever played in the nursery. After Olivia told Ellie in a dream where the lost key was, the children made the room theirs, and they had an imaginary friend named Cherry who played with them. She was a grown-up who wore a long black dress just like people in town said Olivia Beaumont did. The girls could see her, but Jordan couldn't.

He told his staff every incredible detail. Miss Olivia couldn't still be in this house, yet she was. She'd been dead for fifty years, but she attended tea parties with his children. She was evil and she had taken his daughters away. She was a force he couldn't reckon with. Her presence defied all logic. The only thing for certain was that he couldn't leave the children alone in this house for even a moment any longer. When he said those words, Vi and Ellie cried.

"What does all this mean for us?" one of Jordan's co-workers asked.

"At the moment I don't know. I can't afford two houses and two offices, but this is day one of my new plan, whatever that means. The girls and I need a place to stay, starting tonight. That's my project for today. I'll be available by phone if you need anything, and I'll see you Monday."

Lauren's brother was off to New Orleans for the weekend, so she offered to keep the kids. Tomorrow she'd take them to the zoo in Baton Rouge, and he would pick them up on Sunday. That afforded him plenty of time to work things out. The girls loved Lauren and begged their dad to let them go. He gave her the rest of Friday off, told her to keep tabs of her expenses so he could reimburse her, and asked her to check in now and then.

With the girls gone, finding a place to stay had less urgency. Now he needed lodging by Sunday night, not tonight. He could stay here and save the expense. Things would all be worked out by the time he picked up Vi and Ellie.

He looked at apartments. He'd lived in one in college and wasn't happy about doing it again. He walked through some houses that were for sale, but they felt cramped compared to the Arbors. He didn't know why he wasted time looking at homes for sale anyway. Without selling the Arbors first, he'd never qualify for another mortgage.

He checked with the nicer hotels about monthly rates and found them exorbitant — throwing money down a rat hole, in his opinion, just like rent. And he looked at VRBOs, houses for rent by owners on a short- or medium-term basis. A VRBO was a rental too, but some were nicer than apartments. The problem was that none were available for six weeks.

Jordan treated himself to a cocktail and a steak at a nice local place before going back to the place he'd called home. The sun had set as he opened the front door to an empty house. He went into his office, checked email, and found himself feeling tired and ready for bed by nine. His heels clicked on the parquet floor of the rotunda as he walked across the broad area and looked up three floors to the dome high above.

He paused, listening. There was a sound — the creak of a door opening and closing.

That sound would have frightened him once. He was the only living thing in the house tonight, and Olivia's comings and goings in the nursery made him angry now.

He stormed up the stairs, threw open the door, and flipped on the light.

She had done it again. Chairs were overturned, dolls were tossed into corners, and the new tea set was in a thousand pieces. He was glad the girls didn't have to see this.

Like last time, the two cribs were undisturbed, their linens lined up perfectly. They were ready for two little occupants.

"You cantankerous old bitch," he shouted. "You won't win this battle. You may drive us out of here, but this is my house now. If my family has to leave, you'll damned well go too!"

As he turned to leave, he glanced in a corner. Peter, the large rabbit who had joined the children for tea every day, sat propped against a wall. The handle of a steak knife protruded from the middle of his chest and his stuffing was strewn all over the floor. It was the first time she had done something like that, and it reinforced his decision to leave. It also made him uneasy as hell.

That night the hours crept by. Jordan was awake a lot, listening to the usual creaks, groans and raspy noises that made up the ancient mansion. But the night passed without incident.

He rose early and spent two hours cleaning the nursery. He put Peter and his innards into a grocery bag; he'd drop him off today at the alterations lady he used. She could make him good as new by the end of the day. He ordered another tea set, one identical to the most recent one. The kids might not play with it in this nursery again, but he didn't want them to know the second one had been destroyed too. They needed a healthy fear of their so-called friend, but there was no reason to terrify them.

Jordan was in town by ten. He dropped off the rabbit and went to see Harold Emmanuel, a man in his late sixties who was St. Francisville's premier real estate agent. Jordan had crafted a story, one that was believable but also wouldn't hurt the property value of the Arbors.

"So you're thinking about selling the old place?" Harold asked. "You've only been there, what — two years?"

"Around that. You may have heard the news report about my girls disappearing the other day."

The older man nodded.

"Well, it turns out they were roaming around in the house and got lost. The place is huge, you know, and it has nooks and crannies and stairways everywhere."

"I'm sure the experience unnerved them. Are they scared to stay in the house now?"

"Yes, and it's not working for me either. The house is too big for us. It's historically significant and it should be open for tours every day. I've wanted to do that, but after the recent death of a tourist, I stopped doing them. All people would want is to see the ghost.

"I need a smaller place. I hope I can find another one that'll be both house and office, to save on the expense."

Jordan's cellphone rang; he glanced at it and declined the call.

The Realtor said, "I'm surprised. You have the best view in town, situated right on the Mississippi River. You bought the house right and you've fixed it up nicely. The accident was just that — a tragic accident. In fact, old Chérie would be downright proud of what you've done to the place."

Jordan jerked his head up. "*Old Chérie?* Who are you talking about?"

"Chérie. You haven't heard that name? That was Miss Olivia's nickname. People say that's what her two-timing second husband, Bruno, called her — Chérie — 'beloved' in French. Nobody else in town considered her beloved; she never had any friends, far as I ever heard. But the nickname stuck, I guess. Most of the old-timers like me still call her Chérie."

Chérie. Or Cherry, as two English-speaking children would pronounce the French word. He clinched his fists and grimaced. Harold asked if everything was all right.

"I hope you can find something for me. I need to go now; I have to find a place to stay —" He paused, having said too much.

"You're not staying at the Arbors anymore? Is it because of the kids?"

"I'm sorry. I need to return a call. I want to put the Arbors on the market, and I'd like to see what else is available. That's it."

He called Callie back from the car. The moment she answered, he remembered. It was Saturday and she was here at his invitation. She'd gone to the house, but nobody was home. She was waiting at a coffee shop, wondering where he was.

He had invited her to come spend the weekend, and he'd forgotten all about it.

Talk about bad timing.

CHAPTER TWENTY-FIVE

Callie was a good friend, and he was ashamed he had berated her about Landry. She had planned an entire weekend at his invitation, and he couldn't send her away. He still had to find someplace to stay starting tomorrow night, but he decided to look on the positive side. She might help him work things out.

He'd been a skeptic when Callie had told him about Anne-Marie. Back then he didn't believe in haunted houses or spirits, but everything was different today. He'd been converted to a believer in his own home. Because of a woman who'd been dead for decades, he was going to sell the house he loved. What a change, he thought, and what a revelation. The paranormal wasn't fantasy. It absolutely existed and it was as genuine as reality. Because of Olivia Beaumont — Chérie — he believed in ghosts.

He met Callie with a hug and brought her to the Arbors. It surprised her that the girls were gone for the weekend and the house sat empty and quiet. Once she knew everything he was dealing with, she was concerned. Her own situation had been different. Her resident apparition was friendly and helpful, while Jordan's was obsessed with the twins and hostile toward him.

"You're welcome to come stay at Beau Rivage," she said, "but I doubt that works for you. It's an hour's drive each way; with the kids in school, I'll bet it's too far. Anyway, the offer stands."

He thanked her for the generous offer and said he hoped to find a place in town. The girls would be back tomorrow, and he had to find a place to stay by then.

Jordan admitted he had forgotten about her visit, so she offered to go home and let him get things done. But he urged her to stay. Callie was a good friend, and he didn't have many of those these days. The couple of friends he'd had when Claire was alive drifted away after her death. They had lives of their own, and the presence of a widower their own age would dampen the mood of a cocktail party or dinner.

He liked Callie very much. Six years younger, she had been on her own for years, and the success of Beau Rivage was a tribute to her tenacity and business sense. She had overcome adversity and had survived life-threatening dangers.

And, he admitted to himself, she was beautiful. Drop-dead gorgeous, to be honest. He hadn't thought that way about a girl in…well, in four years.

"You're here and I could use an extra set of eyes and ears. I know it's not the relaxing weekend you expected, but if you can help me find someplace to stay, I'd appreciate it. We'll pick up some steaks, and tonight I'll be your grill master."

He thought of something. "I've told you everything that's going on here. I should have asked if you'd be more comfortable spending the night somewhere else."

She grinned. "If you're not staying here, neither will I. I'm not brave enough to be the only living thing in this house at night. But if you're staying, I'm game. I live with a ghost too, you know!"

Not a ghost like Chérie, he thought, happy she was staying. Callie had always been simply a client and a good friend. Now all of a sudden he felt like a teenager fantasizing about how to get a pretty girl alone.

Don't be stupid. You're lonely and you don't know what to do right now. Don't mess up a friendship.

The afternoon turned out to be a marathon. They walked through three rental properties. One required a six-month lease and the others a year. The places were smaller than he wanted, and none was zoned commercial, so his office would have to be somewhere else. That meant double rent. The houses needed work; he estimated it would take a couple of weeks to make them habitable, and even then they weren't right.

Around four Jordan got a lucky break. The Realtor, Harold Emmanuel, called with an idea. He'd thought of something that might work for Jordan's home-office needs.

Harold gave them directions to Savoy Farm, a scenic property a few miles south of St. Francisville on Alexander Creek. It was a working horse ranch with a sprawling main house and several outbuildings. It was a beautiful rural environment with fenced pastures where sleek mares grazed alongside their foals.

He met them at the gate and led them to a log cabin a few hundred yards past the big house. It had a wide, shaded front porch that ran the length of the cabin. It was a warm, inviting place. Jordan felt a peace and calmness just being there. The furnished cabin had six bedrooms, three on one side of a large rustic den and three on the other. One side could be his office, he mused, and the other his family's living area.

The owner was a friend of the Realtor's — a pediatrician who practiced in Baton Rouge and lived in the main house with his wife. An overseer lived in another cabin nearby, and there was a bunkhouse for the cowboys who worked on the place and trained the horses.

The cabin had been rented for three years to two LSU medical students and their wives. Both recently graduated and moved away, and Harold had thought of the empty house after his conversation with Jordan that morning. He'd made a call and explained Jordan's situation — not all of it, but enough. A client needed living quarters and a place for a few people to work. Harold explained that Jordan was a successful architect in town. The owner liked the possibility of another dependable tenant, and he offered a reasonable month-to-month rental rate.

Jordan thought the deal would work and Callie agreed. He said he'd take it and arranged a hotel room for five nights starting tomorrow. That was plenty of time to move their personal items. He'd leave the furniture at the Arbors for now; the cabin had plenty, and when he put the mansion up for sale, it would show better furnished.

He wouldn't move the office right away; although there was plenty of room, he wasn't sure about the rural setting. Clients came often, and an office on a farm didn't seem professional to him. The firm would stay at the Arbors until the house sold or Olivia created a problem. When one or the other happened, he'd be forced to relocate. It would be a huge undertaking, far more involved than moving personal belongings to the cabin, but he'd deal with it if he had to.

That evening at the Arbors, he fixed a glass of Chardonnay for her and a Chivas on the rocks for himself. She sat on the porch while he prepped the grill, and then he walked her out to the family cemetery. They looked at the stones and he explained what he knew about the people buried there. The guardian angel was still a mystery.

He took her hand as they walked slowly back across the lawn. Being with her gave him a warm feeling he hadn't experienced in a long, long time. There was a bit of sadness, but being with Callie felt good. Maybe there was something bright in his future. He gave her hand a little squeeze; she squeezed back and smiled.

She'd been waiting for the right time to broach a touchy subject, and this seemed as good as any. She hoped her question wouldn't ruin what was shaping up to be a wonderful evening.

"Once the girls are gone, would you mind if Landry looked around your house?"

He stopped walking and looked in her face. For a second she thought she'd made a serious mistake, but he didn't seem upset and he didn't let go of her hand.

"Why, Callie? Why is he so insistent on coming to the Arbors, and why do you want it to happen so much? You know what a private person I am. I don't want my family blasted across the TV."

"Don't you think too much has happened already to keep things secret? The disappearance of your girls was just the most recent thing that went public. The media was all over the girl's death a few weeks ago, and they compared it to Olivia's husband's death the same way.

"It's too late to keep secrets. Don't involve Vi and Ellie; just keep the press away from them. There's weird stuff happening here, and with your permission or not, someone's going to blow it wide open. You admit the house is haunted. You have a ghost with an agenda. Wouldn't it be better to let Landry come as a friend than to have strangers poking around? At least you could set the boundaries.

He smiled. "You're still persuasive, aren't you? I'd forgotten how hardheaded you were when we worked on Beau Rivage together."

"So is that a yes? I think you'll be happier you did it your way."

"Not quite. We're not even out of the house yet, so give me some time. You can tell him you put the hard sell on me, and I'm thinking about it, but that's all. And speaking of things I'm thinking about —" He put his hand on her cheek, lifted her face and kissed her.

"My goodness, sir," she said in her best imitation of Scarlett O'Hara. "You take my breath away!"

They walked to the house without speaking, both knowing everything had just changed between them.

He served a 2005 Cabernet Sauvignon with the steaks, one of six expensive bottles he'd bought five years ago to hold for a special occasion. A year later Claire was dead, and he realized that every single day he'd had with her was special, but they were young, full of life, and unconcerned about death. From that day until now, there had been nothing to celebrate. He went to the closet, pulled out a bottle, and poured it carefully into a decanter. He put another on the counter just in case. And between the excellent steaks and the stimulating conversation, both bottles were consumed.

She helped clean up, and they went back outside to finish the wine. "Any news about Mark Streater?" he asked, and she shook her head.

Callie knew Mark from college, and he had been a big help when she inherited Beau Rivage. It had required a lot of remodeling, and he offered to help without charging a fortune she couldn't afford. She came to rely on him for far more than repairs; he helped her arrange a loan to pay for upgrades, and he stood by her when her despicable uncle Willard tried to destroy her. She was attracted to Mark until Anne-Marie helped her see what he really was. He had a vendetta against Callie — something that involved the house itself.

Two years ago on a terrifying night at the mansion, she had learned her friend was psychotic. He forced his way in, committed a horrific crime, and was charged with a felony. He made bail and disappeared. People told the sheriff they saw him in Cabo or Puerto Vallarta, but he remained at large. At some point she had decided to stop worrying and begin living again.

"Mark's gone for good, I'd say. I guess he's in Mexico. If he comes back, he could face life in prison. It's been two years and I've moved on."

"It was a terrible time," he said, and she nodded, remembering how glad she had been to find Jordan. She'd hired him to finish the restoration after Mark's arrest; the two men never met, but Jordan had seen how fragile and shaken she was in those days. Mark had created a hellish situation for her, but Jordan had helped her recover.

Callie finished her wine and said she needed to turn in. It had been a long day and she hadn't even unpacked. Her bags still sat by the front door, where she'd dropped them when she walked in.

He apologized for not working out the bedroom earlier. The time had passed quickly for both of them, and from Jordan's perspective, their time together was wonderful.

"I was hoping for a tour too," she admitted, and he promised it would happen before she left tomorrow.

"You have a choice of bedrooms," he said. "I sleep on the third floor, and there are two guest bedrooms up there. The second floor has three bedrooms. One is the master — Olivia's room. It adjoins the nursery, where all the encounters have happened. I don't recommend staying there, but that's just me. It's your call."

Fueled by a bit too much wine and a delightful evening, she felt adventurous. "If it's okay, I'd like to stay in her room. Maybe something will happen!"

"Seriously? You're more of a risk-taker than I remembered!"

She laughed. "Maybe it's reckless, but I'm no stranger to spirits, you know. I'd like to give the master bedroom a try."

"Okay," he replied. "It's your…"

"Funeral?" She smiled, surprised at his choice of clichés.

"I'm sorry. I didn't mean it that way. You just have to be careful, that's all."

He made sure the bed had fresh sheets and that the adjoining bathroom had towels. He paused at the door and said, "I've had a wonderful time today, and I hope you sleep well tonight."

She put her arms around his neck and gave him another kiss. This one lingered long enough to mean something.

He smiled as he climbed the stairs to his bedroom on the floor above hers. He crawled into bed and fell asleep, thinking of possibilities. It had been a long, long time since he'd had thoughts like this, and it was a nice feeling.

Neither he nor Callie had an inkling what would happen just six hours later.

CHAPTER TWENTY-SIX

Callie had trouble sleeping. Maybe it was the sumptuous steak and more wine than usual. Maybe it was because she couldn't stop thinking about Jordan, a man who'd been a friend but whom she was seeing in a different light after being alone with him and hearing him bare his soul.

She heard the grandfather clock on the first floor chime the hour at midnight. At some point she slept, but around three her eyes flew open and she struggled to recall where she was. Had she heard a noise, something that awakened her? Or was it a dream?

In the shadows across the room, something drifted. It was tall and had substance. It stood in front of the draperies, almost invisible in the darkness, but there was no doubt it was there. It scared her; she reached for her phone to use the flashlight, but she knocked it off the nightstand. Now the specter was closer, standing in the middle of the room. It appeared to be a person, although in the darkness she wasn't sure.

"What do you want?" she cried. "Get away!"

Whatever it was raised an arm. Bony fingers emerged from a sleeve and pointed at the bedroom door, silently bidding her to go there. Somehow she knew she wasn't in danger. This apparition wanted to help.

As she hopped out of bed, she heard a shout. *It's Jordan!* She ran into the hallway.

Moonlight bathed the rotunda and the hallways in an eerie half-light. She saw movement on the floor above her. Jordan stood at the far end, near the railing.

She ran toward the staircase and shouted, "Jordan! What is it?"

He glanced at her. "Don't come up here!" he shouted. He turned and yelled, "Get away!" to someone else.

She bounded up the stairs and ran to his side. Drenched in sweat, he was wheezing.

"What happened? Are you all right?"

"There was someone here, but they're gone. My bedroom's over there, and I heard a noise in the hall. I opened the door and saw a light coming from that bedroom." He pointed to an open door across the rotunda. "I went to check it out, and someone dressed in black ran past me into the hall. I think I yelled —"

"I heard you call out."

"It startled me. The figure came rushing at me, and I yelled for it to get away. I turned my head when I heard you shout, and it disappeared."

She took his hand. "When I saw you, I thought you were about to fall over the banister like the others." That surprised him — in the heat of the moment he hadn't realized he had been at the spot where the girl fell.

They went to the kitchen and she made hot tea. He protested, but she insisted it would calm him down and help him sleep.

"What do you think you saw?" she asked as they sat at the table. "It couldn't be Olivia —"

He snapped, "Why would you say that? Who else could it have been?" He apologized for his tone. In his frazzled state, the last thing he wanted was to push her away.

She wanted to calm him, not make things worse. "Here's what I saw. Something woke me — a figure cloaked in black standing by the windows. It raised its arm and pointed to the door. If it hadn't waked me, I might not have heard you shout. I think it was Olivia, and she was trying to help you."

"Trying to help *me*? Think about what you're saying. I'm more inclined to think she woke you up so you could witness her forcing me over the railing. One more death and one step closer to getting everyone out of her house. I don't think Miss Olivia is a friendly ghost. I think she's evil as hell, and I almost was her next victim."

Callie didn't answer. She was certain of one thing — whatever was in her bedroom was trying to help. She had felt no evil. Quite the opposite, it might have been trying to save Jordan's life.

They sat next to each other, sipping tea and lost in thought. Were there two figures or simply Olivia up to her old tricks? Was Jordan's an intruder?

Around four a.m. they went upstairs. He stood in her doorway for a long moment, and she smiled and patted the side of the bed. Their goodnight kiss was different this time. It was deep and meaningful, something that fired emotions and the senses. He crawled into bed beside her. Nestled in her arms, he was asleep in seconds.

They walked through tallgrass along the river, holding hands and sharing hopes, dreams and thoughts of a future together. The sun broke through tall, billowy clouds. Birds sang, crickets chirped and locusts buzzed, in the discordant, beautiful sound that meant it was summer on the bayou. Shaded by leafy branches of a live oak tree, she put her arms around his neck and kissed him passionately. He smiled, pulled her close and —

A harsh noise jolted him awake. She stirred as his hand fumbled around on the nightstand until he found his ringing phone. It was Lauren and it was 9:30 in the morning. He hadn't slept this late in years.

"Hey, what's up?" he mumbled.

Since she knew her boss was an early riser, his voice surprised her. "Sorry, did I wake you? I was just checking in. The girls wondered when they could come home. Call me back later."

"No, no, it's fine." He cleared cobwebs from his brain as Callie snuggled closer to him. He had to get the kids, but it would have been great to have one more day. "I'll be there. What time's good for you?" They agreed that Jordan would pick the girls up at Lauren's house at twelve, and they'd all go to Sunday brunch at the hotel, a rare treat that Vi and Ellie loved.

He lay back on the pillow and Callie said, "Good morning! I hope you gave us a little time before we have to get up."

The next hour was the best one Jordan had experienced in a long time. They burrowed under the covers, held each other close, kissed deeply, and explored the depths of passion. She took him to a place he'd wondered if he'd ever find again, and in one glorious hour, his years of loneliness were over. He was a new man with a renewed purpose in life. At thirty-seven, he felt like a teenager.

Later he recalled that Claire never entered his thoughts, and that was good. It was what she would have wanted, just as he would have wanted her to experience the joys of life again if he died. Claire was gone; what they'd had was wonderful, but this was his second chance.

Before they left to get Vi and Ellie, Jordan gave her a tour of the house. She was particularly interested in the nursery. He didn't mention how the girls could disappear through the portal. Things were going well, and there was no need to bring up disturbing thoughts.

Jordan introduced his girls to Callie, and they immediately liked her. The girls didn't have proper clothes for brunch, so Callie had chosen outfits for them at the house. They changed in the back seat as they drove to the hotel, and they whispered and giggled when their dad smiled at Callie.

Vi and Ellie skipped through the dining room, took their seats, and told Callie she'd done a great job picking out their clothes. "You did way better than Dad would have," Vi teased.

Jordan didn't mention his visit to the farm yesterday afternoon. Instead, they talked about the things they'd done with Lauren. They'd had a blast and she'd even taken them for a banana split at the ice cream shop after a pizza dinner. "We'll spend the night with her anytime," they added.

They drove to the Arbors so everyone could pack for their stay at the hotel. Callie left around two — Jordan walked her to the car. The girls stood on the porch and watched him kiss her goodbye. They nudged each other and snickered, and after she left, they said Callie was his girlfriend. He laughed and said they should mind their own business, which caused them to burst out laughing.

They were loading their backpacks when Ellie looked up and cocked her head as though she were listening. Jordan looked at Vi, who was doing the same thing.

"She wants us to come to the nursery," Ellie whispered. "She wants to tell us goodbye. Are we leaving forever, Daddy? Cherry thinks we are, and that makes her unhappy."

He looked around the room. "Where is she?" he yelled, startling the children. "Show me where she is."

"She's not here," Vi answered. "You don't understand, Daddy. She isn't here; she's talking to us in our heads. She wants us to go to the nursery."

"Then let's do it!" He grabbed them by the arms, maneuvered them to the stairway, and hurried them down.

Vi cried, "Daddy, don't! You're hurting my arm! You're scaring me!"

He stopped and apologized. "I'm sorry, honey. I'm not trying to scare you. I just want to prove something." He threw open the door to the nursery and took them inside.

Everything was in its place. A newly repaired rabbit sat in his chair, the new tea service was where the old one had been, and Olivia had behaved herself this time.

"Look around, girls. The room's empty. She's not here waiting for you. I want you to see for yourselves that Chérie isn't here. This has to stop, now. She isn't your friend, she's not your playmate, and she isn't here. I can't explain what's going on in this house, but as we can all see, she is *not* in this room."

Vi and Ellie turned to the rocker that sat in the corner, and so did Jordan. It was moving back and forth. The chair was empty, and there was no breeze in the room.

"Is she sitting there?" he whispered.

They nodded, and their father went berserk.

CHAPTER TWENTY-SEVEN

Jordan's phone vibrated in his pocket, but he ignored it. He was too busy screaming orders at his terrified children.

"Get out! Get out of the house right now!" He pulled his daughters roughly down the stairs, ignoring their stumbles and how terrified they were.

As he pushed them into the car, Ellie cried, "Daddy, our backpacks are still in our room! What's the matter? Why are you so mad at Cherry?"

His phone vibrated again, but there was no time for that. "I'm not mad. I'm afraid. She wants to take you away again — don't you understand? We have to get out of here now!"

Frightened and confused, the girls cowered in their car seats as he spun the Tahoe around. Vi whimpered, "Daddy, you left the front door open!"

"I don't care!"

She burst out in a wail of tears and said, "Stop shouting at us! You're scaring me, Daddy!"

He stopped the car and turned off the ignition. He'd done a horrible thing; how he felt inside was one thing, but he was the parent, and he had no right to shift his own fears and doubts to two eight-year-olds. He wasn't like this, and they had every right to be afraid.

He calmed himself. "I'm so sorry. I shouldn't have done that, but all I care about is keeping you safe. You're all I have, and I would do anything to make sure nothing ever harms you. I know that you can see Chérie and you know she's a ghost. That's hard for me to understand, and I know it is for you too. I'm afraid, kids. I know daddies aren't supposed to be afraid, but Chérie wants to take you away for herself. She told you she built that nursery for you, but you know that's not right. She lived and died a long time ago, before I was born. She couldn't have known about you. She never had children of her own, don't you see? That's why she wants you. But I want you, because you're my girls, not hers. We're never spending the night here again."

He saw in their faces that he'd said too much. How could he expect eight-year-olds to understand something he couldn't comprehend himself? The girls were afraid of him, not their friend Cherry. They knew she was different, but they had played with her long enough that she was real to them. They loved the nursery and that strange place she'd taken them.

There was one thing they could understand. No matter what, daddies always told the truth. If Daddy said Cherry was trying to take them away, then he was only trying to protect them. They did understand that, and they told him so.

"We can't ever stay there again?" Vi asked. "Could we go back if Cherry left?"

"Maybe, but I don't think she'll leave her house." Selling the house was his only option. He hated it, but it was what he must do.

He drove back and locked the front door. Then he looked at his phone. The missed calls had been from Callie, and there was a message. Before he listened to it, he called

Lauren and asked if she would go to the Arbors, get the girls' backpacks, and bring them to the hotel. She agreed but wondered why he asked. The hotel was less than two miles from the house. Why didn't he get the backpacks himself? But as oddly as her boss had been acting, she did what he asked without question.

He listened to Callie's voicemail and learned her car had broken down on the highway a few miles south of town. She wasn't asking him to come — she'd called roadside assistance — but he wanted to see her again and it wasn't far. He and the girls drove out to see what had happened.

She said her car was fine, but then it just quit. Fortunately, she'd been in the right lane and pulled to the shoulder without incident.

"Want to take a look under the hood?" she asked, and Jordan laughed, explaining that he knew absolutely nothing about cars except how to fill the gas tank. She sat in the car and talked with the kids while they waited for the repairman.

Ellie's and Vi's minds were reeling with what had happened, and they insisted their dad tell Callie. Afterwards she told the kids that Jordan did a good thing. Even though Vi and Ellie thought of Cherry as a playmate, she wasn't that at all.

"Most people don't believe in ghosts, but we know they're real, don't we? You guys have one in your house, and your daddy's right to worry about her. If she really wants you for herself, then you couldn't ever see your dad again. That would be sad, wouldn't it?"

The girls nodded and, as children often do, simply changed the subject to get off a topic they were done with.

"Are you Dad's girlfriend?" Ellie asked with a mischievous grin. Vi snorted and Jordan told Ellie to stop asking silly questions.

Callie smiled, and Ellie said, "We think you are!"

Jordan got a reprieve as the AAA repairman pulled his truck to the shoulder in front of Callie's car. He looked under the hood for a few minutes and said, "The serpentine belt's snapped. Seems kind of strange in a late-model car like this, and it doesn't look like it frayed from wear. Take a look." He held up the rubber belt and pointed to the place where it had broken. "See how even this looks? I think someone cut it partway through with a knife. That would let your car run for a few miles, but then it would break and you'd be dead, like you are. Not you, hopefully. Just the car. Got any enemies?" he asked, cracking a joke that wasn't funny.

Callie looked at Jordan and he glanced at the girls. They would wait until later to talk. The man replaced the belt, and fifteen minutes later there were more kisses, more giggles and more goodbyes. Jordan promised to call her for lunch soon, and she was on her way south while they headed north to their lodging for the next few days.

CHAPTER TWENTY-EIGHT

Mrs. Patrick refused to babysit the girls inside the house now. She might take them out for a few hours, but after the fiasco, she would never keep them in the house again. That left only Lauren Baxter.

His assistant became Jordan's salvation. She agreed to keep Vi and Ellie weekdays until school resumed in two weeks. When Jordan had office work for her, the girls would sit in the conference room, watching a movie or playing a game, and she'd work next to them. It turned out to be a good solution. Ellie and Vi loved being with her, Lauren received her salary, and she got to be outdoors a lot instead of cooped up in the office.

Once school started, Jordan would get his assistant back. There were after-school activities every weekday, so the girls wouldn't set foot in the house ever again. Jordan would pick them up at five and take them straight to their new home. The girls had seen the cabin, and they seemed excited about living on a farm among horses and cows.

He made several trips hauling clothes, toys, books and kitchen supplies to the cabin, and he enlisted Mrs. Patrick to give it a once-over on the Saturday morning they would move in. She would make up the beds and get everything ready, and that afternoon they'd move from the hotel to their temporary home. He had two days to go, and then maybe things would settle down.

Lauren picked up the girls on Friday morning for a picnic in the park and an afternoon at the movies. She said she'd have them back by five.

It had only been four days, but Jordan found himself missing Callie a lot. With Ellie and Vi in good hands, he called and invited her to lunch. She accepted and he hoped she was as excited as he was.

Since there were no restaurants near Beau Rivage, he suggested one of his favorites — Soileau's in Opelousas — for lunch. From St. Francisville to Callie's house was forty minutes; he picked her up at Beau Rivage, and twenty minutes later they were at Soileau's.

He asked for a booth. She picked a side and laughed when he told her to scoot over so he could sit next to her. She smiled and took his hand, and within minutes they were enjoying great wine and perusing a menu filled with mouthwatering Cajun dishes.

During lunch she mentioned Landry's request again. "Tomorrow you guys are moving and the office will be the only thing left at the house. Have you thought any more about letting Landry do some filming now that you're out?"

He asked her opinion about going public. Would paranormal activity make the house harder to sell? They talked it through; nineteenth-century houses in these Cajun parishes all had ghost stories with varying degrees of scariness. Some were downright gory while others were tender. She believed that a house with a history was intriguing, and she pointed out that when Penny was doing tours at Jordan's house, she'd included the ghost of Miss Olivia in her spiel.

Ask your Realtor, she suggested, and Jordan texted Harold for an opinion. He replied in minutes. His opinion was that in this part of the world, eerie goings-on were an attraction, not a detriment.

Maybe it was the wine, maybe it was the company, and maybe it was her mellowing influence on his psyche. He agreed to let Landry come one evening after his staff was gone.

After the dishes were cleared, they ordered coffee and talked. He revealed all the bizarre things that had happened; she knew some of it already — she'd even been part of it — but he wanted her to know everything behind his decision to tear apart the life they'd planned at the Arbors.

She asked how much she could tell Landry and he answered, "We might as well do this right if we're going to do it at all. Tell him everything. He needs to know what to look for."

The maître d' stopped by their table, apologetically asking if his people could prepare the dining room for dinner. They had lost track of time. It was almost three and they were the last customers in the place. A blossoming romance, good conversation, and excellent food and wine had allowed three hours to pass in a flash. Caught up in each other, they had ignored everything around them, and now he had to hurry back to meet Lauren at five.

As they drove to Beau Rivage, they commented on how much fun the lunch had been. When they arrived, he walked her to the porch, took her in his arms, and said, "I can't remember the last time I had something wonderful happen."

She smiled. "I love every minute I'm with you. Drive safely and let me know how the move goes tomorrow." They embraced and kissed once, then again.

She couldn't stop smiling as she stood on the porch while he drove down the long tree-lined drive and out towards the main road. She watched until his Tahoe was out of sight, and when it was, she called Landry.

CHAPTER TWENTY-NINE

The next Friday night, five people stood in the second-floor hallway of the Arbors. It was after eight p.m. and their mission was to spend several hours and perhaps all night investigating the mysterious goings-on inside the nursery.

Henri Duchamp drove up from New Orleans. He was president of the Louisiana Society for the Paranormal, and he knew Landry well. He was a frequent source on *Bayou Hauntings* shows, and there was a mutual respect between them. Duchamp was a scholarly-looking man in his forties with horn-rimmed glasses and a neatly trimmed goatee. Tonight he sported his usual outfit — a tweed jacket and bow tie that made him look like an absentminded professor. He was perfect for the job; he had a passion for unexplained phenomena, but he was quick to debunk things that weren't.

Landry had asked Callie to join them, and after learning Jordan was coming too, she accepted.

They drove in rain that was heavy at times. Here in St. Francisville it hadn't hit yet, but the storm had been building all afternoon, and the forecast predicted heavy rain and flash flooding in the bayous. Zigzags of lightning illuminated the halls as they entered the house. Seconds later thunder rumbled, a deep crescendo that signaled the rain wouldn't be far behind.

Once everyone arrived, they stood in the hall outside the nursery door. Jordan kept it locked now, and they had to wait for him. Callie, Cate and Landry watched Henri unpack boxes of complicated-looking equipment. There were motion-sensing devices, air-temperature monitors, an ultrasensitive audio recorder, and an electromagnetic fluctuator. He usually included a video recorder, but tonight that was someone else's bailiwick.

A Channel Nine cameraman named Phil sat on the floor, arranging his gear. He would run the cameras and he proclaimed everything ready to go.

Jordan was late. He should have been here thirty minutes ago, and Callie wondered if it was raining at the cabin. Thank goodness he'd given her a key to the house, or else they'd be out on the porch in the rain. It would have been good if the guys could have gone into the nursery and set everything up, but with everything that had happened, Jordan never left the door unlocked.

Once he had been cleared to come, Landry decided he had nothing to lose by calling Jordan to request one more favor. The nursery would be filled with observers and experts. Would he bring his girls for the filming?

To categorize his response as angry was a massive understatement. The only positive thing Jordan said was that he understood why Landry wanted them there. Olivia was more likely to manifest herself with the children, but Landry got the message that using Vi and Ellie as bait was a bad suggestion.

Landry told Callie about how upset Jordan got when he asked about the girls. She already knew it from Jordan himself. He thought Landry was way out of line, and he said he'd almost cancelled the entire thing, but he'd agreed and he intended to keep his promise. He told Callie he'd be there, but he hadn't decided whether he'd set foot in the nursery or just stay in the hall.

It was unlike him to be even five minutes late. She phoned him, but the call went straight to voicemail. She sent a text asking where he was.

A moment later her phone rang.

"Jordan! I was getting worried. Is everything all right?" A pang of fear struck her as she heard noises in the background — wailing sirens and people yelling.

"Ma'am, this is Trooper Lauder with the Louisiana State Police. May I ask your relationship to Mr. Blanchard?"

She panicked. "What's going on? What's happened?"

"There's been an accident, ma'am. Out on Highway 61 south of St. Francisville."

"Is he…is Jordan okay?"

"He's injured, Miss Callie — uh, may I have your last name? And I need to know your relationship to Mr. Blanchard, please."

"I'm Callie Pilantro. He's a…a really close friend. How did you know my first name?"

"I heard his phone ring and saw your name on caller ID. I returned the call because there were two children in his SUV —"

"Oh my God, Ellie and Vi! He has them! Are they all right?"

"The EMTs are working on all three of them, but it looks like the car seats saved the kids from serious harm. Are they his children?"

"Yes. How about Jordan? How is he? Is he —"

He interrupted. "Miss Pilantro, who should I contact about the children? If the EMTs release them here, who can take them? Is there a Mrs. Blanchard?"

"No. His wife died. Are you saying they're not releasing Jordan? What are you not telling me?"

"I'm sorry. Since Mr. Blanchard is your friend, I know this is hard. He's been in a very serious accident, and he's going to the hospital. They may take the girls too, but I can see them; they're up and moving around, so they may be released. If there's no one to give them to, we have to notify Children and Family Services."

"No, don't do that! I'll take them. Jordan's my —" She paused, thinking of the right word. "He's my boyfriend. They know me and I can bring them home and stay with them."

"Can you come now, just in case? Ask for me — Trooper Lauder."

"I'll be there as quickly as I can." She hung up and told the others. Cate asked if Callie wanted her to come along, and she gratefully accepted. There would be no filming tonight. Henri and Phil went back to New Orleans, and Landry stayed until Cate and Callie's return.

He was alone in the house for the first time. He went into the master bedroom — the room where Callie had slept the night Jordan fended off something upstairs. She'd seen an apparition here, and he wanted to experience the room for himself. He stood in the darkness while his eyes adjusted. In a moment he stepped inside and walked to the door that went into the nursery. He was astonished to find it unlocked — they could have gotten into the room after all, but Jordan wouldn't have liked that. He opened the door and walked into the room he'd heard so much about.

It was easier to see in there than in the bedroom because Jordan had removed the draperies. Eerie moonbeams played throughout the room, their light shimmering and pulsating through the gauzy sheer curtains.

There was Olivia's chair, where she rocked back and forth while only the children could see her. There was the *Alice in Wonderland* table, where little girls entertained a ghost for tea. A large rabbit sat in one chair, his waistcoat repaired from the stabbing.

At the far end stood the two cribs he'd heard so much about. Like the others, he wondered why they were here. He stood beside them, his hand on the fragile linen covers, and wondered what all this had to do with the twins who had become Olivia's playmates.

Once Cate and Callie returned, he'd learn about Jordan's condition. That would determine what happened next to his film project. Would he ever discover the true secrets of the Arbors, or was this bewitching idea over before it ever began?

He sat in the dark nursery, rocking in Olivia's chair and hoping something would happen. It was a classic night for supernatural activity. A storm raged, lightning flashed across the skies, and thunder boomed and rolled every few seconds. The old house spoke to him in a melancholy voice — moaning, grinding sounds issuing forth from a building that had weathered storms for one hundred and sixty-eight years. He listened and watched, hoping for something and ready for anything, but Olivia was quiet.

CHAPTER THIRTY

Callie and Cate drove south on Highway 61. As anxious as they were to get to the scene of the accident, it was slow going. Callie hit puddles of water every few yards, and she worried about hydroplaning in the steady rain. Topping a hill, they saw red and blue lights in the distance and the brake lights of cars and trucks in front of them slowing for heavy traffic. Her heart skipped a beat — the crash had happened at the turnoff to the farm where Jordan had rented his cabin. He'd been on his way to meet them.

It took ten harrowing minutes to go the last mile. They reached a place where patrol cars blocked the southbound lane. Troopers were directing cars to the opposite side of the highway to get around the wreck. Callie rolled down the window and explained that Trooper Lauder had called her to come. The officer moved a barrier, instructed her where to park, and showed her who Lauder was.

Shaken and scared before she arrived, Callie screamed in horror now as she walked around an ambulance and viewed the crash scene. The wreckage was so awful that they wondered how anyone survived. The driver's door of Jordan's Tahoe was crushed almost to the console, and deployed airbags lay in the mangled cab. The other vehicle was a pickup — they knew that only because the back half was still intact. It looked as if the driver had T-boned Jordan.

A young African-American trooper walked up to them. "Miss Pilantro? Mike Lauder. I'm sorry to have asked you to come down here — I know it's hard to do this, but it's for the girls."

"Where are they? Can I see them?"

"Yes, ma'am. They're in an ambulance right over here." Vi and Ellie cried when they saw Callie and Cate; as they hugged tightly, there were tears from everyone.

"They won't let us see Daddy!" Vi said. "We're scared! Is Daddy going to be all right?"

The trooper saved Callie from an uncomfortable question to which she had no answer. "The medics are treating your daddy," he said in a soothing voice. "He's going to fly to the hospital in a helicopter. The storm's supposed to let up soon, and then they'll take him to where the doctors can fix him up."

"Why can't we see him?"

Callie held the children's hands as the trooper explained that he couldn't talk to them right now. "They gave him some medicine so he wouldn't hurt, and it made him fall asleep."

Ellie's lip trembled. "Will he ever wake up again?"

The women were impressed at how well the young officer handled the girls. "The medics here are the best, and the doctors at the hospital will be too. He'll probably have an operation and then he'll want to see you all." He turned to Callie and asked if she could stay with the kids while he spoke with the EMT to see if they could go home.

Vi and Ellie were good to go. They had been through a severe trauma and the impact had thrown them to the right side of the rear seat, but the car seat restraints kept them safe. The side air bag had deployed, scratching Ellie's face, but luckily they were on the opposite side from the point of impact. They were bumped and bruised and sore, but nothing was broken.

Cate asked, "What about the other driver? Is he —"

Trooper Lauder shook his head.

He asked the girls if they wanted to go with Callie, and they said yes at once. They were glad to have someone with whom they felt safe and secure. The trooper handed Jordan's cellphone to Callie, took her number, and promised to keep her updated. She thanked him for his empathy with the children.

Trooper Lauder knelt down and hugged Ellie and Vi. "You girls go home and get some sleep. The doctors will take good care of your father, and Callie will take good care of you."

Callie switched the car seats to her vehicle. Policemen helped her maneuver into the northbound lane, and she drove back to the house to drop Cate off.

When the girls realized where they were going, they hoped they were staying at home, but Callie told them they were staying at the cabin, not the Arbors. When she dropped Cate off, Landry told Callie they were heading back to New Orleans. Callie told him Highway 61 was awful because of the wreck. She knew an alternate route to Jordan's cabin that would also work for her friends. Beach Road to Parish Road 965 to Highway 61 and then south, she advised. She locked up the house and they left.

She used Jordan's hidden key to get in. The girls were washed up and in bed before ten. They prayed for their dad, and Callie promised that tomorrow morning she'd tell them any news she got during the night. She discovered that the only other room with a made-up bed was Jordan's. He wasn't coming home tonight, and he wouldn't care anyway. She crawled between the sheets and willed herself to sleep.

The call came at a quarter past eleven. Trooper Lauder sounded exhausted. The medivac chopper couldn't land in the storm, so Jordan had gone by ambulance to University

Medical Center in New Orleans a couple of hours earlier. They were there now and he was going into surgery shortly.

"I'm not supposed to say anything about his condition," Lauder continued, "so please keep this to yourself until you hear it from someone else. I'm sure you're sick with worry — I know I would be — so here's what I heard from the medics. His vitals are stable, but he hasn't regained consciousness. He has several broken ribs, and his left arm is broken. He may have a punctured lung. He left here on a ventilator, but that happens a lot in these situations. They're just being cautious. He's in rough shape, Miss Pilantro. There's no denying that, but at least he's alive."

She asked him if they knew how the wreck happened, and he said the investigators were still at the scene. It appeared Jordan pulled onto the highway in front of a southbound pickup, but he cautioned that might not have been how it was. A team from Baton Rouge was examining the vehicles. When they finished, the cops would wrap up the scene and tow trucks would haul the wrecked cars away. They hoped to have the highway open in time for morning traffic.

There was little sleep for Callie the rest of the night. She called Cate and relayed the information; then she lay in Jordan's bed staring at the ceiling. When she dozed, she dreamed of flashing red and blue lights and car parts strewn all over a rain-drenched highway.

She got up at five and called the hospital. Without a medical authorization, they wouldn't say much, but she learned that he was still in surgery. He was alive, and that was enough for her right now.

Unsure about their morning routines, she woke the girls before seven, told them the doctors were working on their daddy, and asked what they wanted for breakfast.

It was good that the eight-year-old girls were self-sufficient in selecting clothes, preparing lunch boxes and gathering backpacks. She dropped them off at school and said she or Lauren would pick them up at five. Then she drove to the highway and turned south. She'd be in New Orleans in under two hours, traffic permitting.

When she passed the place where the accident had occurred, only one state vehicle remained. An SUV that said Louisiana State Police — Medical Examiner sat on the shoulder, its light bar flashing red and blue. A man in jeans and a polo shirt was walking around in the wet grass, staring intently at the ground. She figured he was wrapping up things, looking for anything they'd overlooked.

She got to the hospital and learned he was in surgical ICU. She went to the nurses' station and explained her situation. The nurse was sympathetic, but without a medical release signed by the patient, the hospital couldn't give her any information.

"There's no way he could sign anything; he's been unconscious since the accident. He'd give me a release if he could. There's no family around here except twin girls, and I'm taking care of them. His wife died several years ago. Please help me. I have to know what I'm facing here — for the children's sake if not for my own."

The nurse turned to her computer, scrolled through several screens, and said, "I know how worried you must be. The doctor's reducing his pain medication. When he wakes up, they want to check for a concussion. If I were you, I'd stick around here for a couple of hours. It might be longer, but my bet is he'll be awake by this afternoon. If the doctor says yes and if he's up to it, maybe you can have a few minutes with him."

Callie appreciated the information and asked if she could give the nurse her number. She'd go out for a while and be back by one p.m., and if he woke sooner, the nurse said she'd give Callie a call.

She called Jordan's office and updated Lauren. She asked her to pick up the girls from school and stay with them until Callie got back, and Lauren promised not to bring them to the Arbors. They'd go straight from after-school activities to the cabin.

Callie drove aimlessly around the Garden District, turned toward the river at Audubon Park, and came back down Magazine Street. She crossed Canal and entered the Quarter, parked the car, walked to Mr. B's Bistro, and sat at the bar. She needed a Bloody Mary, but she was unsure what would happen this afternoon. She ordered a glass of sauvignon blanc and a bowl of gumbo.

She was settling her check when the nurse called. Jordan was stirring and the doctor was on his way. She said she'd be there in fifteen minutes, and when she walked to the nurses' station, her helpful friend gave her a wink.

"You can go in for just a moment," the nurse advised. "Get ready for a shock — he's been through a terrible trauma. He doesn't look good, but his vitals are strong. Put on a brave face for his sake."

Callie was glad the nurse had prepared her, even if the reality was far worse than she had imagined. A doctor was bent over the bed, a stethoscope in his hand. The upper part of the bed was elevated, and the first thing she saw was that Jordan's eyes were closed and his face was covered with scratches and bruises. A tube ran into each nostril, and a clear plastic device with a much larger tube covered his mouth. A ventilator on a stand whisk-whisked quietly, forcing air down his windpipe. His left arm was in a cast. Tears welled in her eyes as she realized how much she cared for him.

"Come over here on the right side and squeeze his hand," the nurse said. "Doctor thinks it might do him good to see a friendly face."

The physician smiled and backed away. "Just for a moment," he said, and went into the hall.

It alarmed her how cool and clammy Jordan's skin was, and she drew her hand back.

"Easy, girl," the nurse said. "Be strong."

Callie took his hand and his eyelids fluttered for a moment. She squeezed lightly; he opened his eyes, saw her, and gave a tiny squeeze back.

"Hey, buddy. You've had a hard time, but they're taking good care of you."

His eyebrows raised and he stared at her intently. She knew what he wanted to know.

"Ellie and Vi are fine. I took them to the farm and spent the night with them. They're at school now. I'll stay with them until you're out of here, and Lauren will help me out. Don't worry about a thing."

A solitary tear rolled down his cheek. As she wiped it away, her fingertips gently brushed his face and he squeezed her hand again.

The nurse moved close to the bed and took his hand. "Mr. Blanchard, Callie here wants to keep up with you. If it's okay for us to give her your medical information, can you squeeze my hand twice?"

Two little squeezes.

"That's good. I understand." The nurse turned to Callie and said, "It may not be a medical authorization, but it's enough to keep you informed."

The doctor returned. "Time for your visitor to go, I'm afraid," he said to Jordan. "She can come back tomorrow if you're improving."

Callie kissed his forehead and said, "I'll be here whenever I can. Hang in there. A lot of us need you to get well fast."

She called Lauren, told her about the visit, and advised she'd be at the cabin in time to handle dinner. It was close to four and the traffic along Interstate 10 was lighter than it would be an hour from now. She suppressed the wellspring of emotion in her gut. Now wasn't the time for letting go — she had to drive, and she had to be strong for the girls once she got to St. Francisville.

She was optimistic with the kids, minimized how awful he had looked, and told them he was working hard to get well. Once the kids were tucked into bed with prayers said for Daddy's recovery, she crawled into Jordan's bed, buried her face in his pillow, and let her feelings out.

She said the words over and over that she hadn't allowed herself to utter, even in the depths of her own heart.

"I love you, Jordan. I love you. Don't leave me. Please God, don't let him leave me."

CHAPTER THIRTY-ONE

Callie called the nurses' station before she woke the girls the next morning. There was a shift change; she was thankful that Bernice, the nurse from yesterday, had put notes in Jordan's record so Callie could get updates.

The good news was that Jordan did not have a concussion. Since he was on a ventilator, he was fed intravenously. His physician had further reduced the pain medication in hopes he could tolerate it. The nurse said things were good so far, and he had requested a slate and a piece of chalk. He had written just one word, and he pointed to it whenever anyone entered the room.

Callie.

"I'll be there as soon as I can," she said, buoyed by the news. "I have to get his girls off to school —"

The nurse interrupted her. "When you come, don't forget what he's been through. You may think he's better, but he has a long, long way to go. You'll only be able to stay with him a few minutes, two or three times during the day. He needs rest and quiet."

Callie knew how frustrating it would be to see him for a moment and wait hours to see him again. But he was alive, thank God, and that was all that mattered. He'd written her name on the slate, and she would do whatever it took to see him.

She checked in with Lauren, dropped the kids at school, and drove south. On the way she updated Cate by phone. She entered Jordan's room at 10:30 for a five-minute visit. Jordan looked the same as yesterday — eyes closed, ventilator chugging away — and she tiptoed over to see two beautiful flower arrangements sitting in the window. One was from his firm and the other from Landry and Cate.

As she sat next to him, she heard a light tap-tapping sound. Jordan's eyes were open and he was hitting the slate with a piece of chalk taped to his right index finger. She jumped up and ran to his side.

"Morning! How'd the night go?"

It was a mistake asking an open-ended question to a man who could only respond by writing on a slate. "Never mind! You're awake and I'm here and that's all that matters."

His weakness saddened her. He moved the chalk slowly on the slate and tapped it to signal he was done. He'd drawn a smiley face.

As the nurse entered to usher her out, Callie leaned down and whispered in his ear, "I realized something last night, Jordan. It made me very happy and it's about us, so get well fast and I'll tell you what it is!" She gave him a peck on the cheek and left.

Callie got two five-minute visits that afternoon. When the last one ended, she told Jordan she was going back to St. Francisville to pick up Ellie and Vi. He wrote on the slate, *Where stay?*

"Lauren or I will have them when they're not in school," she assured him. "I spend the night with them at the cabin. They won't be at the Arbors at all. Don't worry about it."

Thanks, he wrote.

She whispered in his ear again. "I'm sleeping in your bed. It feels good." She smiled and winked. She thought she saw a smile in his eyes.

Four days made a tremendous difference in his recovery process. Tests showed his lung was simply bruised, and the doctor removed the ventilator. Now Jordan could eat soft food and at last he could speak. He transferred to a regular room and his condition was upgraded from fair to stable. Callie settled into a routine. She took the kids to school in the morning and picked them up at five; during the day she was in with him.

He asked about the accident and she explained what little she knew. The human mind has a way to cloud painful memories; Jordan knew he had left the house in a rainstorm, but that was all he could recall. When his mind was clear, he asked Callie to read the preliminary accident report to him.

He had failed to stop at the intersection where the county road to the farm met Highway 61. He had pulled in front of a southbound pickup that T-boned him. Because of the rainstorm, the truck wasn't speeding. On a typical evening it might have been going the speed limit — sixty miles an hour — and there would have been four fatalities instead of one. His Tahoe left no skid marks; the other driver likely never saw Jordan until the moment of impact, and it tore at his conscience that he had killed an innocent person.

Jordan's progress took a major upswing on Saturday. On Friday Callie asked if he was ready to see the girls, and the thought brought tears to his eyes. Ecstatic, they giggled and laughed all the way to New Orleans. She was glad they hadn't seen him before now. He looked a hundred percent better than the first morning she'd come. She prepared them for what to expect, and they performed bravely, looking past the bruises and scratches to see the father they loved.

They spent two hours together, sitting on his bed, holding his good hand gingerly, and patting his arm. They drew funny pictures on his cast, ate ice cream from the hospital kitchen, and it fascinated them that he'd used a slate to communicate.

He asked if Callie and Lauren were treating them okay, and they laughed for a long time. "They love us, Daddy! They'll always be good to us!" They admitted they missed the nursery at the Arbors, but he could see they were accepting that the cabin was their home.

Vi and Ellie asked other questions — difficult, unanswerable ones. They wanted to know what had happened that night, how the people in the other car were, and when he was coming home.

He knew the answer to one of their questions, but he didn't admit it. The innocent man in the pickup that hit him, a twenty-two-year-old unmarried construction worker, was on his way from someplace in Mississippi to Baton Rouge. His death was something Jordan couldn't process himself, much less explain to his children.

Bernice, the nurse who'd been so helpful from the beginning, arrived to whisk everyone away so Daddy could rest. He and his children made a date for next Saturday — same time, same place — and as they walked out, Bernice whispered to Callie.

"I predict he's out of here before then. They don't keep them long these days, especially when they're recovering like Mr. Jordan is. He'll begin in-house rehab on Monday, and when he leaves, they'll prescribe outpatient rehab. You might look into what's available near his home."

This was exciting news. With his injuries, Callie hadn't let herself be optimistic. Now, for the first time since that awful night, she knew things would be all right. On the way back she thought about rehab. She doubted they'd find anything in the town where he lived, but Baton Rouge was thirty miles away. She'd talk to his doctor next week and get the ball rolling.

Callie had an excellent manager at Beau Rivage, but she hadn't been there in a while. Now that Jordan was on the mend, she needed to return to Point Charmaine and check on everything. She took the kids to Lauren's house on Sunday morning, where they'd stay at least through Monday afternoon. Callie drove to Beau Rivage with an upbeat attitude and an optimistic feeling that things were heading in the right direction.

Thanks to Callie's regular updates with Cate, Landry knew about Jordan's progress. On Monday, he went to see the patient. He knocked on Jordan's door, stuck his head inside, and asked if this was a good time to visit. Jordan had expected him to show up, and he invited him in.

They talked about Jordan's condition, the rehab that would start today, and his optimism that he'd be released soon. They talked about Vi and Ellie and how much Callie enjoyed being with them.

Landry had been told Jordan's memory of that night was vague, and he didn't intend to bring it up, but Jordan did it instead.

"I guess you heard I pulled out right in front of that poor guy. He didn't have a chance. It's tearing me up inside, not knowing what really happened. It's coming back to me slowly. I remember the rain, coming to the intersection and seeing headlights, but that's all I know. I killed someone. You can't imagine how that feels."

"I can't, but surely it wasn't what it seems. There's more to it – there has to be. Have the troopers given you any more information?"

"No, and that frustrates me. It's been over a week since the accident. You'd think they'd know something by now."

The cellphone on the nightstand rang. Landry handed it to him and Jordan looked at the screen; it was an unknown caller he presumed was spam, so he declined the call.

The caller, a state police detective, left voicemail saying he had important information.

Jordan laughed. "What a coincidence he calls just you show up."

Landry offered to leave, but Jordan told him to stay. "Whatever it is, everybody'll know it soon anyway."

The detective had a startling revelation. Someone had cut the Tahoe's brake line. He hadn't noticed it between the farm and the highway because he hadn't needed to use the brakes on that sparsely traveled farm-to-market road. The first time he hit the brakes was at the intersection of Highway 61. They failed and he drove right into southbound traffic.

He had entered the intersection without ever slowing for the stop sign. He didn't have a chance to avoid the accident. Unfortunately, neither did the man in the pickup.

"Let's talk about enemies," the detective said. "Can you think of anyone who would want to hurt you?"

Jordan said he couldn't.

"Think about it a few days. This was deliberate, no question about it. We figure someone did this when your SUV was at the cabin. I hoped there were outdoor cameras, but there aren't. I'll give you my number in case you come up with any ideas about all this."

Landry sat by the bed and waited. In a moment Jordan said, "The cop said no matter how far-fetched, okay? You're the ghost hunter. Could Olivia have done this?"

"I'm no expert, but I know one. Henri Duchamp was at your house with me the night of the wreck. He's the head of the paranormal society and he's investigated this stuff for years. With your permission, I'll ask him." Jordan nodded and Landry continued. "In my experience, ghosts haunt places where there's a connection, like cemeteries, buildings or houses. I've never heard of anything like this."

"I think it was Olivia I saw. She tried to push me off the third floor, like her first husband."

"But Callie saw something in the master bedroom at the same time — a spirit that was trying to help."

"Who knows? I'm an architect, for God's sake. I deal in reality, not the spiritual world. I thought all this stuff was mumbo jumbo until she tried to take away my girls. I don't know what's real and what's not anymore. Do I believe in ghosts? A few months ago I'd have laughed at the idea. Now I know something haunts the Arbors, if *haunts* is the right word. Ellie and Vi can see someone, play with her, talk to her, and go places with her — but I can't. Did Olivia cut my brake line? Why not, I guess. It's no crazier than anything else that's happened. I'm sure you know something similar happened to Callie. Somebody cut the serpentine belt on her car. It turned out fine, but it could have been a disaster."

Landry had never heard of a spirit traveling around the countryside doing harm to people by sabotaging their vehicles. He needed expert advice on this one.

Landry called Henri on speakerphone, told him what had happened, and asked his opinion. "If you ask me, this is a criminal act by a real person," Henri opined. "I've been in this business for years. I've never encountered something from the spirit world that could travel several miles from its home and commit a tangible act, using tools to sever a brake line or cut a belt. No, you need to be looking in the world of the living for this one." The call ended with a promise to keep in touch.

That call was a perfect segue into one reason Landry was here. A week earlier, the crew had been ready and waiting for Jordan's arrival at the Arbors. Except for the accident, Jordan would have unlocked the door to the nursery and let them film a segment inside. And Vi and Ellie were with him.

"I have a question that's been nagging at me. That night, did you intend to let your girls go into the nursery?"

"I can't answer that. Yeah, I had the girls with me and, yeah, I was coming to the house. I was going to unlock the door for you, that much I know. The rest is as much a mystery to me as you. Did I intend to go in the nursery too? Would I let my children go? I can't imagine I would have, but why did I bring them? I can't remember any of it.

"Olivia scares the hell out of me. She kidnapped my girls, even though you ghostbusters might have a different take on what happened. She took them away and promised to let them see their mother. Do you know what that means? I damned sure do. If it were just me, that would be one thing. You involve a couple of little girls and that's something else altogether."

There was no rebuttal to that logic. Landry knew Jordan was right to be scared, even though Olivia didn't seem to want to harm the children. But what *did* she want? That was the question no one could answer.

"After all this, are you still willing to let us film in the nursery?"

"Without me and the girls? Sure. Just tell me what you need and I'll do it."

"But you had them in the car last time. You were planning to bring them then. You know the girls are a catalyst —"

He responded with such fury that an alarm went off on the monitors next to his bed. He shouted, "The girls are NOT a catalyst! This is not some kind of experiment. They're little children and she wants them! They're all I have! Don't you understand that?"

A nurse rushed in, looked at Jordan's elevated blood pressure reading, and ordered Landry out. Moments later she walked into the hall, saying she'd given him a sedative.

She was not happy. "What did you do to agitate him? He's in a fragile state. You can't barge in here —"

Landry apologized and said he'd brought up something that upset her patient. Chastised, he left and called Cate, telling her everything about his visit.

It was disappointing that they had missed the chance to film that night. If Jordan had shown up with the girls, would he have let them in the nursery since he'd have been with them? Nobody knew.

Landry tried to convince himself that the girls would have been safe. There had been a roomful of adults, and Cherry couldn't have snatched them. If they had finished up that night, they might know what was really going on at the Arbors.

He was trying to paint a positive picture. Olivia wasn't the only issue; someone deliberately sabotaged both the Tahoe and Callie's car. A living person did that, not a ghost. Was he putting his own quest for a story ahead of a family's safety? He was bending the facts to suit himself.

He sat at his desk and stepped back for a fresh look. He had to see what he knew, what he didn't, and how to deal with everything from here.

When it came to it, everything at the Arbors revolved around the children. The nursery was the focal point, the mirror a portal, and the old toys, books and furniture all clues. Ellie and Vi were the keys, the connection to a long-dead matriarch. Even with them they might never find answers, but without the girls there would be no resolution.

If the answer lay in the girls, could he — should he — keep trying to get Jordan to involve them? Someone had to confront Olivia, but was it right to involve two eight-year-olds, the only family their father had left? What if something went wrong? Landry himself had used the term *bait* — what if he talked Jordan into what he wanted, and the girls disappeared forever? He had no idea what powers Olivia had, yet he still wondered how to get them into the nursery.

Landry had all the questions but none of the answers. He also had a conscience, one which was running on all cylinders right now. He picked up the phone to call Cate, but he hesitated. Always levelheaded, wise and sensible, she would tell him to let this one go. Maybe he should. Maybe it *was* time to drop everything before someone else got hurt, or worse. There were other stories to investigate, so why was this one so alluring?

Instead of Cate, he called Henri Duchamp and asked him to lunch.

CHAPTER THIRTY-TWO

Light rain fell as Henri and Landry sat on the front porch of the Columns, once a grand home in the Garden District and now a boutique hotel and restaurant. The porch was called the Front Gallery. It was a favorite among diners, who enjoyed a quiet drink or a leisurely lunch just steps off tree-lined St. Charles Avenue. Every so often the streetcar clang-clanged its way down the median of the broad street. It was easy to imagine oneself in the 1800s when the hotel and the neighborhood looked much the same as today.

Landry ordered a bottle of Henri's favorite wine — Pouilly-Fuissé — and waved off menus for now. The two hadn't spoken since the night of Jordan's car wreck. He brought Henri up to date on Jordan's condition and described their confrontation at the hospital.

His frustrations were obvious from the beginning. Something unusual was happening at the old mansion — there had been too many curious things, most recently the tourist's death. Like many children, Vi and Ellie had an imaginary playmate, but other than her being a ghost, there was nothing imaginary about Olivia. When the children disappeared from the nursery, Jordan had heard faint voices and a tinkling noise. They returned hours later, thinking they'd been away for a few minutes.

Miss Olivia — for that was clearly who they were dealing with — treated the little girls well, although her occasional reminders that they were *her* children were disturbing. More frightening was her offer to take Vi and Ellie to see their mother.

There was no evidence Olivia had children, so why was there a guardian angel marker in the family cemetery? Were the parish records incomplete? Were children buried there?

He laid out everything — his fear of involving the girls, could they engage the ghost without them, what danger the nursery might hold for them, and how — if — they could ensure the children's safety. He revealed the personal conflict he was experiencing, and he wanted to know if Henri had any idea how they could bring Olivia out without using the children as bait.

Landry's biggest question — the reason he'd offered to buy his old friend's lunch and bend his ear — was what should happen next. There was no one in Louisiana with more experience in the paranormal than the man sitting across from him. Landry leaned in to hear as Henri spoke, offering opinions in a whisper so nearby diners couldn't hear.

"You're in a tough spot. The girls are the connection to the spirit who dwells in the house. Is it Olivia Beaumont? From the evidence, I believe we can assume so, and I was looking forward to seeing what turned up when we were there the other night. The fact is, Mr. Blanchard had the children in the car with him. Did that mean he was going to let them go into the nursery that night? He told you he didn't know. If he had, could we have ensured their safety? That's the real question here, isn't it?"

He paused as the waiter brought salads and poured more wine.

"Landry, you've seen some strange things in the short time you've been doing psychic investigations. The paranormal events you saw at the Asylum in Victory were terrifying. There are many things in this world that defy traditional explanation. I'll give you opinions on your questions about the Arbors. You may not like my thoughts and you may not agree with them, but here's what I think is happening."

"We have two little girls who are the key to dealing with a spirit. The spirit seems to enjoy them, but there are disquieting facts. She built a nursery for children she never had, she calls them her own, and she's enticing them to join her in a place that's beyond reality. Her motives may be noble, but I doubt it. She had two husbands, both of whom she may have disposed of. She also may have caused the recent death of the tourist at the house.

"Olivia was a domineering, powerful and driven woman, and there's no doubt it's her spirit we're dealing with. Everything happening — and everything in the past — is driven by one thing only, and that is children. She fervently hoped for a child, but that wish was denied her.

"Olivia has been dead for over fifty years. Then for the first time she hears a child's laughter echoing throughout her house. She sees happy children playing in her nursery with the toys she carefully and lovingly chose for her own. She interacts with Vi and Ellie, revealing herself to them as a real person, although they soon realize that she isn't like them. They don't *want* to understand why their father can't see her. Do you see what I'm saying? Ghost or not, they want to continue their relationship with an adult who devotes her undivided time and attention to two little girls."

Lunch arrived and they took a break. Their age difference was under twenty years, but Landry considered Henri a mentor. He was scholarly, conservative in his thoughts and words, and he'd been an inspiration to Landry. As they dined, they chatted about Landry's life — the routine assignments an investigative reporter handled, his growing interest in Cate Adams, and his love for unexplained phenomena. Now that he was becoming somewhat of a celebrity, people sent him tips about strange things. As in New Orleans, the bayou country abounded with history, mystery and tales of the supernatural. Landry was having a great time, he told his friend, but this situation — the mystery of the Arbors — was confounding him and he couldn't stop thinking about it.

After the waiter cleared the table, Henri took another sip of wine. "The main takeaway from this discussion is this," he said, his voice again dropping to a whisper. "Olivia wants to take the girls. She was content at first to play with them in the nursery, because that's where her own children would have played. As Jordan became concerned about their welfare, Olivia decided to take them on an adventure into another place — a dimension we don't understand. That was to show their father she was in charge, not him.

"Then there was a tragic accident that could have killed them all. Was that Olivia's doing? I doubt it. I don't think her intent is to harm the girls. Could she travel miles away from the house and cut the brake line on his SUV? From my experience I say it's highly unlikely, although I find out new things about the paranormal every time I take a new assignment."

The rain stopped as Landry poured the last of the wine. Henri apologized for monopolizing the luncheon conversation. Landry said the discussion helped very much, but he still didn't know what to do next.

Henri said, "Consider this before you decide. This is the opinion I told you might be hard to accept, but you asked for my advice, and here it is. Jordan hasn't allowed the children into the nursery for quite some time. They rarely visit the house; when they do, someone else is always with them. That must distress Olivia no end. If we go back to the Arbors for the filming, and if you convince Jordan to bring the girls into the nursery, there's a strong possibility that she might take them away and never bring them back. *Would* that happen? I don't know. But it *could* happen. We've seen it once from her. If you allow her the opportunity, I believe you might never see Vi and Ellie again."

CHAPTER THIRTY-THREE

The Arbors
Spring 1959

Olivia Beaumont's one heartbreaking regret in life was that there were no children. There would be no son to carry on the family name and no daughter to offer love and care to an aging mother. Townspeople saw Olivia as a strong-willed, spirited woman who dominated her husbands and her household. But the consequences of her fate often drove her into utter despair, and she retreated to a place in her mind — and in her house — where she forced herself to confront her emotions. The nursery.

Tonight she sat in darkness in that awful room where tears flowed and her body heaved in agonizing spasms. In this room harsh realities were faced and dreams washed away in a vast sea of wretched hopelessness.

There stood the two cribs adorned with fancy linens and lace. When Olivia sewed the dainty covers, the fabric had been white, but it was yellowing now, even though she never let the sun's rays penetrate this room. Heavy drapes drawn tightly shut covered the windows. This was not a place of sunshine or hope or promises for the future. Here there was only desperation, hopelessness and perpetual gloom.

Olivia rocked back and forth in a chair she'd placed here fifteen years ago, back in 1945 when she was young and full of excitement about the twins she'd soon nurse in this very chair. Bears and dolls stared blankly at her from a couch across the room, where she'd planned to lie at night until her newborn daughters were asleep. A beautiful hand-carved wooden cradle sat on the floor beside her, and a porcelain doll with a fancy dress rested where a baby should have lain.

She was alone, as she had always been. Yes, there had been husbands — two of them. Worthless, spineless bastards who spent her money and gave her occasional companionship, but neither gave her what she required, and now they were gone.

Charles Perrault had been a merchant, selling furniture door-to-door from a catalog. The first time she laid eyes on him was when he had knocked at the Arbors in 1932. Her father had died just a year before, and the mansion was her house now. She was thirty-two, and she had never been in love.

Tonight, as every other time she visited the nursery, she reflected on her loveless life, and she told herself she had no regrets. She had never experienced maternal love; in a savage twist of fate, both Olivia's maternal grandmother and her own mother had died just after giving birth.

Olivia had been raised by an overbearing father with no time for a little girl. The nanny was kind enough, but she offered no loving encouragement or support. Olivia never learned how to love another person, but she desperately sought love in just one thing — a child. That would have been sufficient for her, and she would have given that child her all.

Years ago she'd weep over these memories, but not now. She willed herself to face the demons of her past without the release of sadness. Like a medieval jailer applying the whip, Olivia scourged herself for mistakes. Somewhere deep inside, she understood her transgressions, but she suppressed those thoughts. She chose instead to blame herself for having no offspring.

She recalled when she had first met Charles. Olivia was attractive, intelligent and wealthy, and he was a well-dressed, dashing fellow whose company she enjoyed. He was funny, interested in her, and before long he was pushing her to marry him. She felt nothing amorous, but it seemed the right thing to do. Eight months after they met, she became Mrs. Charles Perrault in the Catholic church in town. She walked herself down the aisle, refused to repeat the usual vows, and instead promised to "accept" her husband into her life. The priest found that strange, but Olivia Beaumont herself was strange — a headstrong woman who was accustomed to having things her way.

Charles would never know that his sole purpose in Olivia's life was to provide a child. He was on the road a good deal of the time, but when he was home, she gave him wild, imaginative sex, hoping to achieve her goal. Sometimes she found their trysts enjoyable, but things didn't turn out well. Becoming desperate as the years passed, she finally consulted a voodoo priestess. The crone sold her one potion after another and gave her specific instructions on what to do in the bedroom. Maybe it was witchcraft and maybe it was positive thinking, but it worked. In 1944, at age forty-three and having been married to Charles for twelve years, Olivia became pregnant. There were complications and frequent visits to the doctor. On one of those visits, the physician listened with his stethoscope and told Olivia she was carrying twins. At her age, he recommended she stay in bed as much as possible until the babies were born.

Olivia had rested a little, but she had a nursery to furnish. She ordered two cribs and enough toys, dolls and games to outfit a kindergarten. Sparing no expense, she prepared for the wonderful days ahead.

Tonight as she sat in the darkness rocking back and forth, the memories flowed through her body and her mind like a raging torrent. Things were always the same in this room, and she came here only when she lost control of her emotions. In those rare instances grief, despair, and helplessness crept into her mind, and she was lured back into the nursery, where everything good had become bad in one horrifying afternoon.

She stared blankly at a half-sized table near the fireplace. When she became pregnant, she had ordered it from a catalog. She painted the top with whimsical scenes from *Alice in Wonderland* that were sure to make a child giggle. There was a worried White Rabbit looking at his pocket watch, a gigantic Alice trying to squeeze through a tiny door, and the Red Queen screaming, "Off with his head!"

There were four child-sized chairs, ready for Olivia to host a tea party with twins who would never come. No child would ever sit at the table. Her hope — her lifelong dream — died that horrible, awful day when the halls of the Arbors resounded with wretched, pathetic wails of misery.

That day, as always, her husband Charles had gone to the country club at noon. Sometime that afternoon, perhaps when Charles was dealing a hand of cards or ordering another cocktail, Olivia had miscarried. She was at home and all alone when two baby girls died, taking her future with them.

The pain had been terrible, the experience excruciating and almost unbearable, but the strong, dominant Olivia worked through it alone, as she did with everything in life.

By the time Charles strolled nonchalantly into the house around five, she knew what she would do. He hadn't a care in the world, but without children, her life was over.

Soon her husband lay downstairs, spread-eagled on the parquet floor in the middle of the rotunda. Life was over for him too. She had paid the price, and now he had as well.

After she did it, she returned to the nursery. She walked to the cribs, arranged the linens just so, and left the room, locking the door behind her as she always did. She walked down the circular staircase, stepped over Charles's body, went into the library, picked up the telephone, and called the police.

"There's been a terrible accident," she reported, her voice as steady as if she were talking about the weather. "My husband fell through an upstairs railing. I think he's dead. Please send someone out right away."

The coroner ruled forty-nine-year-old Charles Perrault's death accidental, the result of a misstep by a man with considerable alcohol in his bloodstream. There was no reason to suspect foul play. Olivia said she was in her second-floor bedroom when she heard a noise, a sound that turned out to be her husband's body crashing through the banister on the floor above. There was no financial benefit to her in his dying — she was the wealthy one in the marriage. Perrault's death was an accident.

As she sat in the nursery today, Olivia thought about Bruno Duval, husband number two. She never took his name. After Charles died, she used her maiden name and would remain Olivia Beaumont until her death.

Hoping for one last chance, she married Bruno in 1950, again with the sole purpose of becoming pregnant. She was fifty, a risky age for bearing a child in those days, but she was determined to try again, and she chose Bruno for one reason — he was twenty-eight, half her age.

She understood why Bruno would marry her. He was an opportunist, a playboy who'd rather carouse than work. He was handsome and witty, and the females loved his company. She knew all that, but she didn't care. He signed up for a ride with a wealthy older woman and he used her, but she used him more. He got the gravy train and she got a young stud, but nothing happened for years. He was virile enough — that wasn't the issue — so it had to have been something with her. Her regret turned to blind rage, all aimed at him.

She began to think how to deal with him. This had gone on long enough. The more months that passed with no pregnancy, the more sullen and morose she became, and the more time Bruno spent at his posh club in town. She knew what he did there — everyone in town whispered about it. He didn't even hide his dalliances from her. People pitied Olivia, and that infuriated her, but she kept her thoughts to herself and she still forced him to perform over and over, desperately trying to make it happen.

The sex came less often as she aged, but she persevered, and in late 1958 she became pregnant again. It was a foolhardy thing to do at fifty-seven, but it was her second chance. She was happy for the first time since her miscarriage, and she didn't need him anymore. He was free to do whatever he wanted.

While he played the field, she sat in the nursery, rocking back and forth and thinking of the future. At last she would have a baby. She'd mourned the twins she lost, but one child was plenty — more than enough. One child would make her life complete.

On January 3, 1959, Bruno arrived home drunker than usual, sneering when she pointed out the lipstick on his cheek. She raised her hand to slap his face, and he hit her in the abdomen with his fist. Maybe he had done it on purpose and maybe not. Maybe he was too drunk to realize what he had done. At that point, what did it matter?

There would be no children for Olivia. This time her life was over. Whatever time left on earth for her would be a meaningless existence.

Tonight, as always when she came to the nursery, she apologized to her child. "I tried, darling," she whispered. "I tried to bring you into this world to live with me, to love me as I love you. Bruno ended that for both of us."

Olivia was a private person, and although friends at the club wondered in the following weeks where the dashing Bruno had gone off to, no one dared ask his odd, reclusive wife about it. She waited a few weeks before ringing the authorities to report that her husband was missing. He had left home on a business trip to Baton Rouge and never returned.

Like everyone else in St. Francisville, the policemen knew Bruno by reputation. They wondered if he had finally dumped his much-older wife and run off with one of the twentysomething girls in whose company he was often seen. Had he started a new life somewhere far away? Probably. Who'd blame him?

After a half-hearted investigation, the authorities filed away the case. The disappearance of Bruno Duval would remain an unsolved mystery.

CHAPTER THIRTY-FOUR

Present Day

Jordan came home from rehab with his arm in a sling. Although his body had been battered and bruised, he grumbled about his slow recovery. He needed a cane for balance, and that frustrated him. At least he was out of the hospital; getting back to work was the best therapy, and he was happy to be doing something productive for a change.

A few days after his discharge, Landry asked Jordan if they could film on Friday after his staff left. He said they might be there until dawn, going where Henri Duchamp directed. They would visit the cemetery too; nothing unusual had been reported there, but a graveyard always spiced up a segment. Landry again promised that nothing would be broadcast without Jordan's permission.

Jordan said yes. He said he'd be there to observe the activities, but, as Landry expected, the girls would not. Jordan said there was no way to keep them safe. After Landry's lunch with Henri, he couldn't argue that point.

He was disappointed the kids weren't coming. It might be a night of wasted time and no paranormal activity, but they would do the shoot in the nursery without Ellie and Vi.

The same people as last time assembled at the Arbors around six thirty. Jordan had stayed at the house to wait for the others. Landry, Cate and Henri drove from New Orleans in one car, and Phil, the Channel Nine cameraman, drove a news truck. Callie was staying at Jordan's cabin, helping get him accustomed to being back home, and she arrived last. She told him Vi and Ellie were home watching a movie and eating popcorn with Lauren, and everyone went upstairs to the nursery.

While Phil set up his equipment, Callie said to Jordan, "I called earlier, but you didn't answer. I guess you were busy."

Jordan felt his pocket. "Damn, I don't have my phone. I guess I left it in the office."

Callie searched the entire first floor but didn't find it.

Henri arranged the delicate equipment around the house while Landry and Phil talked through tonight's plans. "Be ready to move on a moment's notice," he cautioned. "We don't know where things might turn up."

"Like always, boss. Not my first rodeo." Phil laughed. He knew what to expect and how meticulous Landry was. This was the time for discussion, before anything unusual happened. Sometimes phenomena occurred quickly, and he must be prepared for anything.

By the time they finished setup and checked the cameras one last time, the sun had dropped below the trees that bordered the yard. They shot test footage over and over, ensuring that nothing would go wrong when they did it for real. At last the house was ready.

Everything was quiet while they worked in the nursery. The only noises were the ones they made, and there was nothing unusual.

Everything, that was, except for something strange that Henri discovered.

While Landry and Phil were setting up, Henri puttered around the room. Even though he'd heard all about this room, he'd never seen it himself. The newness of everything surprised him, as it did everyone who came here for the first time. Jordan's girls had played in here — there was plenty of evidence of that — but the toys, furniture and everything else was new even though the things were seventy or eighty years old.

He examined books on a shelf and removed a slim leather-bound volume about four by six inches in size. It was a collection of bedtime prayers printed in 1935, and its unusual title was *If I Should Die Before I Wake*. That should scare the daylights out of a child, Henri mused as he flipped through the book. He noticed that the flyleaf bore a handwritten inscription.

"Have you found something interesting?" Cate asked. She'd been killing time too, walking around the room and taking everything in, and she saw him take the book.

"Very. Can you come over, Landry? I want to show you something."

Landry read the title. "What an odd name for a children's book. How did you find it?"

"Browsing. It caught my eye. Look inside and get ready for a shock."

Landry opened the book, read the inscription and turned to Henri, astonished.

"Is this…do you think…"

"Are you asking if it's real?" Henri answered. "I think so. Why wouldn't it be? Jordan said from the time Olivia died in 1965 until just recently, the door was locked and no one entered. What motive could someone have to write those words in a book and put it on a shelf where it might never be seen?"

"Is the camera rolling?" Landry asked Phil, who said it had been on the entire time. This was an important find — prophetic words that made Landry's spine tingle. If a documentary was created, this book would be its opening scene.

Impatient, Jordan snapped, "Are you going to keep it a secret? Read it out loud, for God's sake!"

There were words penned in precise handwriting.

My wife is going to kill me.

She killed her first husband. She would never admit it, but I know she pushed Charles over the railing, because I know her motive in doing it.

Ours has been an unusual marriage. I didn't expect love from someone so much older; therefore I wasn't disappointed when there was none. To be honest, I didn't love her either. There wasn't much to love, but there was plenty of money. I wondered at first what she wanted from me, and I discovered the answer on our wedding night.

We married in New Orleans in 1950. I was twenty-eight; she was fifty. From our first night until today, she never changed. She has always been the same cold, calculating shrew. We have had sex, dear God, countless acts of loveless sex over these past nine years, because that is why she married me.

I have not been faithful, although I doubt it matters to her. As long as I perform, she couldn't care less what I do. I am not ashamed of my activities outside this house. My shame arises from what I do when I'm within these walls. I am her gigolo and nothing more. She orders me to become aroused enough that I can do what she requires. She must wonder how I do it — in truth, thoughts of other women allow me to complete the job.

After almost nine years she has at last conceived, although I question her sanity in bearing a child at fifty-eight. Now that I have given her what she wanted from me in the first place, she no longer needs me in her life.

If I am dead when someone reads this, please inform the police that Olivia Beaumont killed me.
Bruno Duval
December 29, 1958

Something amazing happened the moment Landry read Olivia's name out loud. In one sweeping move and with a resounding crash, the children's table flew upside down into the middle of the room. The four chairs tipped over at the same time. They screamed in unison as they watched the bizarre scene unfold.

"Look at that!" Henri said, pointing to a wispy cloud forming by the upright mirror in the far corner. Within seconds the cloud moved to the center of the room, enveloped the table and chairs, and suddenly the furniture righted itself. Within seconds the vapor was gone, leaving everyone stunned and speechless.

"I think we managed to piss her off," Landry said after a moment, and Henri suggested it was Bruno against whom she directed her fury. He had gone missing in the spring of 1959, and perhaps she hadn't known until now that he left a note accusing her. That was what brought forth her wrath.

The discovery encouraged Henri. In his opinion, stirring things up with Olivia might lead to more manifestations. Landry instructed Phil to take a series of stills of the book and its flyleaf. Later he'd read the words aloud on camera.

It was getting dark, and Landry said they needed to hurry to the cemetery. "I want to do a shoot in the half-light for effect." They walked across the newly mowed grass. Jordan and Callie came last; still recovering, he struggled to keep up with her.

As Phil filmed, Landry walked from one grave marker to another, saying a few words about each one and capturing the eerie setting. He'd do a full voice-over back in the studio.

When they came out of the woods onto the grass, Jordan saw someone standing on the porch. It was too dark to see who was there until they came closer and saw Lauren waving to them.

Jordan's heart started beating wildly. He gripped Callie's arm, and a wave of fear swept over her. This was wrong. What was Lauren doing here? She was supposed to be keeping the girls at the cabin.

CHAPTER THIRTY-FIVE

Waving, Lauren ran down the steps. "Hey, Jordan! I'm excited to see what you found!"

"What I found?" he shouted. "What are you talking about?"

"You texted me! You told me to bring Vi and Ellie!"

He panicked and lost his footing. Callie took his arm to steady him. "What are you talking about? I lost my phone. I haven't had it for hours!"

She turned back toward the house. "Oh, my God. The girls! I sent them up to the nursery!"

"Good God, Lauren! You let them go to the nursery alone? What were you thinking? Callie! Run! Run up there now! Landry, help me get inside!"

Callie flew across the rotunda and bounded up. In seconds she was inside the nursery, and she found everything just as they'd left it. The camera was running, but the children weren't there.

Hysterical, Jordan stood on the ground floor and shouted to his girls. He needed to be upstairs fast, so Landry and Phil got on either side of him, linked arms, and carried him to the second floor. From there he used his cane and joined the others in the nursery.

"Where are they?" he screamed, and Landry shook his head.

He shuffled to the mirror and pounded on its glass as tears streamed down his face.

"Ellie! Vi!" His wails echoed throughout the house, but his children didn't answer.

Lauren came over to him, tearful and apologetic but unwavering as to why she let the children go upstairs alone. "Jordan, you texted me. You told me to bring the girls here. We had just finished dinner. I got them dressed and we hurried over. From the sound of it, everything here was fine. The kiddos were dying to see what you'd found."

"I didn't text you!" he screamed. "Why the hell do you keep saying that? I didn't have my phone! I couldn't have texted you!"

She turned her phone on and handed it over. She had received a text thirty-five minutes ago. A text from Jordan Blanchard.

I've found something exciting that the girls won't believe! Bring them to the Arbors as quickly as you can. Send them on up to the nursery the minute you get here. I'll be waiting for them.

He heard something. He put his finger to his lips and shushed everyone. There were faint sounds — a light, tinkling noise, voices in the distance, and indistinct words spoken by children far away.

He shivered and Callie put her hand on his arm and asked, "Do you feel how cold it is in here?"

Henri said, "It's because of her. It will be coldest by that tall mirror standing in the corner. I noticed it earlier — it's a portal."

Jordan said, "The girls told me this is where she takes them. Where do they go? Where are they?"

"In layman's terms, it's a doorway. I've come across them many times in traditional hauntings. A room, a door sealed up and long forgotten, a piece of furniture like this mirror — they can act as a portal to a different place. Some call it a parallel dimension, but there's more speculation about what it is than hard evidence."

Jordan was frantic. "Are the girls still in this house? Can they come back? Last time they were gone for hours, but to them it felt like minutes."

Henri carefully chose his words. In Jordan's fragile state, he had to be upbeat. "This is where it gets into speculation. They came back before, so we should assume they can do it again. It all depends on Olivia."

"Dear God, I can't lose them! This is all my fault. Why in hell did I agree to let you all come here?"

Callie said, "Jordan, allowing Landry to come didn't cause this to happen. Someone sent Lauren that text. A ghost didn't send it, so we have to find out who did."

The camera had been recording the entire time, and when they reviewed the footage, they saw what Henri had prepared them for. Ellie and Vi ran into the room, shouting, "Daddy! Daddy!" They looked at the rocker and screamed, "Cherry! Did Daddy bring us here so we could see you again? We've missed you so much!"

There was no one in the video except the two eight-year-olds, who paused, listened to Cherry's response, and clapped their hands in delight. Jordan sobbed as Ellie exclaimed, "Yes! Yes, I'd love to go back! I love that place. Are we going to see Mommy this time?"

Then the girls walked to the mirror at the far end of the nursery, looked up and nodded their heads. What happened was unmistakable, even though the video showed only the children. Olivia was standing next to them, talking to them, guiding and reassuring them.

"Watch closely," Henri said as the girls stood in front of the mirror. "This can happen in several ways."

The girls waited for Olivia to pass through, and then they stretched their right arms outward and *into* the mirror. They stepped through and were gone.

Jordan's nightmare had started again. The girls were gone and he was at Olivia's mercy. Where was his phone, and who sent the text?

He asked Lauren what had happened when she showed up at the house.

"When we walked in, I glanced upstairs and saw that the nursery door was open. It's usually closed, so I figured you were in there, like the text said you'd be. I didn't give it a second thought. The kids ran into the nursery and closed the door. Three minutes later I heard voices from the yard. I went to the porch and saw all of you walking toward the house."

He apologized for being angry with her. Once again he was wallowing in despair over his girls, but things had worked out before, and he had nothing but hope to cling to this time. He was helpless; whatever was happening had no logical explanation, no simple fix. It was beyond comprehension. Everything was falling apart again, but none of it was Lauren's fault, and he told her so. It wasn't Landry's fault either, nor the others. Everyone had to work together now. As hard as it was for Jordan, he garnered the strength and resolve to be positive. If he gave up now, he might never see them again.

One floor above the nursery, a person tiptoed down the hallway so those on the floor below wouldn't hear. He entered the girls' bedroom and placed Jordan's cellphone on Ellie's pillow. Then he went back to the place where he'd been waiting and watching for so long. The secret place where no one would look.

Finding the cellphone was critical. Jordan stayed in the nursery to wait for the girls while the others searched the house. Even though Callie had looked on the first floor earlier, Cate and Landry scoured every room. Henri and Phil went to the family bedrooms on the third floor, and Callie inspected the master bedroom and the other rooms on the second floor.

There came a shout from upstairs. Henri had found the phone in the children's bedroom, sitting on a pillow on one of the twin beds. He handed it over to Jordan, who saw the text that purportedly came from him.

CHAPTER THIRTY-SIX

Fifteen hours had passed and the entire team was still at the house. The cameraman stayed up all night manning the camera while Henri, Cate and Landry slept in the guest bedrooms. Jordan refused to leave the nursery, and Callie stayed with him, dozing now and then.

Around seven they convinced Jordan he had to rest. He and Callie went to the master bedroom next door and lay on top of the covers. They were asleep in seconds. Phil went to bed too, and Cate took a turn sitting in the rocker by the portal.

"I've got an errand to run," Landry told Cate shortly after noon. "There's something I want to check. I'll be back later."

As he stepped inside the River View Restaurant for the second time, Landry had a déjà vu moment. *Some things are timeless*, he thought to himself, recalling the other time he had come to the bar looking for Ox Fedder.

Like last time, it was Saturday afternoon. He recognized several of the men at the bar and heard the same loudmouths in the back room yelling for LSU to whip the asses of whoever they were playing.

There was no guarantee Ox would be at the bar, but Landry would have bet a hundred bucks he would be. And sure enough, there he was. He was hard to miss — he sat in the same place, wearing the same wife-beater shirt and John Deere hat. There were no seats next to him, so Landry took a stool across the bar, where Ox would see him.

Landry considered how suitable for him Ox's name was. He was big; he might have been muscular once, but an alcohol-fueled existence had changed that. Regardless, Landry figured he could still hold his own in a fight.

Landry ordered an Amber and tried to catch Ox's attention, but the man looked straight ahead and spoke to no one. He took a gulp of his bourbon over ice, chased it with a Turbodog and let out an enormous belch. In a couple of minutes he did it again.

Landry had neither an afternoon to waste or the desire to spend much time at the River View, so he walked over and tapped Ox on the shoulder.

"Whadda you want?" the man said without turning around.

"I have a question to ask you."

There was such a long pause that Landry thought Ox hadn't heard him. Finally Ox nudged the man next to him and said, "Get down off that stool and go sit somewhere else. This here city feller's gonna give me fifty dollars and buy you a drink." He looked at Landry. "Ain't you, mister ghost man?"

The man grumbled and swore, but he stepped down, got his drink, and moved away. Landry took the stool and scrunched in between Ox and an equally big man on the other side.

"Thanks for getting me a place to sit."

Ox still didn't look his way. He grunted, "Gimme my fifty dollars."

"What do you mean? I didn't say anything about —"

"What you said was you have a question to ask me. Last time it cost you fifty bucks. Since you came back, I guess fifty bucks is a good price."

"I'm not paying anything until I know if you can help me."

"Suit yourself," Ox replied, shifting his huge rump on the barstool and further infringing into Landry's space. "I ain't leavin' til five anyways."

"What do you know about the family cemetery at the Arbors?"

Ox didn't answer. When the bartender came around, he killed the rest of his bourbon and ordered another.

"Did you hear me?"

"I hear just fine, buddy. Ain't no problem with my hearing. You got a problem with yours?"

The bartender brought Ox's drink and he turned to Landry for the first time. "Pay the man," Ox said, and Landry tossed a ten across the bar.

"I know stuff about the cemetery. Gimme my hundred and I'll talk to you."

"Hundred? You said fifty."

"Yeah, but that was before you pissed me off. You think I like sittin' here talkin' to some TV show host? You want to talk, you put a hundred bucks on the bar right now or get the hell outta here."

Landry pulled out a hundred and laid it on the bar. Ox's massive paw closed over it.

"Now we got that part over, what do you want to know?"

"Why is there a guardian angel gravestone in the cemetery? Are there children buried there?"

"You shoulda asked my daddy about that when you had the chance. I never worked there 'til after Miss Olivia died. Daddy was the one what knew about things."

"But so do you. You said you know stuff about the cemetery. Tell me what you know."

"You ain't runnin' this show, slick. You get one more answer. Start askin'."

Ox would do things his way, and Landry had to be patient if he wanted to find out anything. He might know nothing; as he said, he hadn't started there until after Olivia died. But he'd been around when his father worked there earlier.

Landry continued. "There are seven tombstones. Charles Perrault, Olivia and five of her ancestors are buried there. The last stone is an angel. People use those to mark a child's grave. I want to know who's buried under it."

"Why don't you go digging and find out?" Ox laughed and coughed, belching an odor that made Landry almost gag. "Dig 'em up. That's the best way to find out who's buried somewhere."

Landry ignored the stout man's feeble attempt at humor. "Who's buried there, Ox?"

"There's more than one. That's all you get for a hundred bucks. I know more. How bad do you want to hear it?"

"You tell me whose buried there, and I'll pay you another hundred. But you talk first and I pay after."

Ox looked straight ahead again, seemingly lost in thought, and he spoke quietly without turning his head. "A hundred for each one who's buried that you don't know about."

This was news. Landry had expected one child, maybe two considering the cribs in the nursery. How many were there?

"All right. I'm not sure if I have enough money on me."

"How much you got?"

"Four hundred."

"That'll work."

Ox rambled about his father. Carlton Fedder came to work for Miss Olivia as a yard man in 1954. He was in his early twenties, and even though he hadn't finished high school, he was clever and handy. Soon she had him doing all sorts of jobs inside the house and out, and he became indispensable. He was Olivia's only employee from the day he arrived until the day she died in 1965, and she trusted him with everything she needed done.

Mundane jobs and important ones too, as Landry soon learned.

"There are three little babies buried under that angel," Ox said. "My pa buried 'em all hisself."

"Three? Tell me about them."

"Gimme three hundred bucks first."

Landry had no choice at this point. Ox could be lying through his teeth, but the gravestone was there for a reason. There might be something to his story.

Money in hand, Ox continued. "Pa came there in 1954, like I said. After she got to know him pretty good, she told him she wanted him to do a chore for her. He might have got a hundred bucks too — who knows?" The thought made Ox laugh out loud.

"And?"

"And she gave my daddy a little wood box and told him to go bury it in the cemetery. She had a marker too — it was out in the garage all covered with dust and stuff. Pa said she must have had it for a long time, waiting for someone she could trust. Anyhow, he went down to the cemetery and done what she wanted. He buried the box and set that angel marker on top of it."

"Did he look in the box?"

Ox laughed and took another swig. "Sure he did. Wouldn't you? There was two little babies in there. Real tiny, Daddy said, and it surprised the hell outta him. Weird, like they wasn't ready to be birthed yet or somethin'. He said they was all shriveled up and dry-lookin' like they'd been in there a long time. He didn't ask no questions. He done what she asked and that was that."

"He showed them to you too, didn't he?"

"What makes you think that?"

Because you're a bunch of Coon-ass rednecks, Landry thought. "I just figured he did. Did they scare you?"

"Maybe. Like I said, they was little and kind of creepy lookin'."

"Were they Olivia's children?"

"You think Pa would've asked her that?"

"I'm asking what you think."

"I was just a kid, so what I think don't matter. My pa figured they was hers. She'd fixed up the nursery, bought a couple of cribs, all that stuff. Made sense they was hers. But it wasn't his place to ask."

"So your father buried a small wooden coffin in the ground and erected the marker on top of it. You said there were three children."

"The other one came a lot later on. Right about the time Miss Olivia's second husband Bruno disappeared. He left town one day, people said. Just up and left, but Pa said she didn't give a damn."

"What about the child?"

"It was maybe five years after he buried them other two. She told him to make a box like the other one. She put something in it and told him to bury it beside the first one."

"Did you see it too?"

"Naw, but he said it was scary lookin'. Not even a baby. Just a bunch of goop or whatever. He didn't know about them things. He buried it and that was that."

The money had been well spent. Now Landry knew much more about Olivia Beaumont and why she was obsessed with Jordan's twin girls. She'd lost twins of her own and likely a third child as well.

He called for the tab and thanked Ox for the information.

Ox turned to him and muttered, "Wanna spend that last hundred you brung with you?"

"You told me about the three children."

"Yep. That I did. But I know somethin' else. If my pa wasn't dead and gone, I'd never be tellin' it. Ain't gonna hurt him now. Her neither. There's a big secret you ain't gonna believe."

He had Landry's attention. Maybe it was all a lie, but Ox didn't seem to have the brains to make up a story on the fly. Landry pulled out the last bill and handed it over.

Ox's raspy voice dropped to a hoarse whisper. "I told you a lie about Mr. Bruno a minute ago. I said he disappeared, and that's what everybody in town thinks. But accordin' to my daddy, he didn't run off at all. He's still there."

Landry's eyes widened in fascination. "What are you talking about? He's still where?"

"Still at the Arbors. My daddy boarded him up in a wall."

"Did Olivia kill him?"

"Ain't nothin' more to tell, mister ghost man. That's all I know, and that's all I'm sayin'." He turned his back to Landry and his attention to the football game.

CHAPTER THIRTY-SEVEN

On the short drive back, Landry had a thought — a long shot and maybe useless, but there might be another way to reach the children. He drew Callie aside and explained. She agreed it was far-fetched but worth a try.

Jordan was in no shape to hear what Landry had learned from Ox. With his girls having been missing for twenty hours, his moods vacillated wildly. At one moment he was sullen, withdrawing into his own dark thoughts. The next, he was out of control — shouting curses at God, Olivia and himself. Having been out of the hospital only a few days, he was physically fragile, and the trauma he was experiencing now took a toll on his body.

He was on the verge of a breakdown, and Landry couldn't blame him. He couldn't imagine the torment and grief Jordan was experiencing. The man had lost his wife, and now the two people who connected him to Claire — his beloved twin girls — were missing too.

Landry asked Henri to join him in the kitchen for a cup of coffee. The paranormal investigator had plenty of experience with unmarked graves and secrets hidden in old houses. His views on Ox's wild tales might somehow help them find Ellie and Vi.

"Ox Fedder told me there are three children buried in the cemetery — a set of twins and another one, maybe a miscarriage. The twins died first, a few years before the third child. He said that's the reason for the guardian angel marker."

Henri furrowed his brow. "They're Olivia's children?"

Landry nodded, explaining how Ox's father had followed Miss Olivia's orders. She gave him a box to bury; he opened it and saw desiccated twin corpses. He did what she asked, and he erected the marker over the graves. Later on he buried another coffin.

Landry had saved the most bizarre revelation for the end. "He told me something else. His father boarded up Bruno Duval in a wall."

Henri's eyebrows shot up. "Now that *is* interesting. Was Bruno alive when he was interred, à la Edgar Allan Poe, or had someone killed him?"

"He didn't say."

Henri thought for a moment. "Well, well. This changes things, and I don't think it's good. If this is true, we have Miss Olivia haunting the mansion and a nursery ready for twins who are instead buried in the cemetery. Some years later Olivia miscarries, and a third child is buried beneath the guardian angel. Her playboy husband disappears but actually never leaves the house. Instead she has the handyman wall him up. And then Jordan's twin girls come along."

"And that's why Olivia wants to play with them?"

"I'm beginning to see the entire picture and it's not a pretty one. Olivia doesn't want to play — it's far more dire than that. She *wants* them. She has her twins at last. This ratchets up the stakes tremendously."

"Are you saying —"

"I told you at lunch there was a chance she might not let them come back. They should never have come back here. I think they're gone, Landry. Maybe gone for good this time."

———

Callie had spent most of last night and today at Jordan's side. He refused to sleep, snapped at her and everyone else, and slumped in the rocker beside the mirror. Every few minutes he called their names and pleaded with Olivia to bring them back. Since last night there had been no sounds — no muted voices, youthful laughter or faint wind-chime jingling.

Callie took Jordan's hand and said, "Cate will sit with you for a while. There's something I need to take care of. Until I'm back, she and Landry will be here with you."

He stared into the mirror; she didn't know if he had heard what she said, and he didn't ask where she was going.

It was hours later — around ten p.m. — when she returned. Landry and Cate were in the kitchen; when Callie texted she was on the way, they waited up. They had convinced Jordan to rest by promising that someone would stay beside the mirror every minute. Jordan went to the master bedroom and crawled into bed. Cate looked in on him and said he was asleep in seconds.

Callie asked who was keeping watch in the nursery.

"Cate set up shifts. Phil's on from now until midnight, Henri comes in until three, and I'll sit up from then until daybreak. You're off for tonight — you must be as tired as Jordan is."

She admitted that her entire body ached, and she'd almost fallen asleep on the hour-long drive she'd just made. She sat at the table with them and put her head in her hands.

"Did you do any good?" Landry asked, wondering if his idea had worked.

"Time will tell, I guess. I saw her, if that's what you're asking. But will anything come of it? You never know. If it happens, it happens." She stood. "Please forgive me, but it's all catching up. I have to sleep before I fall on the floor." She walked out.

Landry smiled at Cate. "With everything bad that's happened, I'm glad you're here with me." She squeezed his hand and they went upstairs too.

The alarm on Landry's phone buzzed at five 'til three. He put on sweatpants and a T-shirt, went to the kitchen, fixed a cup of coffee, and walked to the nursery. Henri was awake; he'd pulled an armchair over by the mirror, and he rose when Landry entered the room.

"Anything new on the children?"

He shook his head. "I call to them now and then, but everything is quiet. I switched chairs. Jordan had Olivia's rocker over here, and for an hour I sat in it myself, in hopes I could entice her into appearing. She was not happy. I could feel negative vibes every time I rocked. To get a little peace and quiet, I moved the rocker back to the corner."

"If I rocked in it, could I make her angry enough to come back?"

"That would be a mistake. We need her on our side, at least until we get the children back and Jordan can move away. How we lure her here is the question." He stood, stretched and yawned. "I'll leave it with you. See you in the morning."

Engrossed in a book on his phone, Landry didn't notice the hall door open and Callie slip inside.

"What are you doing up? I thought you were asleep —"

She whispered, "It's happening."

"What's happening?"

Callie pointed to the far end of the room. A blond-haired girl in a blue dress stood in the corner. Landry wondered how long she'd been there; he hadn't seen her, but then he hadn't been paying attention.

"She came, Landry. This is what you wanted. She appeared in my bedroom a few minutes ago and woke me. You need to go now. I'll stay here with her."

He understood. As he opened the door, he turned to the child and said, "Thank you for coming, Anne-Marie."

Her pale face was impassive. When he left, she walked to Callie and said, "He's going to hurt you."

Callie knew not to take her words literally. They could be about something or someone else entirely, although this time she seemed to be talking about him.

"That's Landry, Anne-Marie. He's my friend."

The child shook her head and said two chilling words. "Not him."

Still groggy from lack of sleep, Callie let it go. She pointed at the mirror next to her and asked Anne-Marie if it was a portal.

"You can go far away," the girl answered. "A very long way."

Callie had gone back to Beau Rivage at Landry's suggestion. She sat in the library for nearly an hour, hoping Anne-Marie might appear. Every few minutes she called to the child, begging her to come out. About to give up, she said, "I wish you would help me one last time."

From the opposite side of the room had come a familiar voice. "I'm here."

Callie knew a great deal about Anne-Marie, but there was far more she didn't know. She asked if Anne-Marie could go to other places. The child had nodded.

Callie told her some of what was happening at Jordan's house. When she finished, Anne-Marie turned and walked out of the room. A few minutes later, Callie drove back, unsure if the child would help.

She had come, and Callie explained everything. "There are two little girls, younger than you are. Vi and Ellie are their names. A woman took them in there." She pointed to the mirror. "She wants them for her own, but their father needs them back. Their mother died, and they're all he has."

"That's very sad."

"Can you go in there? Can you find them?"

Anne-Marie laughed and stood just inches from the mirror. She put her hand through the glass, then her leg, and just walked inside.

"Anne-Marie! Can you hear me?" Callie asked anxiously. There was no response.

At a quarter past six Landry opened the nursery door. Callie sat in the chair, her head resting on her chest. He looked for Anne-Marie, but no one else was in the room.

When he touched her arm, she jumped up and said, "Is she back?"

"I don't think so. It's just us. What happened?"

"She went into the mirror, and I fell asleep waiting for her to come back. She left two hours ago. What if she can't come back?"

"I wouldn't worry about it. Look how long Jordan's kids have been gone. Time means nothing on the other side. And Anne-Marie's not like us, as you know. She's — well, she's like Olivia, a spirit. She came when you asked, and that was what I was hoping for. Now we have to pray she'll find them."

Callie thought for a moment about Anne-Marie's words. She had said, "He's going to hurt you." She'd used the same words before, back when Callie was in trouble at her own house. But what did Anne-Marie mean this time? Surely she wasn't talking about Landry. It had to be someone else. Who else could it be?

She replayed the conversation in her mind. *I told Anne-Marie that Landry was my friend, and she answered, "Not him." What did she mean?*

"Help me! I need some help!" The words came from somewhere outside the room. They ran out and heard the call again, from the master bedroom next door.

They found Jordan in bed, the cast on his broken arm twisted up in the bedsheets.

"God, Jordan! You scared the hell out of us," Callie said. "I thought you were in trouble!"

"I am. Dammit, I can't get my arm loose. I need to use the bathroom, and then I want to go to the nursery. Anything happen since I fell asleep?"

Landry glanced at her. Revealing Anne-Marie's arrival wasn't his tale to tell. The child was the resident ghost of Beau Rivage — *Callie's* ghost — and if anyone told Jordan, it should be her.

"No news," Callie answered. "Nothing yet." It was the truth, but it was only part of the story. Landry thought it right to stay mum about Anne-Marie's trip through the portal; there was no need to build Jordan's hopes until they knew something.

Jordan walked close to the mirror and called out, "Vi! Ellie! Can you hear me? Are you there? Please come back!"

There was no answer.

CHAPTER THIRTY-EIGHT

The man glanced up and down the third-floor hallway to be sure he was alone. He went into a mechanical closet and closed the door behind him. He scrunched around an air-conditioning unit from the forties that hadn't seen use in decades. Behind it was a much-smaller door.

When he first saw it, he thought of the tiny door in *Alice in Wonderland* that Alice couldn't go through. He found it interesting that a similar door was painted on the children's table in the nursery.

He wouldn't have known it was there except for a lucky break at the historical museum in New Orleans. A dusty archives room held floor plans for many old buildings in southern Louisiana, and he'd found the one he wanted — the original set for the Arbors. That was how he had discovered the maintenance room and stairwell.

He pushed his body through the door; a larger man couldn't have done it. With his chest pressed against one wall and his back on the other, he climbed steep, narrow stairs that led to the dome at the top of the house. Given the amount of cobwebs and dust, he knew no one had been up here since Olivia died in 1965. Jordan didn't know about this secret place, and that made it perfect.

The first time he visited the Arbors was as a tourist. As the guide ushered his group through the house, he looked everywhere for something he needed. He was about to give up when he had an idea.

When the tour ended, he walked into the office, leaned over the front desk, and asked a young man in the back for directions to the restroom. He left with a key ring he'd palmed off the desk. He went to town, had copies made, and returned just after midnight. The house was dark and still as he crept onto the porch and tried the keys. The third one worked and the front door opened silently. He went into the office, tossed the key ring under the desk where someone might have dropped it, and left.

From that day forward, he'd come to the Arbors every night, crawling up into the aerie at the top of the house. On every visit he brought things — items he needed to carry out his plan. He also stashed snacks and bottles of water since this all might take a while. Window-like openings encircled the cupola, offering a means to clean the glass, and he could view most of the house from his perch. The nursery was of special interest to him, and he had a clear shot of its door. Early on, he discovered something helpful. If he left the small door at the foot of the stairs open, he could hear everything in the nursery through the air-conditioning vents.

He roamed the house freely once everyone was asleep, learning what rooms Jordan and his kids lived in and finding other hiding places. Most of what he observed was of no use, but a few things infuriated him. When she spoke tenderly, when she stayed for hours in his bedroom, when she played with those little girls — her public displays of affection, her lovey-dovey stars-in-the-eyes attitude — it made him want to teach her a lesson. Thinking how he'd do it always calmed his anger.

Be patient. She'll beg for mercy before this is over. Then you'll get your revenge.

The first day or two he stayed for only an hour but later until daybreak. Emboldened, he now sometimes watched from his perch in the daytime too, taking note of the children, their father and the employees who worked downstairs in the office. It was more exciting when people were up and about. He found eavesdropping a thrilling experience — one could learn so much about people when they didn't know anyone was listening. He heard Jordan's concerns about the make-believe playmate his daughters enjoyed. He watched the film crew coming and going, and he saw the concern when the girls mysteriously went missing. He couldn't see inside the nursery, so he didn't know exactly what had happened. One minute the children's voices echoed through the vent, and the next minute there was silence.

After the girls disappeared, he wanted to look inside the nursery, but for some reason people stayed there all night long. Were they waiting for the children to return? It frustrated him that he didn't know where they had gone.

One morning around six he was almost caught. After spending the night in the dome, he opened the closet door into the hall and stepped out. Thirty feet away Jordan's bedroom door opened; he was up an hour earlier than usual. The man darted back into the closet and waited until he heard Jordan go in the bathroom and turn on the shower. Then he scurried to the place through which he came and went. He made it across the yard and into the woods just as the sun was rising. The close call only made him more determined to succeed. He was on a mission fueled by rage and revenge, and nothing would stop him.

———

Jordan continued the vigil in the nursery, sitting next to the mirror and waiting for Ellie and Vi to pop back through it. Usually Callie was by his side, offering silent encouragement in a situation with an unpredictable outcome. Jordan didn't realize that Callie's watchfulness wasn't just for his children. She was also waiting for Anne-Marie.

It was early afternoon when Callie's head jerked up. She must have been dozing. She glanced at Jordan; he was asleep too. His head lolled back in the chair and he snored lightly.

"Here I am."

The quiet, melodic voice came from the other end of the room. She looked up and saw Anne-Marie near the door. Callie ran to her.

"How long have you been here?" she whispered.

"How long was I gone?"

"Since last night. You were gone almost a day, Anne-Marie."

She broke into a rare smile. "Hmm. It never seems like a long time when you're there."

"Did you see them?"

"They are nice girls. I played with them."

Her indirect answers were frustrating, especially in a devastating situation like this one. Callie remained calm and let the child do things her way.

Jordan was awake now. "Who are you talking to?" he asked as he walked to them.

Callie introduced Anne-Marie and explained why she was here. "I didn't tell you earlier because I thought it was better to wait until we had news."

"This is the child you've told me about — the ghost from Beau Rivage?"

Anne-Marie's eyes flashed. "Don't call me that!"

"I'm sorry. I don't understand how these things work. Miss Olivia, the woman the girls call Cherry — she's a ghost, at least that's what I call her. I can't see her. Only they can. But I can see you. Why is that?"

244

"I saw them."

"Who?"

Callie said, "She saw Ellie and Vi."

"You saw them? Dear God! Where are they?"

"I played with them. I like them."

He shouted, "I don't care about that! How do I get them back?"

Anne-Marie frowned, and Callie said, "Jordan, please don't raise your voice. Why don't I handle this?"

The girl spoke quietly to Callie. "That man I don't like. He's here, you know."

"Who's she talking about?" Jordan asked, his voice calm.

"Landry."

Anne-Marie shook her head. "He's going to hurt you."

Their disjointed conversation irritated Jordan. "What does that mean? Can we talk about Vi and Ellie?"

Callie knelt in front of Anne-Marie. "You've helped me so very, very much. Jordan's a nice man, a good father. He wants his children to come back. Can you do that for us? He loves those girls so much."

"Cherry loves them, and they love her too. She's good to them."

Jordan couldn't help what happened next. Given the situation, it had been inevitable. Later he'd apologize and worry and kick himself and spend another sleepless night, but at this moment her oblique comment infuriated him. His emotions burst out and he screamed, "They're MINE! They're MY children, for God's sake! She's evil, don't you know that? She took my girls from me!" He buried his head in his hands and sobbed. "I have to get them back. Can you please help me?"

There was no response. He raised his head; Callie was there, but Anne-Marie had disappeared. They wouldn't see her again for twenty-four agonizing hours.

CHAPTER THIRTY-NINE

Yesterday afternoon the man had been listening and watching. He heard them talking in the nursery, and he knew Anne-Marie was here. Months had passed, but the mere thought of her infuriated him.

Things were beginning to make sense. Olivia had taken the girls somewhere, and Callie had asked Anne-Marie to bring them back. How appropriate that Callie sent her to whatever netherworld the girls were in. Having the ghost child as part of the rescue effort only made him more determined that her plan would fail. Olivia Beaumont had Jordan's children, and he'd do whatever he could to make sure they never returned.

By ten everyone was in bed except for those keeping watch in the nursery. Every other room in the house was dark.

It was time to go. He'd been here for a long time, and his bones ached. He was hungry and thirsty and he wanted some sleep. He shifted out of his hiding place, took the narrow stairs down carefully, and opened the door into the maintenance closet. He slid around the AC unit and gasped in surprise. Standing two feet from him in the dimly lit closet was a girl in a blue dress.

"I won't let you," she said.

"Anne-Marie, we meet again. I knew you were here."

"You are a bad man, Mark Streater. Why won't you leave her alone?"

Her words made him smile. "I thought I killed you. I shot you point-blank. But it's not that easy with your kind, is it? You're like a pest that's hard to get rid of. Like a rash or something."

"I won't let you hurt her."

"There's nothing you can do. You protected Callie from me last time, but it won't happen again. Now get out of my way."

Mark raised his hand to push her aside, but she vanished. He crept into the silent hallway, tiptoed down the stairs, and left.

Now that the damned child had come, Mark's plans had to change. He had to move quickly.

No problem, he thought to himself. *There's a score to settle. Doing it sooner rather than later works for me.*

———

Everyone worried about Jordan. After forty-eight hours without the girls, he lashed out at everyone, and the torment in his mind kept him from sleeping. He had eaten almost nothing; he stayed by the mirror, alternating between wails of grief and shouts into the portal demanding Olivia release them. Jordan was becoming impossible for them to deal with. Even Callie, who remained steadfast during his tirades, had to get away now and then. She would go into the master bedroom next door to rest, but with his ranting a few feet away, sleeping was impossible.

Those around him sympathized. He might well have seen his daughters for the last time. What a horrific way to lose your children, through a portal that led to another dimension. As sad and gut-wrenching as it was, one could deal with the rational — accidents or even fatal illnesses — but having two little girls snatched away by a malevolent spirit was unfathomable.

Callie told Lauren what was happening to him, and she wouldn't let Jordan go to the office until things were better. The staff didn't need to see him like this, and Callie said she'd give Lauren updates so she could keep his worried employees informed.

Callie was resting in the master bedroom when she thought she heard Jordan talking to someone. Then he shouted to her.

"Callie! Callie, come here now!"

She ran to him.

Jordan pointed at the rocker, where Anne-Marie sat.

"Hi! Where have you been?" Callie asked in a soft voice as she sat on the floor by the chair.

"She won't let them come back yet."

Those words were the last straw for a frazzled, beaten-down father. Jordan wailed, "Do something, then! You're the ghost — the whatever — who's supposed to help us! Make her stop this madness!" As tears of grief streamed down his face, Callie rushed to console him.

Callie glanced at the rocker and was glad Anne-Marie hadn't gone. She said, "What will happen next?"

"I talked to that man. He wants to hurt you."

"Who, Anne-Marie? Who are you talking about?"

"He has a secret place —"

Jordan muttered to himself, "There are secret places all over this accursed house. Can we concentrate on finding my children?"

Anne-Marie frowned. "I won't let him hurt you," she whispered. "I want to talk to the lady. I'll be back in a minute." She walked to the mirror and went away.

Callie prepared for the hours that would pass before Anne-Marie reappeared. Jordan slumped in his chair, and this time he didn't protest when she took him next door and put him to bed.

Two hours later Callie, Cate and Landry were talking in the nursery when they noticed Anne-Marie in the rocker.

For her own peace of mind, there was something Callie had to settle. She took Landry by the hand and led him across the room.

"Is this the man you said was going to hurt me?"

Landry looked astonished, while Anne-Marie gave her typical response. "I told him I wouldn't let him hurt you."

"Who are you talking about? Landry? This man?"

Landry was confused. "Me? What do you mean? I wouldn't hurt you!"

It came to Callie in a moment of understanding. How could it have taken so long for her to realize what she meant?

"It's Mark! You're talking about Mark. Is he somewhere nearby?"

Anne-Marie frowned. "I saw him upstairs."

"In this house? When?"

"He watches."

Landry asked what she meant, but Anne-Marie didn't answer.

"Please tell us what's going on," he urged, but Callie told him to be patient. "She's talked more in the past two days than since I've known her. Anne-Marie and I would do anything for each other, wouldn't we, darling?"

The child smiled.

"She never answers directly. But everything she says is important. You just have to figure it out."

She looked at the girl. "It *is* Mark, isn't it? That's who the bad man is."

"You must be careful. When I'm in there —" she pointed toward the mirror "— I can't help you."

Landry asked if Anne-Marie would take them to the place where the man hid, but as usual, she changed the subject.

"Ellie and Vi said to tell their daddy hello. They are having a wonderful time."

"What do they do there?" Callie asked, thinking what a bizarre conversation this was.

"They're her little girls now, like the ones she lost a long time ago."

The twins, Landry thought. *She's talking about the twins Carlton Fedder buried in the cemetery.*

Callie spoke in a calm, serious voice. She'd held back playing her last card, but there was no time left. It was good that Jordan was asleep in the other room, because she was about to say things they'd never discussed. She had to convince Anne-Marie to rescue the children, and this was her last hope.

"Anne-Marie, I want to tell you something. Jordan, the children's father, is a wonderful man. I'm falling in love with him, and I think someday he may ask me to marry him. If I did, I would be Vi and Ellie's stepmother. Do you see what a wonderful thing for everyone that would be? But if the girls never come back, I think Jordan will die from grief. I would be sad too — sad for him but also for me. I love those little girls. Please help me, Anne-Marie. Please convince Cherry to bring them back home."

Anne-Marie's face was impassive. She stared straight ahead and rocked for what seemed like an eternity. At last she stood, and for the first time ever, she hugged Callie. Taking her hand, she pointed to Landry and said, "Come with me. Bring him."

Anne-Marie took them upstairs to the maintenance room and pointed to the narrow space behind the air-conditioning unit. Landry scooted around it and said, "There's a small door back here. Should I open it?"

The child said nothing. Callie knew Anne-Marie well; nothing she did was frivolous. The door was where she had led them, and Callie told Landry to do it.

"There's a stairway and there's light at the top. It's very narrow — I can't fit in it unless I go up sideways."

He ducked through the door and sidled up fourteen narrow risers. *Thank God I'm not claustrophobic,* he thought as he maneuvered through the cramped space. *Or overweight.*

He assessed the situation and returned to them.

"Somebody's been up there; there are empty water bottles and snack wrappers. It's a walkway that goes all around the dome. There are openings all along that look like window frames. If you lean through them, you can touch the glass in the cupola. It's a perfect spot for spying — nobody downstairs can see you, but you have a clear view of the entire house, from the top all the way down. There's an echo effect since the rotunda is open all the way to the top. I could hear conversations on the first floor."

Callie asked, "Anne-Marie, does this place have something to do with Ellie and Vi?"

For once, she gave a direct answer. "Mark. It's his hiding place."

"How do you know that?"

Anne-Marie smiled. "I told him I wouldn't let him hurt you."

————

The camera in the nursery recorded twenty-four hours a day. There was a time it would have upset Jordan, but now nothing mattered. He hardly knew where he was, much less that the camera standing in a corner was functional.

It was important to capture everything. Regardless of the outcome — and Landry hoped the girls would return quickly — this was a supernatural experience unlike anything even Henri had witnessed, and he was the expert.

A dominant spirit kidnaps two children and takes them to a parallel dimension. There's a battle to bring them back. But what kind of battle? They couldn't fathom what they were up against. Could they prevail against Olivia Beaumont? *Would* they?

Two of their group left on Saturday morning. Cate went back to Galveston; as office manager of her father's medical practice, her absence created extra work for others. Landry walked her to her car. Watching through a window, Callie saw Cate give him a big hug and kiss. Callie smiled, knowing she wasn't the only one with new feelings stirring inside.

Phil had to go too. Since nothing was happening, the station manager brought him back to New Orleans. Landry, however, was instructed to stay on site while things played out.

Three were left — Callie, Landry and Henri. They would stay with Jordan, although each knew that the story might have already ended. There could come a time — a week or a month from now — when they gave up and admitted the girls were gone forever. For now, for the sake of Jordan, Vi and Ellie, they would cling to hope.

CHAPTER FORTY

The length of time the girls had been gone was measured in days now, not hours. If it hadn't been for the people working in Jordan's office downstairs, the house would have been as quiet as a tomb. The boss hadn't set foot in his office in the four days since the girls left. Hoping to keep his mind off them, Lauren came upstairs from time to time to ask him questions, but even that had ended for now.

Jordan was sinking into a quagmire of despondency. Depressed beyond imagination, he stared for hours into the corner where the portal lay. His shoulders slumped and his body shuddered as his gut wrenched in spasms. The others helped him eat and drink when he couldn't hold a glass or spoon in his trembling hands.

In his deteriorating mental state, Callie doubted even with Landry's help she could get him to a doctor. Jordan didn't have a primary physician, and even if he had, house calls were a distant memory. She asked Lauren for ideas and learned a close friend's mother was an internist in Baton Rouge. She was coming to St. Francisville this weekend, and she agreed to stop by and see him.

The twenty-four-hour vigils by the portal had stopped. Sitting in a chair struggling to stay awake was hard on everyone, and Jordan had stopped asking them to do it.

On Friday afternoon of the fourth day since Ellie and Vi left, Callie walked past Jordan's bedroom and heard him mumbling. She looked in; he was sitting on the edge of his bed, a pistol in his shaky hands. He was looking down at it, his words unintelligible.

Careful to avoid startling him, she moved closer until he noticed her. He looked up and she murmured, "Why don't you let me keep that for you?"

"I may need it."

"You have to be strong, Jordan. You have to be here for your girls."

"Do you think they're coming back, Callie? Can you look me in the eye and honestly tell me you believe I'll see them again? She took them to be with their mother, and now they're gone just like Claire is." He played with the gun, moving it back and forth until the barrel was facing him.

She sat next to him on the bed and put her hand on his. She could feel his finger resting loosely against the trigger.

"Lauren's got a friend whose mom is a doctor. She's coming by tomorrow to check on you." He let her take away the pistol.

"I don't need a doctor. I need Ellie and Vi. I'm going crazy without them."

"You can't do everything alone, Jordan. No one could expect you to. I can't imagine how you feel, but please stay brave and believe they'll be back. Be positive for them — and for yourself."

He was exhausted; she helped him into bed and fluffed his pillow. Once he was asleep, she took the gun and went into the hall. She'd been strong for him, but now she collapsed on the carpet and sobbed. If she hadn't been there, he might have killed himself.

She composed herself, hid the gun in her bedroom, and went downstairs. There were things she needed to tell Landry and Henri, and with Jordan sleeping, now was a good time.

After Anne-Marie's revelation about Mark's hiding place, Callie had to tell them everything she knew. She hadn't mentioned Mark when Cate and Landry were at Beau Rivage. She didn't know them well then, and she wasn't comfortable discussing it.

The incident with Jordan's gun would be her secret for now. Her heart was breaking for him. She missed the children too, but he was dying inside. She'd tell the doctor tomorrow, but there was no reason to bring it up with the others.

She joined Landry and Henri in the kitchen, and she revealed everything about Mark, including his trying to murder Anne-Marie by shooting her point-blank in the back.

Landry knew some of Mark's history because of the publicity surrounding his disappearance. He was a psychopath who had been released on bail only because he was charged with manslaughter instead of murder. He'd disappeared the moment he was free. Anne-Marie claimed he was watching everyone from the rafters of the Arbors.

Should they believe her? Callie trusted Anne-Marie, but her odd way of answering questions left you wondering what she meant. Landry had more experience with otherworldly events and apparitions than most people did, but he still didn't know what to make of Anne-Marie.

She appeared dedicated to Callie. She had saved her from Mark before, and he believed she would try to do it again.

CHAPTER FORTY-ONE

"Is there a pistol in this house?"

Landry's question startled Callie, and she wondered if he knew about Jordan's episode.

"This isn't my house, and in Jordan's condition, I wouldn't recommend asking him."

"Agreed. But you haven't seen one yourself?"

"Why are you asking this? After what I told Anne-Marie yesterday, you may have the wrong impression of my relationship with Jordan. I don't know much about him or this house."

"No need to explain about you and Jordan. It's none of my business. I say do whatever it takes to get the girls back."

Her eyes flashed. "You don't understand. What I told her was true. I'm headstrong, independent, and a man will never push me around again. I learned that lesson from my uncle Willard and from Mark. After all that, I vowed to run my life and Beau Rivage with no outside help or interference. I knew Jordan already; we had a working relationship. I was sorry that he'd lost Claire and was raising two girls alone, but his personal life wasn't my business. Then you and Cate came along, I introduced you to Jordan, and here we are today, facing the biggest battle anyone should have to fight.

"I've realized something as we've gone through this. I'm thirty-one and I have my whole life ahead of me. Maybe being alone is right for me, but why shouldn't I explore my options? All men aren't like Uncle Willard and Mark. Until now I hadn't found the other kind. I've discovered feelings that were locked away. I told Anne-Marie I loved Jordan, but I don't — not yet, but I see possibilities. Am I going to marry him? Who knows? That's not what I told her. I said someday he *might* ask me. And someday, he just might. Did I tell her that so she'd help get the girls back? Absolutely. Was it a lie? Not at all."

Landry took her hand and said, "I haven't known you for long, but I see the look in your eyes when you're with Jordan. We all know you have strong feelings for him. You've already been a source of comfort and strength to him through his trials — maybe the only source he has now. I wish you both luck however this turns out. And I pray constantly for the girls to come back."

"But in the meantime, you want a pistol. Why?"

"I want to catch Mark. When I do, I have to be ready."

"Ready for what? To kill him?"

"To control him until the police show up."

"Landry, you're not a cop —"

"Au contraire, my dear," he answered in a Rhett Butler voice. "Once upon a time, I was a deputy sheriff in Iberia Parish."

"You were a deputy sheriff? I didn't know that. But you're not now. Call the police and let them handle it."

"We know Mark watches the house. If he sees the police here, it'll send him deeper into hiding instead of bringing him out. I don't know when or how he comes and goes, but this has to end. Please help me. Is there a gun in the house?"

"Yes," she admitted, fudging her answer. "Jordan has one. I took it because of his mental state. I'll give it to you, but please don't do anything rash. I know what Mark's capable of."

She brought him Jordan's fully loaded .357 Magnum revolver. As she handed it over, she brushed away a tear and left the room without saying a word.

Half an hour later, Anne-Marie said goodbye to Callie and went into the portal. She didn't mention Callie's plea for help, and she didn't say when she'd return.

Henri left for a day trip to New Orleans. After hearing Ox Fedder's wild tale about a body boarded up in a wall at the Arbors, he needed extra equipment. He went by his office, loaded his car, and treated himself to lunch at Galatoire's before heading back. He was on the road by two, at the Arbors by four, and setting up equipment an hour later.

The house was enormous, full of nooks, crannies and rooms that led to other rooms. If there was a body inside a wall, it could be anywhere. Examining every square foot would take weeks they didn't have. Henri started in the logical place, the room where everything happened — the nursery.

"When you don't know where to look, one place is as good as another," Henri commented, telling Landry since the mirror was the pivotal point in the room, he would start by examining the walls behind it. He stacked two machines on top of each other, ran an extension cord to the closest plug, and moved two black devices up and down the walls from the floor as high as he could reach. The things he held looked like wireless remote controls, and the machines emitted low humming sounds as Henri worked his way around the room.

Henri explained that one machine detected anomalies — hidden recesses. The other identified organic matter.

The doctor stopped by that afternoon. She spoke with Callie first, asking what was going on with Jordan. Callie told her about the missing children and Olivia Beaumont. The woman didn't bat an eyebrow at the supernatural tale she revealed. Maybe Lauren had prepared her, or perhaps she was a native Louisianan who was accustomed to crazy stories.

After Callie told her about the gun incident, they went into Jordan's bedroom. The doctor stayed with him for thirty minutes and rejoined Callie. She said he was emotionally and physically drained. He wasn't eating or sleeping properly, he was fixated on his children's dilemma, and it was taking a serious toll on him.

"I know you're worried sick," she told Callie, "and I think things are even worse than you think. Taking away the gun may have saved him for the moment, but a person bent on suicide will keep at it until he finishes. He needs to see a psychiatrist as soon as possible. I know a good one in Baton Rouge. If I call, maybe he could see Jordan tomorrow or Monday at the latest."

Callie agreed and the doctor made the call. Her friend would return Sunday night from New York, and he would see Jordan in his office at 8 a.m. Monday. She gave Callie prescriptions for a narcotic to let him sleep and an antidepressant.

It was time for dinner. Callie helped Jordan down the stairs to the kitchen. Landry fixed sandwiches for everyone.

There wasn't a word said about what Henri and Landry were up to. If Jordan knew one was looking for a body and the other was stalking a killer hiding in the house, it would have sent him into further mental anguish.

Jordan had asked to go to his office earlier this afternoon, but he'd done nothing productive. Now he slumped in his chair, picked at a sandwich, and grunted when they tried to talk to him.

Landry cleared the table and drove to the drugstore. Henri went back to work, and Callie took Jordan upstairs. He wanted to sit in the nursery a little longer, and she stayed with him, afraid to leave him alone in the evilest part of the Arbors, the room where his girls had disappeared. The nursery.

CHAPTER FORTY-TWO

Another day dawned without the return of the three children. Thanks to the medication, Jordan slept well for the first time since the debacle began, and he seemed somewhat improved when Callie woke him at six. He needed a shave and a shower, but he said he wasn't up to it. She helped him dress and they left the house shortly after seven for his appointment with the psychiatrist in Baton Rouge.

Henri's search of the nursery was almost finished. All that remained was the closet, which was still loaded with boxes.

He and Landry unloaded the closet. In the back was a tall clothes wardrobe stuffed with new store-tagged dresses, their fabrics faded and torn after all the years hanging there. They removed the clothes and pulled the wardrobe aside.

Behind it was another half-sized door like the one in the mechanical closet upstairs. This one was locked, and none of Jordan's keys would open it. Henri ran his detection equipment over the door and wasn't surprised there was a room behind it.

Henri's second machine, the one that detected organic matter, emitted a shrill beep. Something behind the door was — or had been — alive. It could easily be a dead animal. There was no way to tell without opening the door.

Landry wanted to break through, but that was Jordan's call, and he didn't know they were looking for Bruno. They had to wait until he and Callie returned. In the meantime Henri moved his equipment to the master bedroom next door. Maybe Olivia had walled up her husband there to keep the rascal nearby even in death.

Callie and Jordan were back before ten. Upbeat and alert, he reported that his session with the doctor had been productive. The big takeaway was that hope overcame fear. Jordan needed to remain focused and positive. There might be other ways to bring the children back, and with a clear mind he could help.

Even though he worried that Jordan would nix the search, Landry had to tell him about their search for Bruno's body. He asked if they could remove the door or break through it.

Jordan was in better shape than he had been in days, but like before, he refused to allow them to damage the door. Find the key or leave it alone, he said emphatically, leaving them with no way to proceed.

———

A late-afternoon thunderstorm moved in. The lights in the house flickered as streaks of lightning flashed across the sky. Jordan napped in his bedroom while Callie sat in the nursery, praying for the safe return of all three girls. With a yawn and a stretch, she walked to the windows that looked out upon the Mississippi River. A massive container ship a thousand feet long chugged downstream in the driving rain and wind that whipped through the oak trees on the shoreline. She watched them sway in a hypnotic dance that mesmerized her and rescued her from her thoughts.

It's time to give it up. She'll come back when she wants. His girls, I'm not so sure about, but I can only pray Olivia will let them go. Lost in reverie, it startled Callie when the house went dark. After a few minutes, she decided to go downstairs. As she turned from the window, she glimpsed something out there in the rain. It was a black shape that blended with the trees and was hard to see in the fierce storm. Then it was gone, and maybe it hadn't been there at all. The trees whipped about, low-hanging fog was moving in from the river, and with the rainstorm it was hard to see across the yard. She squinted her eyes but saw nothing. She'd been wrong.

Callie walked through the nursery and grasped the doorknob as something in the corner caught her eye. Olivia's chair rocked back and forth. Anne-Marie was back.

Callie dropped to her knees. "I'm so glad to see you! I've missed you so much! Are the girls coming back?"

She looked at Callie, her face as unreadable as always. "He's here. I came to help you."

Callie's eyes widened in surprise. "Mark is here? Now?"

"I won't let him hurt you."

"Anne-Marie, you must answer me. Is he hiding up in the dome?"

"What you need is hidden in the closet."

"What do you mean? I don't understand. You're confusing me!"

"The key. It's in there." Callie turned as she pointed to the closet. She looked back, but the girl wasn't there.

They went over every square inch of the closet, but there was no key. Anne-Marie had said, "The thing you need is hidden in the closet," and that it was a key.

Landry wondered if they were looking in the wrong place. Maybe it wasn't in the closet but in the cartons stored inside it. They rummaged through them.

There were scads of clothes, dolls and toys. Callie found dozens of children's books from the 1940s and 1950s in front of her, and she thumbed through each one.

Her diligence paid off. She held up a tarnished brass key and a folded piece of paper stuck inside a Bobbsey Twins book from the 1940s.

"This makes perfect sense," Henri exclaimed. "If Olivia killed her husband and hid his body, it's a logical place for the demented woman to keep the key — in a book about twins. That was her obsession. Still is, I might add."

Landry opened the paper and saw old-fashioned flourishes of penmanship with fancy curlicues. "It says, 'Rot in hell, Bruno Duval. Matthew 5:38.'"

"What does that verse say?" Callie asked.

Landry looked it up and read it out loud. "Ye have heard that it hath been said, An eye for an eye, and a tooth for a tooth."

Henri shook his head and smiled. "If I were a betting man, I'd lay odds we've found the final resting place of Olivia's missing husband."

The key slid into the hole. Landry jiggled it right and left; there was resistance, but at last it turned with a solid click.

"Should we tell Jordan?" Henri asked, but Callie said no. It worried her that he might still refuse.

"He said if you found the key, you could open it, so let's do it. There may be nothing back there worth looking at anyway. What if the organic matter is a nest of dead rats?"

Henri smiled but said nothing. His machine showed him the size of what was behind the door. This was no nest of rats.

The hinges were rusty; it took effort to get the door started, and it creaked mightily as they tugged and pried. At last they pulled it open.

They waited while Landry moved the camera into position and directed a bright light into the darkened area. Callie stepped in first, let out a scream and stumbled backwards into Landry. Her hand over her mouth, she pointed speechlessly at the opening, and Landry looked in. After reading Olivia's clue, what he saw didn't surprise him.

The space was tiny — only three feet wide and two deep. It was an access cabinet with pipes running up the back walls. The desiccated body of a man wearing a sports jacket and tan slacks was curled into the fetal position on the floor. No one doubted who he was. They'd found Bruno Duval at last.

Henri examined the inside of the closet door, running his fingers along a series of deep gouges in it. Then he knelt to examine the corpse, careful not to touch anything. They'd call the police next, and the medical examiner would do a full investigation.

The face looked like a mummy's, its skin drawn tight and the lips pulled back in a grimace. There was a veneer of gray mold and the eye sockets were empty. "The insects had a feast," Henri murmured as he worked.

The fingernails appeared to be long, but he explained that was an illusion, a result of the skin withdrawing.

"My God," he whispered. "Look at his fingers."

Landry looked closely and drew back in horror.

The man's fingernails were ripped and broken off below the quick. Dried blood covered his fingertips. He had scratched and clawed at the locked door until he gave up. Who knew how long it had taken for him to die, from starvation or lack of water or madness?

Olivia had loathed her husband enough to do this horrific thing. She'd taken his life for taking her child away.

"You mentioned Poe the other day," Landry said. "I forget which story it was."

"It's 'The Cask of Amontillado,'" Henri replied. "The word is *immurement.*"

"Immurement? That's a new one to me."

"Olivia did what Poe's villain did. She *immured* Bruno — she entombed him alive.

CHAPTER FORTY-THREE

Mark was drenched. He'd sat in the dense trees all afternoon, waiting for an opportunity to get back inside the house. Two of them had left the house, but the others were still there, so he couldn't get in. The raging storm had taken out power in parts of St. Francisville. If it happened here, he could sneak in. If not, he had to wait hours until everyone was asleep.

Getting in was simple from the first day. When the architect designed the house, he'd included a handy feature next to its two massive fireplaces. Three-foot-square inserts through the walls allowed servants to load firewood from outdoors. Logs sat dry and ready behind a decorative interior door. Mark found the storage bins, saw the simple padlocks, and made them his way of entry. When he crawled through, the only potential danger would be if someone was in the room. He typically came late at night, and he'd never had a problem.

There was a jagged bolt of lightning and a deafening crash of thunder, and every light in the house went off. *Perfect!* He waited a moment and walked to the edge of the trees, ready to make a run across the yard. He took a deep breath, adjusted his poncho against the driving rain, and glanced toward the upper floors of the Arbors. Someone was there, staring out a window! He darted back into the trees and looked again. It was her! It was Callie gazing out at the storm and the broad expanse of grass he'd almost dashed across.

That was not only close — it could have been a disaster. Had she seen him already? It was unlikely, but if he'd started across the yard, it could have ruined everything. He retreated deeper into the woods to wait. What difference did a few hours make when his plans were about to come to fruition?

———

There was another dead body at the Arbors and they had to call the authorities once again. Before the call they had to get Jordan ready to face the police. In his improved state, the matter of Bruno Duval wouldn't be a problem. But there was a more powerful issue — the missing children. The police didn't know about that, and Jordan insisted it stay that way.

When Jordan awoke and went into the nursery, he found them in the closet and learned about the body. His eyes gleamed with interest; even a gruesome distraction from worrying about Vi and Ellie seemed a positive thing.

They briefed Jordan on the notes they'd found, the statement by Ox Fedder that his father had walled up Bruno Duval, and how Henri's equipment led them to the hidden room. He seemed prepared and ready to talk to the authorities, but Callie said one important thing remained before they called.

"I hate to break the news to you," she chided, "but you must clean yourself up. You want to keep the girls a secret, but everyone will wonder what's wrong if we don't get you into the shower. You look like you've spent a month in the backwoods."

Callie went with him to his bedroom, and he explained why he hadn't showered earlier. The antidepressant was giving him vertigo; he'd almost fallen several times.

"I need your help," he said, and it surprised even her how quickly she said yes. More expectant than uncomfortable, she undressed Jordan, helped him shower and shave, and dressed him in fresh clothes.

She found herself with interesting thoughts as she watched him shower. *Not a bad body. I should stop looking,* she told herself, but she didn't.

Jordan called the police. His words were direct and clear as he explained what the others had found.

Chief Kimes, another officer, and the medical examiner arrived. They examined the closet and saw the note Olivia had left with the key. They also read the accusation Bruno had penned on the flyleaf of the book.

Bruno's note was dated December 1958, and there was no reason to believe this long-dead corpse wasn't him. The ME asked what year Olivia died.

"In 1965," Jordan replied. "He's been in there for over fifty years."

The dead man's pockets held receipts for lunch and drinks at a club in town on January 3, 1959. There was a gold Dunhill lighter, a pair of glasses and a package of Certs breath mints. There was also a wallet with ninety dollars in cash, a Diners Club card, and a 1957 driver's license issued to Bruno Duval, whose address was the Arbors, St. Francisville, Louisiana. On the floor were a dozen butts and an empty Old Gold cigarette pack. Landry imagined him frantically chain-smoking every one as he pondered his fate.

There was little doubt whose body it was, but the ME required positive identification if possible. Fingerprints might work, or DNA. The policeman asked Jordan about next of kin, but he didn't know anyone. When the cop was finished, the ME brought in a stretcher and took Bruno's body away to the parish morgue. If no family turned up, Jordan offered the family cemetery. After what he had suffered with Olivia, he thought it fair to do so.

It was after midnight by the time everyone retired. Mark waited until the house was dark and then maneuvered his way through the wood bin and into the parlor. Tonight would be a critical one. The time for hesitancy was over. He had spent the afternoon creating the final act in the drama of the Arbors, but first there was something he had to know about.

A few hours ago a police car and the parish medical examiner's SUV had arrived. He had crept to the house and peered through the windows. He counted heads — Callie, Landry, Henri and Jordan. All present and accounted for. So who died?

He thought at first it was the children, but the officer and ME were only in the house for an hour — not long enough for a full-blown investigation — and no one seemed the least bit excited about things. At the end they carried a sheet-draped body on a gurney out to the SUV.

Whose body was it?

Mark tiptoed into the nursery and saw the closet door standing wide open. He looked at the wardrobe they'd pushed aside and the small door in the back with an old key in the lock. The tiny room was musty and there was a large imprint on the dusty floor. There were also plenty of fresh footprints.

The body had been on the floor! That realization gave him a great idea. Now his clever plan would be even better. He looked around the room and saw lots of pipes and wires. Where the dust had been disturbed, he found a line in the floorboards as if a saw had cut it. He followed it with his finger and realized it was square, but what was it? He used his pocket knife to outline the edges and realized he was looking at a trapdoor. Underneath was a two-foot-high crawl space. He didn't know why it was there, but it was perfect.

At last the time for waiting was over. Mark went up to his aerie and felt behind a wall stud. His fingers closed

274

around a spray bottle of isoflurane, the first thing he had purchased when he planned his revenge. Buying it in the States would have been difficult, but he'd fled his home country. As with many other drugs, purchasing the stuff in Mexico was no problem. He'd bought it from a vet, saying it was for his hundred-pound dog. Since he didn't have a dog, Mark tested it on himself to get the dosage right. That had been a trip, but a successful one. After being out cold for ten minutes, he'd awoken with nothing more than a dull headache.

He'd hidden the isoflurane and his other supplies days ago. Back then he hadn't known how long he'd be waiting, but his patience had paid off. Tonight was the night and Mark was ecstatic. He put a roll of duct tape in his pocket and crept out into the hall. He tiptoed to Callie's bedroom and went inside.

Callie was asleep. He clamped his hand over her mouth, shot a spray of isoflurane into each nostril, waited sixty seconds for the powerful anesthetic to work, and picked up her inert body. He carried her to the new place, that room in the nursery closet. He placed her carefully on the floor, duct-taped her hands, feet and mouth, and eased her down into the cramped crawl space. With the floorboards replaced and dust swept around the edges of the opening, no one would see it.

He left the key in the lock as he had found it, closed the closet door, and went back to his perch to wait for the action to begin.

Anne-Marie's remarkable powers were ineffectual on the other side of the portal. When she stepped back into the nursery thirty minutes after Mark had left, she knew something was terribly wrong. She felt sadness and dread. But since she'd been away, she didn't know what had happened.

Anne-Marie had developed a bond with Callie. It was her first attachment with a living person in almost two hundred years. She found the strange emotions in her mind unfamiliar and disconcerting. She had returned tonight with important news for Callie and the others, but this new development disturbed her very much.

She went into Callie's bedroom. The bedcovers were in disarray and she wasn't there. There were people in the house; she could sense their life forces, and she wondered if Callie could be someplace else.

Landry's room was next along the hallway. He awoke with a start as he realized someone was standing by his bed.

"What the hell —"

Anne-Marie asked where Callie was.

"I have no idea. Don't you know?"

"I came back from the other side. I want Callie."

"Her room's next door," he said, but the child shook her head.

"Do you want me to come with you?" he asked, and she stared into his eyes without responding. He got out of bed, embarrassed at first to be wearing only boxers, but remembered this was no child. He donned a shirt and sweatpants, and they went into the hall.

The house was as quiet as he'd expected at four a.m. She walked to Jordan's room and paused. Landry knocked, and at last he opened the door, groggy from the effects of the narcotics. Landry asked if Callie was with him, and he shook his head.

In a few minutes Jordan joined them, worried that along with the children, his friend Callie was missing too. They woke Henri next. She wouldn't have been in his room, but they had to eliminate every possibility.

Mark could hear them shouting Callie's name. It was exciting to watch them rushing all over the place, looking here and there on every floor. He observed things unfolding as though he were a theater patron watching actors perform a play he'd written himself.

It was Landry who searched the nursery. He looked around the room, opened the closet and the small room where Bruno's body was discovered, but he didn't find her. She heard his footsteps on the boards just above her face, but she couldn't move and she couldn't shout. Then things were quiet again and she cried.

Mark was pleased to see Landry leave the nursery empty-handed. She'd be awake by now, but she couldn't have made a sound.

They combed every square foot of the house, and soon they would look in the dome. He waited as he watched their fruitless searching.

This was act three of his stage play; it was his grand finale and the anticipation made him giddy.

CHAPTER FORTY-FOUR

Anne-Marie opened the door to the maintenance closet and saw the dim light behind the air-conditioning unit. She sensed his presence. He was there, and she realized she'd broken her promise to Callie.

She had gone into the portal, a place where she couldn't help. Trying to bring Ellie and Vi back, she had left her friend alone. And Mark had hurt her.

Mark heard something down below. Someone had come in the maintenance closet. Anne-Marie knew about his post, but had she told anyone else? Maybe not, because no one shuffled around the machinery and came up the narrow staircase. In a moment he heard the door close again and everything was quiet.

Anne-Marie confirmed Mark was hiding up there. She closed the door, found Landry, and brought him to the maintenance room.

Landry went in first and slipped behind the unit. Seconds later Anne-Marie appeared too, on the other side of the open door and inches from Landry. He looked inside and saw a man at the top of the stairs. It had to be Mark Streater, and Landry ducked back out of sight.

"Where is Callie?" Landry yelled, and he heard a maniacal laugh.

"She's gone. She paid the price for what she did to me."

"You'll never get away with this!" Anne-Marie moved into Mark's view and stared up at him.

"I knew you'd show up to help your friend, you little bitch," Mark sneered. "I've got bad news for you. Even a spook can't save her this time!"

Anne-Marie stared up at him as if she were in a trance.

"What have you done to her?" Landry shouted.

"All I wanted was to help Callie, but in return she took my inheritance and she ruined my life. Now I've gotten justice! Her life is over and so is her boyfriend's. You want to know who texted from Jordan's cellphone? I did! I lured the girls back here so Olivia could take them away forever. Who sabotaged the cars? I did! They should both have died, but they didn't. Now Callie's gone for good and Jordan's life will be pure hell. If I can't have her, neither can he!"

Anne-Marie began walking up the stairs.

"Don't come up here! If you do, you'll never know what happened to her!" Landry looked up the stairs, but Mark had moved away. Anne-Marie reached the top step and turned. There was a muffled scream and then silence.

Landry scooted up the stairs and stuck his head into the open area that ringed the dome. No one was there. He looked through one of the window slots and saw a body spread-eagled on the parquet floor three stories below.

Mark Streater was dead, and Anne-Marie was gone.

The Arbors became a house of chaos. Jordan, Henri and Landry sat around the conference table and gave statements to Chief Kimes, who was again personally handling the investigation. The medical examiner got to work, snorting that these deaths were becoming a little too frequent.

Mark Streater had been found, but if what he said was true, there was another missing person now. The chief and his men searched the house, including the room where Bruno's body had lain for decades. They failed to see the trapdoor, so they missed Callie.

Callie had been bound and gagged for over twenty-four hours. She had no idea where she was; all she knew was that the narrow space was very dark. She was terrified that it was a coffin. She was sandwiched between two layers — her back lay on boards, and her stomach touched ones above her. She panicked; with her mouth taped shut, she tried to suck in air through her nostrils and hyperventilated. Forcing herself to be calm, she occasionally dozed off. One thing was certain; without water she'd die soon. If she was underground in a coffin, death couldn't come quickly enough.

There was only one thing that might save her. She channeled her energy and her thoughts into one focused plea for help. In her mind, she called out to Anne-Marie. Time and again she appealed to her spiritual friend to save her life.

As Henri, Jordan and Landry sat at the kitchen table discussing what to do next, Anne-Marie walked in. When Jordan saw her, he jumped up so quickly his chair fell backwards. He ran to her side, tears streaming down his cheeks.

"Thank God you're back! Do you have any news?"

"She needs me. I heard her, and I came to help her."

"Vi? Ellie? Please, Anne-Marie. Stop talking in riddles. Who are you talking about?"

Landry said, "Easy, Jordan. Stay calm. Let me talk to her." He asked what she meant.

"She's upstairs."

"Take us there."

She led them to the nursery and pointed to the closet. Jordan threw open the door and said, "Where are they? Where are the girls?"

"They're gone. Forever."

Her unemotional statement sent Jordan back to the depths. He collapsed, sobbing and beating his fists on the floor. Henri consoled him, helped him up, and took him to his bedroom. He gave Jordan the quick-acting sedative that put him to sleep in minutes.

"Where is she?" Landry asked, and Anne-Marie pointed to the small door at the back of the closet. He opened it and they both stepped inside. The child stood still for a few seconds. There was no sound except for Landry's breathing. Anne-Marie cocked her head to one side, knelt on the floor, and traced a square in the dust with her finger. He saw the outline of a trapdoor.

Landry threw it open. Stuck beneath the floorboards, her eyes wide open in panic and relief, lay Callie Pilantro. He lifted her out and removed the duct tape. She fell into his arms, exhausted and relieved.

"Thank God you heard me. I was calling for you in my head!" she said to Anne-Marie, who smiled. "How did you know where to look? I thought you couldn't help me from the other side."

"I came back to tell you something. Something important. That's when I heard you calling me."

"What did you want to say?"

She shook her head and vanished.

Landry and Henri helped Callie walk to her bedroom. She gulped down water too quickly and vomited. Then she laughed and said, "I've never missed a drink so much in my life." This time she took it slowly and kept it down. The men left her to a hot bath and a change of clothes. By the time she returned to the kitchen, Jordan was awake and waiting for her.

He held her as they kissed over and over. "I thought I'd lost you too," he murmured. "I'll never let you go again."

Finding Callie had calmed Jordan a little, even though Anne-Marie's devastating admission had scarred his very soul. He told Callie his beloved Vi and Ellie were gone forever.

"I have nothing to live for," he cried. "Nothing."

Even though it might be false hope, Callie said, "Anne-Marie speaks in riddles, Jordan. What she says isn't always literal. Like the doctor said, keep hoping until we can talk to her again."

"She won't ever let them come back," came a voice from behind them. Jordan cried in despair as Anne-Marie walked to Callie's side.

"How do you know that?" she asked.

"She lost her own children. Now she has them back."

"But these aren't her children. She's taken someone else's. She's hurting other people. Ellie and Vi are Jordan's girls. And mine." Jordan's head jerked up when he heard her, but he said nothing.

Neither did Anne-Marie.

Landry walked to Callie and whispered something to her. When he finished, she paused for a moment and then she nodded.

Landry said, "Anne-Marie, may I talk to you in the nursery?"

He sat at the *Alice in Wonderland* table and she took a chair beside him. He talked to her for a few minutes. She kept her thoughts to herself, saying nothing. The door opened behind her. Callie stuck her head in and asked if things were okay. As he nodded, he realized Anne-Marie was gone.

Callie asked, "Do you think your idea worked?"

"I don't know. I wish I could have thought of something better. Jordan won't like it, but to get his girls back, I think he'd agree to anything."

Landry had asked Anne-Marie to offer Olivia a compromise. If she let the children come back and she never took them again, Jordan would promise to live in the house. Vi and Ellie could play in the nursery and she could see them whenever they were at home. It would be just like those early days before Jordan realized what horrors his daughters were involved in.

In order to get Ellie and Vi back, he would have to agree to let Olivia be a part of their lives. But it hadn't happened, and now they waited to see if Anne-Marie could — or would — do what they asked.

CHAPTER FORTY-FIVE

When Anne-Marie returned, Callie and Landry went to the nursery to hear what had happened.

"Did you ask Olivia?"

"She doesn't like their father. If she brings them back, he will take them away from her."

"No! To get them back, he'd promise they could stay."

Anne-Marie looked straight ahead and said nothing.

Landry tried next. "Callie wants the girls back. She told you how much they mean to her. Can't you help her?"

"I did help her."

"What do you mean?"

Not a word came from Anne-Marie's lips.

Callie touched the girl's arm. It was the first time she had touched her since the night at Beau Rivage when Anne-Marie saved her life. Expressions of love weren't part of this specter's disposition but today Callie was desperate, and Anne-Marie didn't resist.

Callie murmured, "Please tell me how you helped me."

"I did that." Anne-Marie pointed to the mirror just as Ellie and Vi emerged from the portal, laughing and jostling each other.

"Hi, everybody! We spent the night with Cherry! Did you miss us?"

They'd been gone for six days.

Callie ran to them, hugged them, and took them downstairs to see their father. Landry and Anne-Marie remained seated at the little table.

"I thought you said she wouldn't let them come back," he said. "Can they stay?"

She nodded.

"Is Cherry coming back?"

She shook her head.

"Then how —"

"You gave me an idea and it worked. I want to talk to Callie." Just then her friend walked into the room.

Callie sat next to Anne-Marie and said, "I can't thank you enough. I thought you said Olivia wouldn't let them come back. How did you make this happen?"

As usual, Anne-Marie showed no emotion. She was the most enigmatic, no-nonsense girl in the world. Callie's mind was flooded with feelings for this child who wasn't really a child, although Callie couldn't help thinking of her as one. She looked like a girl, but that was it. She was — she was an unexplainable thing, something you shouldn't wrap your feelings around. But Callie had found that impossible.

Anne-Marie's face was expressionless. Her eyes stared at something in the distance and she spoke in a low monotone. "She wants a little girl. I told you that already. She wanted Vi and Ellie."

The child pointed to Landry. "He told me what to say. I told her she couldn't keep them. I told her you loved them. She let them come back."

Confused, Callie looked at Landry. "What did you tell her to do?"

Anne-Marie said, "I have to go now. With her."

"With *her?* What are you talking about?"

Callie's heart sank; Anne-Marie's words could mean only one thing. She had bartered a deal with Olivia. She had traded herself for the twins. *She* would be Olivia's child.

She trembled and brushed away another tear. "Cherry's not a good person. I don't want you to go with her."

"She let his girls come back. She didn't have to do it, but she did."

"That doesn't make her good. She killed her husband, Anne-Marie. She walled him up in the nursery! She's a murderer! I'm begging you, please don't go with her! Please don't leave me!"

"You're safe. He can't hurt you anymore." The tone of her voice changed as she spoke. It was low and distant, and they heard an eerie tinkling sound. "Olivia and I won't be back. It was either me or them. I have to go."

Callie and Landry sat mere inches away, riveted in broken-hearted fascination as Anne-Marie transformed. Her face became hazy as a thin cloud of white vapor swept up and around her body. She whispered, "I love you, Callie. Goodbye," and faded away.

"No! God, no! Please don't leave me!" Her wails echoed throughout the nursery, her pain as deep as though she'd lost her own daughter. Anne-Marie wasn't Callie's; in fact, she was far, far older than Callie herself. But she had been Callie's friend and protector, and she had saved her life.

Callie would always cherish the special relationship with this wise soul who occupied a little girl's body. She had lost something amazing, something she'd never have again. That awful thought ripped a hole through Callie's heart.

CHAPTER FORTY-SIX

One Year Later

It took time before Callie could discuss Anne-Marie with Landry. She understood the logic of a trade. Anne-Marie wasn't a living person, but Jordan's children were. It made sense, but the loss was as tangible and permanent as if she had died.

When they talked, Landry reminded Callie that he had suggested something different than Anne-Marie accomplished. His idea was that Olivia would return the girls and never take them away again. In exchange, Jordan would stay at the Arbors and let them play with her. They had never discussed it with him, but Callie knew he'd agree to anything to get Vi and Ellie back.

But Anne-Marie had chosen another angle. Callie had asked her to get the children back, and Anne-Marie had traded herself for them.

Much had happened in the months after the traumatic events. Jordan and Callie married in the same Catholic church in St. Francisville where Olivia and Charles Perrault wed many years earlier. Cate and Landry were maid of honor and best man, and Jordan's twin daughters were flower girls.

Anne-Marie had promised Olivia wouldn't return, and that had proven correct. When she left, she took the negativism with her, and Jordan moved the family back into the house he loved. His office was still on the first floor, but he'd expanded since he'd won one of the two major contracts he'd bid on. His staff had doubled, and the place was busier than ever.

It was Callie's suggestion to turn the Arbors into St. Francisville's newest bed-and-breakfast, and six months ago it had come true. A steady stream of guests kept the five second-floor bedrooms rented every night.

The nursery was the house's star attraction. Tourists stood in line to see the room that had been featured on a Landry Drake *Bayou Hauntings* episode. With no ghostly hand to interfere, the nursery door stayed open these days. Visitors could peek in the room without entering; a velvet rope across the door allowed them to look at the cribs, the toys and the children's table without disturbing what was a real playroom for Jordan's nine-year-olds.

When they weren't in school, Vi and Ellie often held tea parties in the nursery while tourists watched. Everyone who saw Landry's show knew the story — two children abducted by a matriarchal ghost who murdered her own husbands, locking one in a closet to die in terrible agony. Some people who watched the kids play believed the tale. They whispered how sorry they felt for the helpless children and how lucky it was that they were safely back.

The skeptics — and there were many who found the story too far-fetched to accept — wrote the whole thing off as a publicity stunt concocted to bring tourism revenue to St. Francisville and the Arbors. If there was a ghost, a dead body inside a closet, and children buried beneath the guardian angel in the cemetery, what father would allow his children to stay here? Those visitors took the tours as if they were in a Halloween spook house. They refused to believe the truth because it was too bizarre.

This segment of *Bayou Hauntings* had been Landry's most incredible because he was personally involved from the start. He had experienced the roller-coaster ride as two children disappeared for days at a time. He saw grief, terror, torment, laughter, relief and sadness in Jordan's three weeks of horror at the Arbors. This wasn't a detached report on a haunting; this was an emotional situation in which he was a participant, not an observer.

Vi and Ellie hadn't appeared in person on the TV show. He told the story and used their names, but Jordan refused to let Landry show their faces. Regardless, they were celebrities themselves now, and some of the visitors waved and spoke to them as the girls reveled in their newfound fame and poured imaginary tea for Peter.

It didn't take long to close the matter of Bruno Duval's death. The "eye for an eye" note Olivia left and Bruno's fateful prediction that she would kill him was enough for Chief Kimes, and fingerprints proved whose body it was. Olivia Beaumont murdered her husband. Carlton Fedder was an accessory. Since both were dead, the matter was closed. There were no relatives, and now he rested in the cemetery. Jordan could have buried him next to Olivia, but he chose to inter the hapless husband near the guardian angel instead.

The two who'd started this journey — Cate and Landry — became closer than ever, although he traveled more these days. They discussed feelings, dreams, and talked about moving in together, but it hadn't happened. She loved her work and Galveston was her home. Sitting alone every night in a French Quarter apartment while her boyfriend hunted ghosts wasn't what she wanted. For now they would see each other several times a month in New Orleans or Galveston or Houston. What did the future hold? Only time would tell.

MAY WE OFFER YOU A FREE BOOK?

Bill Thompson's award-winning first novel,
The Bethlehem Scroll, can be yours free.

Just go to
billthompsonbooks.com
and click
"Subscribe."

Once you're on the list, you'll receive advance notice of
future book releases
and other great offers.

Thank you!

Thanks for reading *The Nursery*.

I hope you enjoyed it and **I'd really appreciate a review on Amazon, Goodreads or both.**

Even a line or two makes a tremendous difference so thanks in advance for your help!

Please join me on:
Facebook
http://on.fb.me/187NRRP
Twitter
@BThompsonBooks

Made in the
USA
Monee, IL